"Unique, witty, and hilarious, Carrie's voice shines throughout *Woman in Shadow*. The perfect mix of intrigue, mystery, and danger, *Woman in Shadow* is most definitely a book for my keeper shelf."

—DANI PETTREY, BESTSELLING AUTHOR OF
THE COASTAL GUARDIANS SERIES

"Danger and drama abide in this tale that takes a walk on the perilous side. With a flair for the macabre, the story will linger in your head long after the last page."

—STEVE BERRY, *NEW YORK TIMES* AND #1 INTERNATIONALLY
BESTSELLING AUTHOR, FOR *RELATIVE SILENCE*

"*Relative Silence* is one of the most engrossing suspense novels I've read in a long time. Pitch-perfect pacing and characterization along with Parks's knowledgeable hand with forensics kept me on the edge of my seat. If you enjoy suspense with a light touch of romance, you must read this one!"

—COLLEEN COBLE, *USA TODAY* BESTSELLING AUTHOR OF
ONE LITTLE LIE AND THE LAVENDER TIDES SERIES

"The perfect beach read! *Relative Silence* is an expert mix of family drama and slow-burning thriller, leavened with Parks's trademark humor. You'll be pulling for Piper and Tucker as the story builds toward a hurricane-force climax."

—RICK ACKER, BESTSELLING AUTHOR

"With skill and her ever-present wit, Carrie Stuart Parks has arranged puzzle pieces and woven story threads into an engaging and quick-moving read with tantalizing questions, quirky characters, and . . . oh yes, some well-placed fictional curve balls along the way. Enjoy!"

—FRANK PERETTI, BESTSELLING AUTHOR, FOR *RELATIVE SILENCE*

"What a great book! Carrie Stuart Parks has done it again. *Relative Silence* offers us characters we care about, a convoluted and clever plot, and hours of reading pleasure. Highly recommended."
—GAYLE ROPER, AUTHOR OF *LOST AND FOUND* AND *HIDE AND SEEK*

"*Relative Silence* has all the bells and whistles. A relatable character in Piper Boone, a plot that keeps moving forward, and a surprising finish. It was hard to put down. A completely satisfying read. I highly recommend it!"
—NANCY MEHL, BESTSELLING, AWARD-WINNING AUTHOR

"What a compelling story! I rarely read a book all in one sitting, but Parks's combination of intriguing plot, vivid setting, and characters you can't help but root for kept me turning the pages right through to the very satisfying ending. I highly recommend this excellent read!"
—MARLO SCHALESKY, AWARD-WINNING AUTHOR OF *WOMEN OF THE BIBLE SPEAK OUT*, FOR *RELATIVE SILENCE*

"Parks has it all in *Relative Silence*—mystery, romance, and a subtle message about God."
—RICHARD L. MABRY, MD, AWARD-WINNING, BESTSELLING AUTHOR OF *CRITICAL DECISION*

"I love Carrie Stuart Parks's skill in writing characters with hysterical humor, unwitting courage, and page-turning mystery. I hope my readers won't abandon me completely when they learn about her!"
—TERRI BLACKSTOCK, *USA TODAY* BESTSELLING AUTHOR OF THE IF I RUN SERIES

"[An] appealing inspirational thriller."
—*PUBLISHERS WEEKLY*, FOR *FRAGMENTS OF FEAR*

"Without fail, Parks delivers stories that reel me in and keep me turning the pages until I'm done and craving more. *Fragments of Fear* is sure to make you a Carrie Stuart Parks addict as well!" #CSPaddictandproudofit
—LYNETTE EASON, BESTSELLING, AWARD-WINNING AUTHOR

"*Fragments of Fear* is a romantic suspense roller-coaster ride not to be missed. Parks has mastered the art of drawing in the reader and gripping our imaginations in a way that keeps us turning the pages."
—KIMBERLY ROSE JOHNSON, AWARD-WINNING AUTHOR

"Parks skillfully blends a lovely yet treacherous locale into the very dark deeds of its human inhabitants. Readers will want to see more of the mysterious and sympathetic Murphy."
—*PUBLISHERS WEEKLY*, FOR *FORMULA OF DECEPTION*

"The sinister tone of this fast-paced story line creates an almost unbearable tension that will keep readers glued to the page. Acclaimed author Parks draws on her career as a forensic artist to imbue her stories with a true-to-life accuracy that will fascinate readers of CSI-type fiction."
—*LIBRARY JOURNAL*, FOR *FORMULA OF DECEPTION*

"Parks (herself a well-known forensic artist) is a seasoned writer of inspirational 'edge-of-your-seat' suspense and mystery. Her latest title is a carefully researched and thoughtfully executed novel that will leave readers begging for more. Fans of Dee Henderson, DiAnn Mills, and Brandilyn Collins will flock to this suspenseful series."
—*LIBRARY JOURNAL*, STARRED REVIEW, FOR *PORTRAIT OF VENGEANCE*

"Parks has created an intriguing female sleuth with depth, courage, and grit. The well-developed characters are complemented by a unique setting."
—*PUBLISHERS WEEKLY*, STARRED REVIEW, FOR *PORTRAIT OF VENGEANCE*

"Rich characters, a forensic artist's eye for detail, and plot twists—Carrie Stuart Parks hits all the right notes!"
—MARY BURTON, *NEW YORK TIMES* BESTSELLING
AUTHOR, FOR *PORTRAIT OF VENGEANCE*

"The compelling crimes, inscrutable community, and resilient heroine propel Parks's latest thrill-packed installment in the chronicles of no-nonsense Gwen Marcey."
—*PUBLISHERS WEEKLY*, FOR *WHEN DEATH DRAWS NEAR*

"Besides having a resourceful and likable heroine, the book also features that rarest of characters: a villain you don't see coming, but whom you hate with relish. Moreover, you think said villain's crazy plans for world domination just might work. *A Cry from the Dust* will keep you hoping, praying, and guessing till the end."
—*BOOK PAGE*

"Renowned forensic and fine artist, Parks's action-packed and compelling tale of suspense is haunting in its intensity. Well researched and written in an almost journalistic style, this emotionally charged story is recommended for fans of Ted Dekker, Mary Higgins Clark, and historical suspense."
—*LIBRARY JOURNAL*, STARRED REVIEW, FOR *A CRY FROM THE DUST*

"Parks, in her debut novel, has clearly done her research and never disappoints when it comes to crisp dialogue, characterization, or surprising twists and turns."
—*PUBLISHERS WEEKLY*, FOR *A CRY FROM THE DUST*

"A unique novel of forensics and fanaticism. A good story on timely subjects well told. For me, these are the ingredients of a successful novel today and Carrie Stuart Parks has done just that."
—CARTER CORNICK, FBI COUNTERTERRORISM AND FORENSIC
   SCIENCE RESEARCH (RET.), FOR *A CRY FROM THE DUST*

WOMAN
IN
SHADOW

ALSO BY CARRIE STUART PARKS

Relative Silence
Fragments of Fear
Formula of Deception

THE GWEN MARCEY NOVELS

A Cry from the Dust
The Bones Will Speak
When Death Draws Near
Portrait of Vengeance

WOMAN
IN
SHADOW

CARRIE STUART PARKS

THOMAS NELSON
Since 1798

Woman in Shadow

Published in Nashville, Tennessee, by Thomas Nelson. Thomas Nelson is a registered trademark of HarperCollins Christian Publishing, Inc.

Thomas Nelson titles may be purchased in bulk for educational, business, fundraising, or sales promotional use. For information, please email SpecialMarkets@ThomasNelson.com.

Scripture quotations are taken from the Holy Bible, New Living Translation. © 1996, 2004, 2015 by Tyndale House Foundation. Used by permission of Tyndale House Publishers, Inc. Carol Stream, Illinois 60188. All rights reserved. And from the New King James Version®. © 1982 by Thomas Nelson. Used by permission. All rights reserved. And from the King James Version of the Bible. Public domain.

Publisher's Note: This novel is a work of fiction. Names, characters, places, and incidents are either products of the author's imagination or used fictitiously. All characters are fictional, and any similarity to people living or dead is purely coincidental.

Library of Congress Cataloging-in-Publication Data

Names: Parks, Carrie Stuart, author.
Title: Woman in shadow / Carrie Stuart Parks.
Description: Nashville, Tennessee : Thomas Nelson, [2021] | Summary:
  "Bestselling and award-winning author Carrie Stuart Parks combines her
  expertise as a forensic artist and her ability to create a gripping story in this
  web of trust and values"-- Provided by publisher.
Identifiers: LCCN 2021004051 (print) | LCCN 2021004052 (ebook) | ISBN
  9780785239840 (paperback) | ISBN 9780785239826 (epub) | ISBN
  9780785239833
Classification: LCC PS3616.A75535 W66 2021 (print) | LCC PS3616.A75535
  (ebook) | DDC 813/.6--dc23
LC record available at https://lccn.loc.gov/2021004051
LC ebook record available at https://lccn.loc.gov/2021004052

Printed in the United States of America
21 22 23 24 25 LSC 5 4 3 2 1

To Mom and Dad. I wish you could have been with me on this journey.

CHAPTER 1

TARGHEE FALLS, IDAHO

W hy are those dogs barking?" I pointed across the wooden picnic table toward two obviously upset canines yelping nearby.

A man staring at a clipboard didn't look up. "They're dogs. That's what they do. Are you Darby Graham?"

"Yes."

The man checked something on his clipboard. "Good. You're all here." He had to speak up to be heard over the commotion.

Before I could ask about the dogs again, he turned and strolled toward the nearby general store.

Although the man seemed unmoved by the dogs' distress, the other people seated around me on Adirondack chairs or at picnic tables had stopped speaking to each other and were staring. The dogs—a black Lab cross with hound-length ears, and a huge Great Dane mix—both had their tails tucked between their legs and were howling.

1

The picnic table trembled.

I lifted my hands off the rough pine surface but could still feel the movement under my body. A flock of birds burst from the treetops. Pinecones dropped to the ground from the towering ponderosas.

Earthquake.

I was seated near the general store, just below a plate-glass window. The glass rippled, then rattled.

Heart thudding, I dove under the table. The ground rolled under me like ocean waves. A low rumbling was followed by car alarms going off from the parking lot on the other side of the store.

The black Lab flew under the table and landed in my lap. I wrapped my arms around the quivering dog, feeling the prominent bones of her spine and rib cage. "It's okay there, girl. You're safe. Your big buddy isn't so scared—"

The second quaking dog joined us, his large body pressing against my back.

The earthquake ended.

"All over." I reached around and scratched the Dane's chest, feeling more bones. Didn't anyone ever feed these dogs?

Both dogs seemed content to stay put, but the weight of the Lab—even though she was too thin—was still more than my leg was used to and it was rapidly going to sleep. "Come on, sweet girl, time to get up," I whispered.

Both dogs took the hint.

On the other hand, here under the table seemed a nice

place to stay. Tucked into the shadows, I didn't need to worry about anyone staring at me. I had room to stretch out and could smell the cut grass. I'd be prepared should another earthquake come. And my assignment was to maintain a low profile. Sitting on the ground under a table seemed to be as low profile as I could get.

Two legs appeared next to me. "Miss Graham?"

Flapperdoodle. Mr. Clipboard found me.

I crawled between the bench and table, sliding onto the seat, then glanced around. Several other people had taken similar action. Only Clipboard had noticed my reluctance to leave my hiding place.

One by one, the car alarms stopped. The slight breeze stirred the fragrance of fallen pine needles.

Mr. Clipboard stared at me for a moment, then turned toward the others. He was holding a number of fabric bags imprinted with *Mule Shoe Ranch.* "Don't be worried, folks. The town of Targhee Falls is less than fifteen miles from Yellowstone. The national park routinely has between one and three thousand quakes a year—"

"Excuse me, but I've heard most of those quakes aren't noticeable," a gray-haired woman in a denim shirt said.

"Obviously some are." The man gave her a rueful half smile and started handing out the bags after checking the attached name tags. "I'm Sam, owner of the general store over there." He nodded toward the building featuring a two-story false front and wooden sidewalk. The peeling sign said Sam's Mercantile. "I provide Mule Shoe with transportation, supplies, and assistance during team-building exercises. Inside these bags you'll find a great deal of information about your stay at the ranch. The owner, Roy Zaring, wanted you to have these while you're waiting for your transportation—"

"When will that be?" asked a handsome teen with flawless olive skin and a thick lock of black hair. "I'm not getting any cell service here." He held up his phone. An impeccably dressed man and woman sitting at the same table gave each other sideways glances.

Sam finished handing out the bags, turned, and looked at the youth. "Those your folks?" His gaze flickered to the two people sitting with the young man.

"Yeah."

"And I'm guessing your mom? Dad? Both? Told you they were here to take a team-building—"

"Watercolor workshop."

"A five-day art class in the wilds of Idaho, right?"

"Yeeeaah."

"Son, the Mule Shoe Dude Ranch is a primitive facility. No Wi-Fi. No cell reception. No television, radio . . . no electricity. You'll have a cabin with a fireplace, a composting toilet, and a lantern at night."

The color drained from the young man's face. "What?" he whispered.

"That reminds me," Sam said. "I'll collect your cell phones and will keep them here and charged for when you return."

I reached into my purse, took out my phone, and placed it on the table for Sam to collect. *Whose brilliant idea was it to send me on assignment to a primitive facility when they know I need my computer and electricity?* And five days with all these strangers? I wouldn't even need to unpack.

"Don't worry." An attractive older woman sitting on a wooden Adirondack chair grinned at the boy. "There's plenty of hot water for showers, courtesy of the natural geothermal environment. The water's gravity fed and the food is world-class." She looked around at all of us. "I've had an interest in the Mule Shoe and was here last summer, although I have to admit, I prefer to visit this time of year. Late September is perfect. You all are going to love it."

The young man's lips compressed into a thin line, and he seemed loath to let go of his cell. Sam kept tugging the phone until the youth relinquished it. "But what is there to *do*?" he asked no one in particular.

"Most of us are here for the art lessons." Denim Shirt reached into her bag, pulled out a piece of paper, and held it up. "Listen." She read from it. "'You'll find trail rides, fishing, canoeing, gold panning, mineral collecting, archery, photography, hiking, campfires, swimming—'"

"That's what I mean." The young man ran his hand through his hair. "There's nothing to *do*."

I tugged out the same brochure. *Welcome, honored guests. We look forward to serving you during your stay with us. Your experiences here will be unforgettable for all the*

5

right reasons! You should bring to Mule Shoe your mindset for success.

Yeah, right. I'd like to set my mind on getting in, getting done, and getting home. "Sam, you mentioned transportation . . ."

"Horse and wagon."

I was afraid of that. "Do you have a regular timetable?"

This time Sam actually focused on me. "No. The horse and wagon are available on an as-needed basis, mostly to transport new groups and supplies."

From bad to worse. I was stuck. Now would be a good time to find a bathroom. Riding a bumpy, horse-drawn wagon would be uncomfortable enough without a full bladder. Besides, if I left now, no one would notice my slight limp. I normally wanted to be invisible, to disappear into a crowd. When Scott Thomas, my counselor, told me not to stand out, to blend in, he didn't have to say it twice. *Your final assignment before leaving us here in Clan Firinn is to check out Mule Shoe Ranch. We've heard rumblings that something's not right. You'll be registered as a guest. I'll tell you more once you get there.*

I was irritated at being sent out like this with no idea of what was expected. *I now know why.* Had I known I wouldn't be able to use my computer programs or the internet, I would have put my foot down. I was fortunate to have a good memory for words.

I'd heard through the Clan Firinn grapevine that those getting ready to leave—"graduate" as they called it—would have a project that would test their progress toward wholeness. I figured they'd find out soon enough that I wasn't ready to leave.

I rose, picked up my purse, and made my way to the general store. A cowbell jangled as I entered. "'I got a fever,'" I muttered. "'And the only prescription is more cowbell.'" The line made me smile. Why worry about earthquakes, lack of electricity, and the inability to do my work when the world needed more cowbell?

"What?" A young, freckle-faced woman with a smear of dirt on her nose stopped replacing items on the shelf.

"Iconic *Saturday Night Live* line—more cowbell?"

"Huh?"

"Never mind." The interior had old oak floors, a tin ceiling, and a long counter with a glass display case. The sun through the window spotlighted twirling dust motes. Various cans still littered the floor, courtesy of the earthquake.

"Just let me know if ya need something."

"Powder room?"

"Huh?"

"WC?"

"I think we're sold out."

"John? Head? Loo? Restroom?"

"Toilet?" She nodded to her right.

Fortunately, the primitive conditions did not include the store bathroom. Returning to the store, I picked up a can of soup that had rolled near me. "Do you know anything about those two dogs?" I handed her the can.

"Why are ya asking?" The woman placed it on the shelf.

"They just seem thin, that's all."

"Yeah, well." She adjusted the display. "Sam's been feeding 'em, but that's gonna stop."

My neck tingled. "I don't understand." I gave her a steady gaze.

She paused her work and looked around. We were alone in the store, but she dropped her voice to just above a whisper. "He's just waitin' for all of you to leave to the ranch."

The tingling grew to an itch. My years of training as a forensic linguist kicked in, even though I was rusty. I grew very still and waited, listening for more clues in her language.

She gave up straightening the cans. "It's like this: The dogs were owned by an old lady. I bet she was, like, at least forty."

"Positively ancient. One foot in the grave." I gave her a slight smile.

"Right. Her name was Shadow Woman. That's what everyone called her. Well, that's the nice name anyway. She was, like, a hermit, but a pretty good artist." She jerked her thumb at a drawing on the wall behind the cash register.

Were owned, was. Past tense. I widened my smile to encourage her. "Why did everyone call her Shadow Woman?"

The clerk gnawed on a hangnail for a moment. "I guess 'cause she was weird, ya know, like she lived in the shadows. Creepy. Always showed up here at the store at dusk or when it was dark. Sam said she could sneak right up next to you in the shadows and you'd never see her. And her face was weird."

"Weird how?"

"Like, really weird."

"Ah, that clarifies it. Where did she come from?"

"Sam said she ran away from a group home near Smelterville."

"I can't imagine why."

"Right, you know? No one wanted her. Anyway, she owned Holly—that's the Lab mix—and Maverick, the Anna-toolian sheepdog."

"Anatolian? From Anatolia in Asia Minor?"

"Yeah, that's what I said."

"Of course. I thought the big dog was half Great Dane, half mastiff."

"Nope. Sam looked it up. Anna-whatevers are super-expensive livestock guard dogs from Turkey or France, I forget which."

"They are such similar countries," I murmured.

"Right. So anyway, Sam was surprised that Shadow Woman had one."

Sam looked it up. Looking for value? *Surprised that Shadow Woman had one.* Not just a hermit but poor? Broke? "I see." I leaned slightly against the shelving unit. "You mentioned Shadow . . ."

"Right. Um . . . so Shadow Woman came to town like once a month with her mule, like I said, always after sunset, and bought stuff, like Spam. She'd usually pay her bill about every other month. The dogs always came with her. Six months ago, you know, she stopped coming."

"Let me guess. She owed Sam a lot of money."

"Right. Boy-howdy was he steamed about it. Then he, you know, got a check and note from the old woman to pay her bill, but the check bounced higher than a buckin' bronco."

"Did anyone follow up, call the police?"

"Not right away 'cause the dogs moved in, first Holly, then Maverick. So, you know, Sam started to feed them. And . . . I think someone changed his mind on what to do with the dogs."

Cluster of *you knows*. Sensitive topic. I kept my gaze on her and nodded again.

She glanced down and plucked a piece of lint from her sleeve. "Sam always said he'd get his pound of flesh from her, whatever that means."

"I'm sure it originated in Turkey or France."

"Right. Foreign-like. Um . . . Sam finally got close enough to Maverick to see he'd been spayed."

"Neutered?"

"What?"

"Never mind." A neutered dog was of zero value, and Sam stopped feeding them. I made an effort to unclench my hands. "How have the dogs survived?"

"You know, folks around town feel sorry for them . . ."

The cowbell jangled.

The clerk straightened and glanced in that direction.

Her cheeks flamed and her tongue flickered out to moisten her lips.

I turned.

A sheriff's deputy charged to the bathroom, disappeared for a few moments, then reappeared and sauntered toward us, replacing fallen items on the shelves. His ordinary brown hair was the only average thing about him. He was otherwise a walking modern-day Adonis, his face chiseled by a master carver. He finally looked up and smiled at the clerk, exposing more teeth than the Osmond family, and seemed to enjoy her reaction to his arrival.

My hand automatically reached to fluff my hair. I stopped and squared my oversized glasses instead.

He looked at me, his eyes widening. "Hello there. I'm Bram White."

"I'm—"

"Leaving," the clerk said. "Goin' to Mule Shoe. She's a guest."

"Darby Graham." I glanced at his holstered pistol, then out the window at the two dogs lying under a tree. Check bounced. *Sam's been feeding 'em, but that's gonna stop. Pound of flesh.*

Deputy Bram glanced at his watch.

My neck was crawling with reasons to scratch it.

"Can I get you a Coke or somethin'?" she asked me. "It shouldn't be long." The clerk moved toward an ancient cooler. "I'd bet the wagon got slowed down by the earthquake."

The two dogs began barking.

"See? I told ya. Betcha that's the wagon now." The clerk moved toward the front of the store, brushing past Bram. "Excuse me," she said. At the window, she glanced out, then looked at the officer. "Yep. The wagon's here." Without taking her eyes from Bram, she said to me, "You can go now."

Sam stuck his head in the door. "Miss Graham? Time to leave." He spotted Bram and gave the man a quick nod.

I gave in and scratched my neck. This was none of my business. No need to get involved. No reason to draw attention to myself. Low profile. *Right.* I straightened. "I think I'll wait here. Catch the next wagon." The words came out without my thinking, but they seemed right.

Sam moved into the store. "I'm sorry, Miss Graham, there won't be a next wagon. It's quite a distance to the ranch and it's getting late. You'll need to leave now." He wiped his hands on his slacks, glanced at the clerk, then at the deputy.

The itch was now a full-scale conviction. "Your clerk here—"

"Julia?" Sam glared at the clerk.

"Was telling me about Shadow Woman. And her dogs."
Bram folded his arms.

Sam opened the door behind him and waved for me to exit. "Miss Graham, I really see that as none of your business."

Go now. Run. You have nothing to offer. Well . . . almost nothing. I slowly walked over to the counter. "I know

12

Shadow Woman's check bounced. How much money did she owe you? And how much to cover all the dog food?" I opened my purse.

"How many times have I warned you to keep your pie-hole shut!" Sam said to Julia.

"I didn't say nothin'!" Julia crossed her arms. "She figured it out on her own."

Sam closed the door and approached me, both hands held out as if to show goodwill. "I don't know what it is that you figured out, Miss Graham, but—"

"Please don't try lying to me, Sam." I pulled out my checkbook. "You figured the Anatolian dog would pay Shadow Woman's bill, but when you saw he was neutered, he had no more value to you. The minute I leave, you're going to have Deputy White here shoot both dogs. Your pound of flesh." I stared into his eyes. "I intend to stop you."

CHAPTER 2

There were times when Bram hated his job. Rarely, as he'd wanted to serve in law enforcement his entire life, but today was one of those loathe-my-work days. Shooting stray dogs was wrong. They didn't have rabies. Hadn't bitten anyone. No threat to domestic animals. Not chasing wildlife. The dogs just needed a good home, but Sam wouldn't listen. The owner had been sent several letters with citations for letting the dogs run and for lack of rabies vaccinations, but she hadn't bothered to show up in court. The sheriff had given Bram the court orders for the dogs' destruction. He'd spent the entire drive from St. Anthony trying to figure out a solution. Sadly, only Sam could reverse the decision.

Dispatch alerted him to the earthquake as he pulled up in front of Sam's Mercantile. Nothing seemed to be disturbed, and the usual group of guests waited outside the store for transport to Mule Shoe. He pulled out a file and looked at a photograph, then compared it to the two dogs lying under a pine. The big dog was memorable and a perfect match. Unfortunately.

He backed into a parking spot, straightened his uniform, and stepped from his cruiser. The black Lab mix spotted him and raced in his direction. Was this dog attacking? How could the dog know why he had come? He reached for his pistol as the lab launched herself at him, placed two dusty paws on his chest, and landed a sloppy, wet tongue across his cheek.

"Uck! Down." He pushed the eager canine off, then brushed the dirt from his crisply pressed uniform. Small black hairs had managed to tangle in the material. He plucked them out as he strolled into the store. He knew where the restroom was and aimed for it, where he grabbed a paper towel and wiped the dog slobber off his cheek. A quick inspection showed most of the canine's damage had been taken care of. He returned to the store. The earthquake had sent a variety of cans to the floor. He reshelved them as he passed, making sure the labels were turned outward and they were evenly placed. The Campbell's and Progresso soups had been mixed together.

He resisted the urge to rearrange the display, turned, and spotted *her*. Thick, shoulder-length, light-brown hair, perfectly brushed. Flawless complexion. Slender but well-toned body. Large eyes behind oversized glasses. The glasses put him off slightly, but they didn't seem to be overly thick. She looked like a cross between Audrey Hepburn and Demi Moore.

"Hello there. I'm Bram White," he blurted.

He knew she was a guest, she'd soon be heading up

to the ranch, and she was in a financial stratosphere out of his reach. The cost of staying at the Mule Shoe was almost a thousand dollars a night. But for the first time in a very long time, he wanted to get to know a woman. This woman.

———

The loud clang of the cowbell over the door took everyone's attention away from my checkbook. A young man in his early twenties entered wheeling a handcart of crated sodas. "Hi, all, your friendly neighborhood Coke dealer is here." He grinned at his wit, but his smile faded when he looked around. "Someone die?"

"Not now, Liam," Sam said without looking at him.

The young man wheeled his load to the old cooler and began stocking the unit.

The cowbell rang again and a lanky man in his late thirties strolled into the store. His worn jeans, battered cowboy boots, freshly pressed blue-plaid shirt, and Stetson hat reminded me of a young Sam Elliott. He stopped as soon as he entered and looked from face to face. His gaze finally arrived at me. Nodding slightly, he touched the brim of his hat. "Ma'am. Time to leave for the Mule Shoe." Underneath his bushy mustache, he seemed to be smiling.

"Ran into a bit of a problem here, Wyatt," Bram said to the wrangler.

"That so?" Wyatt waited.

Everyone spoke at once. "I think you should—"

"This is just a—"

"You've come to the wrong—"

Bram raised his hands, then glanced at my tightly clutched checkbook and pen. "This may take some sorting out. Wyatt, why don't you take the other guests and their luggage to the ranch. I'll see to it Miss Graham gets there before dinner."

Wyatt raised his eyebrows, opened his mouth as if to say something, then touched his brim again and left.

Bram stepped over to the counter. "Sam, seems you have a good solution for your dog problem. Why don't you settle Shadow Woman's account and let her take them? I don't particularly like shooting innocent pets, with or without a court order."

Sam jabbed his finger at the officer. "Yeah, but I got that court order. I'm within my rights—"

"No one's saying you don't have the authority," Bram said. "But if the press gets hold of this, well, you know folks won't be breaking their legs to shop at your store."

Sam scratched his jaw and glanced around.

"I'll double what Shadow Woman owes you," I said.

The words had barely left my mouth when Sam headed for the counter. He reached under, yanked out a file, and opened it. Julia gave him a disgusted look and went back to replacing cans.

"The old lady's balance as of six months ago was two hundred fifty-seven dollars and forty-two cents. Her check for that amount bounced, as I'm sure you heard." He shot

Julia a nasty glance. "The dog food, at forty-six eighty-five a month for six months—"

"Three months," I said. "You stopped feeding them a while back."

Sam didn't bother looking up. "So, three hundred ninety-seven dollars and ninety-seven cents doubled is . . . seven hundred ninety-five dollars and ninety-four cents." This time he looked at me and smirked.

I wanted to punch him into Turkey or France but instead opened my checkbook, grateful that no one could see my shaking hand. I had the money, thanks to the disability payments, but I was supposed to be invisible. Now I had everyone's attention.

After writing the check, I handed it to Sam, then stepped away from him. I knew my limp would be more pronounced. It always was when people were watching me. And Bram was watching.

Why should I care that Bram was watching? *News flash, officer, this model comes dinged, shopworn, and as is.*

"I've added another fifty dollars for dog food to take with me." I turned to the deputy. "Looks like there will be three of us heading up to the Mule Shoe."

Bram grinned at me.

He didn't get the "shopworn" memo.

"Sam, can I borrow your wagon?"

Or maybe he did. "I'm perfectly capable of riding a horse." I tamped down the unwelcome memory of my competitive horseback-riding days. I hadn't been on a horse, let alone raced around any barrels, roped a single calf, or done any other timed event, for five years. I wasn't even sure if I could *stay* on a horse.

"You might be, but fifty pounds of dog food, not to mention the food dishes and bones Sam is about to give you, won't fit on the back of a horse."

"I think the dogs and I can manage."

"But there's more." Bram glanced at Sam. "Since Miss Graham paid Shadow Woman's bill, you need to give her the scrip."

"Script?" Julia paused her tidying up.

"Scrip. No *t*," I said to her. *Stop showing off.*

Bram rubbed his mouth to hide his grin, then said to me, "Shadow Woman used her drawings in lieu of money—"

"A practice called scrip, which is a substitute for legal tender," I said to Julia. Her brows furrowed in confusion.

"Yes," Bram said, "at least for the past year or so. You made that suggestion, right, Sam? So because Darby here has paid her bill, she gets the art. Right again, Sam?"

Sam walked stiff-legged into a back room, returning shortly with an oversized battered file folder. "Here." He shoved it in my direction.

"One more." Bram pointed at the drawing on the wall.

Sam took it down and shoved it into the file folder.

"There's another two small drawings in the phone book." Julia gave Sam a defiant look.

"Who said you—" Sam slammed his hand on the counter and glared at the clerk.

"She needed food, you were gone, and you know how she could become crazy-mad at the drop of a hat." Julia put her hands on her hips.

Bram ignored both of them and stepped into the back room. He returned with an old phone book, which he handed to me.

Sam looked as if he was going to have a heart attack. He finally sputtered, "I'll go hitch up the wagon."

Bram grinned.

Crash!

I jumped.

Julia had dropped several cans.

Bram turned and headed toward her. The woman gave me a snarky grin.

I wiggled my fingers at her as I aimed for the door. *"Vous avez de la saleté sur le nez, arkadaşım,"* I said in French and Turkish. *You have dirt on your nose, my friend.*

Now I really am showing off. If Julia had her sights on Bram, she had nothing to fear from me.

The dogs were stretched out under a pine but rose when I appeared. I sat on the edge of the wooden sidewalk and let them approach and check me out on their terms. Holly, the Lab mix, wasted no time establishing her eagerness to become my dog. She sat beside me, leaned close, and wagged her tail in the dirt so hard she created a cloud of dust. Maverick stood back and watched.

"I don't blame you, big guy," I whispered. "I'm a bit wary

of strangers as well." Now that I could see him clearly, I noted a crumpled ear, healed scars across his muzzle, and a missing patch of fur on his side. "Looks like you're as battered as I am. Well, we'll do our work here, then we'll head back home to Clan Firinn."

The young deliveryman exited the store.

I concentrated on the dogs, hoping he wouldn't come over.

"Hey there."

No such luck.

Holly shot toward him. I turned. He'd parked his handcart beside the door and was talking to the dogs. Maverick stood back and watched. "Hi there, fella." The Anatolian remained out of reach. The man produced two dog biscuits. Holly snatched hers from his hand and raced away. He placed Maverick's cookie on the porch and moved backward. The dog kept his eyes on the man as he gingerly picked up his treat, then sauntered to a nearby tree.

"I'm Liam Turner."

I nodded at him.

"I heard what you did for Shadow Woman's dogs. I didn't realize what Sam was planning, or that he'd stopped feeding them. I would have taken them . . . well, I would have taken them once I got my own place. My mom doesn't like dogs."

"You live with your mother?"

"For now. Say, if you're not busy tomorrow night, maybe we can have a few beers together? Things are usually pretty quiet at Mule Shoe in the evenings. Do you like bro-country music?"

"Bro-country? A country music subgenre about pickups, beautiful women, partying, and the consumption of beer?"

"Yeah!"

"So tempting, so very tempting, but alas, I'll be penning memorable squibs."

"Ah. Okay. Well, keep me in mind. Anyway . . . um . . . thanks." He swung away, then turned back. "You look familiar. Have you been to Mule Shoe before?"

Before I had to answer, a wagon prominently labeled Sam's Mercantile came around the corner, pulled by a chestnut Belgian draft horse with flaxen mane and tail. The dogs scattered. Sam got down from the high seat. "Don't you have to be somewhere, Liam?"

Liam's eyebrows drew together. "Just leaving." He grabbed the cart and stalked away.

"Good luck getting those dogs to go anywhere with you. And remember, if they stay here I got a court order to shoot 'em. And you're not getting your money back." He stomped into the store.

"He's just one step away," I whispered, "from calling out the flying monkeys."

Alone on the street, I walked over to the Belgian and stroked his silky nose. The horse nodded and gave a soft nicker. "I'm sorry I don't have a carrot or apple for you. I didn't pack for organically powered transportation." I moved to the wagon. The bed was high, and climbing up would be awkward, but I didn't want, or need, help. Or sympathy. I tucked the folder of drawings into the bag of information on Mule Shoe, then placed the bag and my purse on the wooden bed. I scrambled up and had just settled in when Bram appeared with a bag of dog food over his shoulder. Julia followed with an array of food dishes, water buckets, and dog treats. Bram effortlessly dropped the kibble onto the wagon bed next to me, then took the items from Julia and added them to the supplies.

"I'm not sure how you're going to get the dogs to follow you." He moved toward the spring seat.

"Holly. Maverick," I called.

The two dogs trotted over and leaped into the wagon bed beside me.

"Well I'll be!" Bram scratched his head, then climbed into the seat.

"You don't have to take me to Mule Shoe—"

"Ah, but I want to. And I'm officially off-duty. Sure you don't want to sit up here with me?" He patted the seat.

"I'm okay."

"Are you sure? You're awfully quiet."

"I'm fine. I'll use the time to ponder the most captivating hook to a bro-country song. 'Chew tobacco, spit' kinda tugs at my heart." I really wasn't fine. Though Maverick was pressed against the wagon as far from me as he could get, Holly had sprawled across my lap. The bed was as hard as cement and the evening was starting to get cold.

Bram clicked his tongue at the horse and we headed up

a steep trail into the mountains. I held on to the side of the wagon until we crested the first hill, then the road leveled somewhat.

The mountains marched into the distance like a stack of torn paper, each layer lighter than the previous one, ranging from deep viridian to soft lavender. The struts creaked in rhythm with the *clop, clop, clop* of the horse.

Thin air from the almost-eight-thousand-foot elevation carried the scent of pine needles . . . and something else. I inhaled deeply. Smoke. "Is there a forest fire around here?"

Bram turned, then sniffed the air. Pulling up the horse, he stood, looked around, then checked his watch. "Right on time. Dirtbag."

"Excuse me?"

He sat down and clicked at the horse before answering. "It's not a forest fire. Don't worry. We should be arriving at the ranch soon."

Not a forest fire, and he checked his watch. "So Targhee Falls has a serial arsonist?"

Bram whipped around so fast he startled the dogs. "What? How did you know? Have you been reading the papers? Online news?"

Why didn't I keep my mouth shut? "You said as much. 'Not a forest fire' means another kind of fire. 'Dirtbag' means an individual. 'Right on time' means this has happened before, and probably fairly often. All that pointed to an individual setting fires."

"Are you Sherlock Holmes disguised as . . . as Audrey Hepburn?"

"Hardly."

He fell silent as if I might clarify. I made a point of scratching Holly behind the ear. The happy canine rewarded me with a sloppy lick on the wrist.

We climbed at a steady pace before passing through a narrow, rock-lined passage only slightly wider than the wagon. Beyond it, the road seemed to cling to the mountain with a sheer wall on my right and a dizzying drop on the left. It reminded me of Glacier Park's Going-to-the-Sun Road, but without the low retaining wall. I closed my eyes and held on to Holly.

"You can open your eyes now." Bram's voice held a lilt of humor.

Tell him you were just resting your eyes.

"Don't tell me you were just resting your eyes."

My mouth dropped open and I gawked at him.

He grinned. "You may be Sherlock, but I'm a mind reader." He urged the horse to move a bit faster. "Actually, everyone gets a bit queasy as we go through the Devil's Keyhole—that's the narrow spot back there—and over Devil's Pass."

"I'm sure it's perfectly safe."

He didn't answer.

Significant pause? What was he holding back? "Isn't it?"

"Um . . . one would need to be careful, of course."

My neck itched. "I see. And at some point, 'one' wasn't careful."

He glanced at me before returning his attention to the road. "Has anyone ever said you're spooky-accurate catching verbal clues?"

My stomach gave a small lurch. I was inaccurate once, and it had cost me everything.

And I was supposed to be undercover.

He clicked at the horse. "About six months ago a couple of hikers probably tried to climb up, or maybe down, the cliff side of the pass. They didn't have the proper gear. Their bodies wouldn't have been found for quite some time, but thanks to an observant fish and game officer looking for some poachers, they were discovered before . . . um . . ."

"Before?"

"The critters had time to get to them and drag them off."

I tried to keep my too-vivid imagination from running wild.

Without a case outline defining what Scott wanted me to do, I wasn't sure what questions, if any, I should be asking the deputy. And I was pretty sure he'd pick up on even the slightest indication that I was anything more than a tourist.

The grassy road started a gentle downward angle, and the burble of a fast-moving stream grew louder. Soon we were level with the small river. The road widened, then opened to a lush green meadow. We stopped at a rustic gate with a log arch holding a Mule Shoe Ranch sign. While Bram opened the gate, curious horses in the nearby pasture gathered at the fence to check us out. Soon after we passed through, a large log-and-stone lodge appeared on the left. An unpainted barn in shades of gray-brown lay ahead, and a series of small cabins were on the right. Steep, pine-covered mountains pressed in on all sides, framing the idyllic scene.

"The lodge is the center of the resort." He pointed left. "Inside is the dining hall, gift shop, classroom, and lobby. Behind the lodge are the staff quarters, which you can't see from here. Guest cabins are over there." He nodded right. "You should have your cabin assignment inside that bag Sam gave you. We can drop the dogs and food at your cabin, then go to the lodge. Dinner will be served soon."

Shifting Holly enough to reach the bag, I felt around for a key. I found a blue water flask with the Mule Shoe logo, a blaze-orange baseball cap, and a batch of papers. I pulled out the papers. Art camp information, team-building projects, corporate retreat ideas, and a map with one cabin circled. "It looks like cabin twelve, but I don't seem to have a key."

"No keys. It's not as if anyone could get away with stealing around here."

If the "something's not right" that Scott wanted me to investigate was theft, the lack of security would be a plus for the thief.

I just hoped my two new pets would prove to be watchdogs.

Bram guided the horse to the last cabin in the line and pulled up. The dogs didn't wait for an invitation. Both leaped out to investigate the new surroundings. I followed suit, grateful to stand and stretch. Bram jumped down, lifted the dog chow over his shoulder, stuck the box of canine cookies under his arm, and entered the cabin. Snatching up the food dishes, water bucket, purse, and bag, I trailed him inside.

The interior held a large fireplace on the far wall with two cowhide-covered wingback chairs facing it. A small fire took the chill out of the room. On my right, a king-sized bed with a barn-wood frame had a Pendleton blanket bedspread. On my left was a rustic kitchen featuring a hammered copper sink and small gas stove with a gray enameled coffeepot. A rustic bookshelf held regional books on everything from plants and wildlife to western lore. A copper-topped dining table held a basket of dried fruit, chocolate, and bottles of wine. Next to that was a pair of binoculars and bird-identification book. My luggage—a suitcase and large duffel bag—rested on a built-in shelf against one wall.

"This. Is. Fantastic."

"Yeah, Roy knows how to treat his guests." He placed the bag of dog chow in a closet. "And, of course, you're paying for it."

Not really. I dropped my purse and bag on one of the chairs and peeked into the bathroom at the back of the cabin. A shelf holding a variety of candles and bath salts lined an oversized, cast-iron claw-foot tub. Light came from a window above the tub. A blackout shade offered privacy.

The bowl sink rested on an antique, marble-topped dresser. A glassed-in shower held a shower chair. Taking a bath would be more like going to a spa.

I picked up the water bucket Bram had brought in, filled it at the sink, then set it outside the door. Bram filled both dog dishes with kibble and set them next to the water. The dogs didn't need to be called. They sucked down the food like a pair of vacuum cleaners. "Do you think they'll stay around if I go to dinner?" I asked.

Bram was trying to remove Holly's fur from his slacks. "Are you kidding? These two would follow you into the Valley of Gehenna itself."

"A cross between Greyfriars Bobby and Hachikō?"

"Huh?"

"Not much for dog literature?"

He plucked more hair off his slacks. "You could say that." He jerked his thumb at the wagon. "Ready for your chariot to take you to dinner?"

"I can walk. How about you? Are you heading back to Targhee Falls?"

"Not in the dark I'm not. Remember Devil's Pass? Roy will expect me to grab some chow and bunk in the staff area tonight as usual. I'll head out in the morning."

"'As usual'? Do you come here often?"

Bram climbed up onto the seat before answering. "You don't miss much, do you?"

"And you didn't answer my question."

CHAPTER 3

The resort was cradled in an emerald-green alpine meadow surrounded by rugged mountains. The road from the outside world split the resort down the middle, ending in the distance at the barn, with attached corrals and a field of grazing horses. I crossed the road as I walked the short distance between my cabin and the lodge. Left of the sprawling building, a dense forest of fragrant cedars bordered a stream. Widely spaced trees with pine needle–covered paths gave the area a park-like feel.

I expected the dogs would settle down at the cabin and stay with their food dishes, but apparently they preferred staying with the source of the kibble. Both dogs trailed me.

Bram drove the wagon to the barn, disappearing inside. I would have rather gone to the barn and stayed with the horses. I was still far more comfortable around critters than people. Instead, I stuffed my hands into my pockets and continued to the lodge. When I told the dogs to stay outside, Holly lay down by the door and Maverick paced. Entering, I found myself in a generous room with the guests from Sam's Mercantile talking and sipping drinks. Most had changed into what they considered casual attire, though Gucci polo shirts in the eight-hundred-dollar range seemed hardly typical of Idaho ranchers. Pools of golden light from oil lamps scattered around the room created an intimate feel in spite of the soaring ceiling. The river-stone fireplace on my left held a crackling fire ringed by a set of cowhide sofas. On one side of the room, french doors opened to a registration desk and gift shop. On the opposite side was a matching set of doors leading to a dining hall. A large map of the area hung on the wall.

The wrangler who'd picked up the guests—William? Waylon? No, Wyatt—held a tray of glasses and moved among the guests. Though looking as if he stepped out of a roughstock rodeo event—bronc or bull riding—he seemed equally at home serving drinks. He spotted me and immediately approached.

"See you made it, Miz Graham. Something to drink?" He held out his tray. On his right hand, tattooed between thumb and forefinger, was a series of five dots.

I knew that pattern. The four dots forming a square represented prison walls. The dot in the middle was the prisoner.

I had one myself, albeit tattooed on my heart.

When I looked up, Wyatt was staring at me. A vein throbbed in his temple.

I rested my hand lightly over his tattoo. "Thank you. Just water, if you don't mind. No ice."

His face relaxed. "Good choice. Alcohol, dehydration, and altitude don't mix. Be right back."

I tried to snake my way to a dark, unoccupied corner, but an elderly man with a crown of white cotton-candy hair snagged my arm.

"Darby Graham? I'm your host, Roy Zaring. Welcome to Mule Shoe."

"Thank you, Mr. Zaring."

"Call me Roy. How did you find your cabin?"

"Everything so far seems exquisite."

Roy beamed. "If you need anything, my dear, just let my staff know." His gaze drifted to my left leg. "And if you want or need help—"

"I'm fine." I made an effort to relax my clenched hands. Obviously Roy was aware of my background.

"A package came for you from Scott Thomas at Clan Firinn. While you're at dinner, I'll have someone deliver it to your cabin."

"You can just give it to me now." I really didn't want anyone sauntering into my cabin.

Roy looked around at the mingling guests. "It might be more discreet . . ."

Did it come in a Depends box? "Of course. You're right. Is everyone here for the art class, or do you have other guests?"

"This week is the art class, though we specialize in team building. But not . . . it's . . . well . . . you know . . . I heard you rescued Shadow Woman's dogs."

A you know and a change of subject. Interesting. "Considering you don't have a phone, email, or internet, you seem remarkably well informed." I smiled. "Maybe carrier pigeons?"

"Close." He took a small black radio from his pocket. "Here on the ranch, we use walkie-talkies. For outside communication, we maintain a two-way radio for emergencies. At any rate, I liked the old woman and I'm just glad someone is taking care of her dogs."

"So you knew her. What happened?"

"I don't rightly know. About six months ago she came here for something. She seemed upset but left before anyone could figure out what she wanted. A month or so later, her mule wandered in. I contacted Sam at the store, figuring he would be the next to see her when she came in for supplies. I wanted him to let Shadow Woman know her mule was here and she could come and get him. Then I started to worry that something happened to her. I was about to call the sheriff for a welfare check when Liam told me she'd moved to Pocatello. Liam's a gossip monger. The next time I went to town, Sam showed me her bad check. Everyone assumed she'd taken her dogs, so it was a shock when they showed up in town."

"I see."

"In retrospect, you know, when she came here, she may have been looking for someone to take her dogs. Like I said, she was upset. She was . . . odd, so I gave her the benefit of the doubt. It could be she placed them elsewhere and they ran away. And she could have just turned her mule loose."

Was this why I was here? To look into an odd woman, a wandering mule, and a couple of stray dogs in the Idaho wilderness? If so, I'd certainly ace Clan Firinn's graduation test. Probably would graduate magna cum laude in my class of one. "I see. Is there any way I can contact her? Tell her the dogs are safe?"

Roy rubbed his chin. "Not that I know of. I don't even know her real name."

"Would anybody know more about her?"

"You might ask Bram. If he doesn't know, maybe he could find out. And if Sam still has the note and check, that might give you more information. Obviously she didn't leave a forwarding address or Sam would have tracked her down for his money. He's rich, but one of the stingiest men I've ever met."

A tinkling chime sounded. "Ah, dinner. Allow me, my dear." He put out his arm to escort me into the dining hall. The room had several square tables set for four. The two women I'd seen in Targhee Falls, Denim Shirt and her friend, were already seated. I'd barely taken my place when Bram joined us. He'd changed from his uniform into a sharply pressed western-cut shirt and jeans. He'd combed his hair, but an unruly lock tumbled to his forehead. He looked a little like the actor Matthew McConaughey. I tried not to stare. Or drool. *Stop it!* I had no place in my life for the complications of a relationship. Single, simple, sane. No saliva.

"Hello, I'm Dee Dee Harris." She held out her hand to Bram. Dee Dee had long gray hair held back by a turquoise and silver clip, denim shirt over a white shell, ankle-length skirt, and enough Native American jewelry to open a store. A very expensive store in Carmel-by-the-Sea. "You're the policeman from Targhee Falls."

"Technically, sheriff's deputy with Fremont County." He shook her hand. "Abraham White. Call me Bram."

"Hello, Bram." The second woman with short gray hair and wide shoulders—bearing a striking resemblance to the character Dorothy Zbornak in the television show *Golden Girls*, snagged his attention. "I'm Grace Tabor."

"Ma'am."

Grace looked at Dee Dee. "Oh, men are so polite here."

"I told you so," Dee Dee said.

The two dogs outside started barking. Before I could get up to see what the problem was, the room gave a *thump* and a shake, sending the hanging oil lamps swaying. Conversation ceased. This earthquake was brief. Thankfully.

Dee Dee, aka Denim Shirt, asked *Golden Girl* Grace, "That's two noticeable earthquakes in one day. Is that significant?" She turned to me. "Grace here was once a science teacher. She knows about earthquakes in general and Yellowstone in particular."

Grace sat up a bit straighter. "Well now, the Mule Shoe is less than five miles from the Yellowstone caldera, the so-called Yellowstone supervolcano."

Several young women in jeans and western-cut shirts started serving salads. Grace waited until everyone was served and she again had our attention. "A supervolcano, by definition, must eject at least 240 cubic miles of material and is capable of measuring a magnitude eight or more on the Volcanic Explosivity Index."

I braced for a pop quiz.

She noted Bram's furrowed brow. "The VEI is rather like the Richter scale for earthquakes. It's logarithmic, with each level representing a tenfold increase. Compared to the Mount St. Helens eruption in 1980, Yellowstone's would be two thousand times larger, and the worldwide devastation would be unimaginable." She took a delicate bite of lettuce, chewed on it a moment, then said, "One possible sign that the volcano is waking up is an increase in seismic activity. More earthquakes."

I put my fork down and shifted in my chair. The salad was unappealing juxtaposed against worldwide destruction. Whatever happened to less upsetting topics like politics or religion?

Dee Dee gave a forced chuckle. "I guess forewarned is forearmed. If we feel a big earthquake, it means the volcano is about to explode—"

Grace shook her head. "If the volcano explodes, we'll all be wiped out immediately."

All of us stared at her, then silently returned to our salads.

"Well now." Dee Dee cleared her throat. "Volcanos seem

to be a conversation killer. Bram, I know you're a police officer—"

"Sheriff—"

"Right. What do you do, Darby?"

"You first, Dee Dee." I smiled at her.

"I don't do much of anything except spend my late husband's money." She returned the smile. "And indulge my love of art, classical music, and Native American jewelry. Back to you!"

Flapperdoodle. Maybe I could steer the conversation to dog literature.

Our waitress, a young woman whose name tag said Zofia, with *Poland* underneath, returned and cleared our plates, then brought the main course. Each plate had a rustic plate cover, which the waitresses removed with a flourish. "Elk steak medallions." Zofia spoke with a thick accent. "With huckleberry red wine sauce, twice-baked Idaho potatoes, and roasted vegetable medley."

I hoped everyone would dive into their dinner and forget Dee Dee's question.

After taking a bite, closing her eyes, and moaning, Dee Dee repeated the question.

"I work for a company called Clan Firinn."

"Clan Firinn?" Dee Dee asked.

"Scottish Gaelic for 'Family of Truth.'" I felt Bram's gaze on me. Looking down, I pleated my napkin.

"I'd bet your career has something to do with words," Bram said.

I glanced at him quickly, then looked down again. The last thing I wanted to do was talk about me. "Something like that."

An awkward silence followed before Dee Dee gave up and changed the subject. While Dee Dee and Grace chatted, I took the opportunity to speak quietly to Bram. "Roy told me you might know something more about Shadow Woman."

"I'd never heard of her before I was given the order to shoot the dogs," he said discreetly.

"Wasn't she named in the court order? And maybe also her address?"

"You're right, she was. I'll see what I can find out."

"Thank you." I glanced at his tumble of hair. I wanted to brush it off his forehead.

He noted my glance and swiftly smoothed his hair.

The rest of the meal passed uneventfully, with Dee Dee and Grace expounding on art, Idaho, and the Mule Shoe. I could feel Bram's gaze on me, but I concentrated on my meal, acknowledging the others with an occasional head bob and grunt.

After dinner, Roy stood. "Good evening and, once again, welcome to Mule Shoe. This particular parcel of land was originally owned by the railroad tycoon Edward H. Harriman of the Union Pacific Railroad. He and the Guggenheim family owned other lands in Idaho, but they always referred to this location as their 'hidden gem.' Early on, the Harrimans gave this ranch to my family as a thank-you for their dedication to conservation. John Muir, in fact, visited here in 1913 and convinced the Harrimans to make wilderness conservation a condition of ownership."

Grace gave an approving nod and there was a smattering of applause.

"Now I'd like to introduce a few people. First of all, the woman responsible for the smooth day-to-day running of the resort. She started out as our cook and now is our general manager. I'm sure she has another name, but we all call her Cookie."

Another round of polite applause greeted the broad-shouldered, rangy woman in western garb and an unbleached muslin apron. "Thank all of you and welcome! I know you'll love Mule Shoe as much as I do. Please come to me if you need anything at all." She gave a brief wave and returned to the kitchen.

"You've all met Wyatt," Roy continued, "our wrangler." Wyatt nodded from the side of the room where he was leaning against the wall. He glanced at me, then away.

"Our three female staff members are all from Poland. Meet Zofia, Maja, and Alicja." The three women nodded or waved as they continued to clean up the dishes.

"Finally, Angie, do you want to stand and introduce yourself?"

A cheerful round woman in her forties with short, curly hair rose from her seat. "I'm Angie Burton, your watercolor instructor." Her booming voice echoed around the room. "I invite you to take a peek at the art room before you head to your cabins. Just follow me down the short hall next to the gift shop." She smiled and strolled from the room. The rest of the diners stood and started to make their way after her. I joined the throng, with Bram in front of me.

Roy approached and caught Bram's arm. "Got a moment?" Roy asked quietly.

I wanted to pause and listen, but Dee Dee came up beside me. "Are you an artist? You'll love Angie. She could teach a rock to paint." She continued to prattle on as we walked.

———

Bram turned to Roy. "What's happening?"

Roy waited until all the guests left the room. "The fire marshal called on the two-way. Said the arsonist burned a barn just outside of Targhee Falls on East Canyon Road. No one hurt, and they got the animals out in time, but he wants you to go there tomorrow and secure the place before returning to St. Anthony."

"Did he mention anything about the sheriff?"

"He said he tried but couldn't get through. The insurance company called him about the fire."

"How about you? Have you had any more . . . incidents?"

"A broken pipe in one of the cabins. Those folks left early. A mix-up in registration made two couples cancel out." Roy rubbed his jaw. "A few other things. Could be simply a run of bad luck. That's why I decided . . . Well, anyway." He shook his head, then took a deep breath. "We have a pretty full house this week. I keep hoping." He turned to leave.

"What's the story on Darby Graham?"

Roy paused. "What do you mean?"

"She mentioned at dinner that she works for a company, a Clan something—"

"Firinn."

"Yeah, that's it. Most of your guests are, quite frankly, stinking rich. Like they *own* companies like Amazon or Microsoft."

"The Gateses enjoyed their stay."

Bram smiled. "I'm sure. But Darby doesn't seem to fit that mold."

Roy slowly nodded. "Darby's special. Her . . . employer is a friend of mine. He sends me, um, guests on occasion. Folks that really need to be here." His eyes had become unfocused as he spoke. Now he sharpened his gaze on Bram. "This time I asked for a bit of help. Do me a favor. Keep what I just told you under your hat."

Now it was Bram's turn to slowly nod. "One last question. What does she do at Clan Firinn?"

"From what I've been told, she has something to do with words. Deception through language. Things like that."

———

The art room was as spacious as the rest of the lodge, with long tables covered in white paper, a single chair at each table, and a stack of art supplies. A smaller table with an angled mirror overhead for demonstrations took up one end of the room, with a set of chairs in front for the students.

Against one wall was a line of wooden lockers with our names neatly printed and placed into a holder. Each locker had a coat hook, a set of shelves, and an empty Mule Shoe backpack.

After everyone checked out their locker, selected a seat, and properly admired the new art toys, Angie again got our attention. "Class starts at nine thirty, right after breakfast. See you all in the morning."

Still shuffling along with the throng, I left the room and headed outside, then stopped. Since I'd been at dinner, the sun had set. It was dark.

I hated the dark.

As I turned to the lodge, Bram appeared beside me with a flashlight and held out his arm. "May I see you to your cabin, madam?" he asked in a bad British accent.

Flashlights were narrow beacons of light in the vast darkness. "Um . . ."

Wyatt appeared at my other side, also with a flashlight. "Looks like you have a full entourage escorting you."

My hands were already shaking and I knew my face would be drained of color. Darkness was one of my triggers. *Come on, Darby. It's been five years. Get over it.* "Um . . ."

A screen door slammed somewhere nearby and Cookie rounded the corner of the lodge carrying a lantern. She strolled to a bear-proof bin and tossed a paper bag inside, then turned to us. "Evening, Wyatt, Bram, Miss Graham." She peered closer at me. "Wyatt, why don't you take my lantern and let me have the flashlight. You can see a whole lot better." She grinned. "And I know you two good-looking fellers want to keep an eye on each other while escorting Miss Graham to her cabin."

My face grew warm.

Cookie and Wyatt exchanged lights, then the three of us moved toward my cabin. The dogs followed, Maverick at a wary distance. The silence made me feel awkward. The two men acted like I was some kind of prize. Like I was still desirable.

I wanted to tell them about the last five years, what I had done, why I was here.

Words abandoned me.

The very things that had once defined my life were gone.

The cabin was a warm haven after the evening chill. Someone had lit several lanterns, stoked the lively fire in the fireplace, and turned down the bed. Both men paused at the door, sending irritated glances at each other.

"Thank you both."

Slowly I closed the door. I listened for their retreating footsteps across the small porch. In a few moments the *click, click, click* of dog toenails was followed by a low whine. I opened the door to Holly and Maverick. Holly found a spot on the braided rug in front of the fireplace. Maverick tucked himself into a corner where he could observe the room.

I was suddenly too tired to unpack but still had my

exercises to do. While both dogs watched, I pulled my exercise mat from my suitcase, grabbed a pillow off the bed and a towel from the bathroom, then slipped off my slacks and shirt. I found my tattered FBI T-shirt and baggy shorts and pulled them on. Removing my heavy glasses, I placed them on the bedside table.

Sitting on the bed, I tugged off my prosthetic left leg, attached below my knee, and propped it beside me.

CHAPTER 4

I crouched beside the rear bumper of the truck, my heart hammering in my ears. Churning blackness swirled on the other side of the vehicle. I had to kill this bleak presence of evil, but I was unarmed.

It's a dream. Wake up!

Wait. I had a pistol. But something was terribly wrong. I looked around, but only tall grasses surrounded me. *Wake up!*

He yelled my name.

I turned and ran. His voice retreated in the distance. *Coward!* The earth rushed up to meet me. The raw smell of dirt filled my nose. Reaching forward, I dug my nails into the ground and pulled. I gained a few inches. Again I clawed forward. I tried to go faster, but something held my leg. Twisting around, I looked behind me.

The swirling blackness crept up my leg. I screamed.

Something wet touched my face, shoved against me. I pushed it away. It came again, more insistently. The scene faded, but the solid feel of the creature continued.

Opening my mouth to scream, I felt something wet slap against my teeth. I jerked upright, gasping.

Holly was on the bed, licking my face and nudging me awake.

The nightmare clung to my brain like pine pitch, reluctant to let go. I pushed Holly away from her frantic concern and sat up. My T-shirt was soaked. The sheets wrapped around my right ankle. The lamps I'd left flickering sent eerie shadows dancing around the cabin.

I needed to clear my head. A shot of whiskey would hit the spot, but I'd been on the wagon for three years now. And the easy fix of popping pills was no longer an option. I wasn't going back there.

I left my oversized glasses beside the bed. I didn't need them to see. They were only a prop I allowed myself to discourage unwanted attention.

Getting around in the middle of the night was a challenge for any leg amputee. The options were hopping, crawling, or crutches. Putting on and taking off the prosthesis was very involved for a simple trip to the bathroom. My solution was an iWALK, an exoskeletal temporary lower-leg prosthetic. The device was a crutch-like lower leg with a curved top where I put my knee. It was held in place by Velcro straps that went up my thigh and around my residual limb. From the front, I looked like I had a crutch from the knee down. From the side, my residual limb stuck out behind. Not very attractive, but very useful. The dogs watched with interest as I strapped on this mobility device.

I moved to the kitchen area. A pot of tea might calm me. The kitchen was fortunately stocked with both Yorkshire Gold and Taylors Organic Chamomile.

Confronting Sam about shooting the dogs, or maybe simply being somewhere new, had triggered my PTSD dreams. I hoped this episode would be short-lived.

While the water heated on the small gas stove, I found the package from Clan Firinn and placed it beside one of the chairs. I started unpacking my suitcase and hanging up my clothes. A large duffel bag, in addition to my suitcase, held my work materials and iWALK. With all my luggage, I always looked like I was moving in for a month.

The teapot sputtered and started to whistle. I dropped a tea bag into a cup, added the hot water, then brought it to the overstuffed chair by the fireplace. The fire had dropped to just glowing embers. After I added a small log and stirred the coals, the log caught fire.

Something moaned behind me.

I turned.

Holly had snagged the pillow, somehow crawled under the blanket, and was stretched out on my bed. Maverick, on the other hand, lay on the hard floor, pressed against the door like a giant draft stopper.

"The original odd couple," I said to both dogs. "A hedonist and an ascetic. An extrovert and an introvert." Curling up in the chair with my tea, I watched the dogs until the nightmare completely dissipated.

I set my tea aside and opened the package. On top was a cover letter.

Darby,

Roy Zaring has been a longtime patron and supporter of the work we do here at Clan Firinn. He's invited a number of our people to stay at the resort in the past. He's getting up to retirement age and is thinking about selling the ranch but is concerned about some random events that could become a problem. His letter is enclosed.

We thought this small assignment would be an easy way for you to reenter your field, and Mule Shoe is always a great experience. Study the papers, talk to a few people, then give us a report. We'll follow up with Roy.

Scott

I set Scott's note aside and pulled out Roy's letter.

Dear Scott,

I hope this letter finds you well. As I told you the last time we talked, I'm thinking of selling the family ranch. I do so reluctantly as it's been in my family for generations. Over the past few months, however, a series of "accidents" has made me wonder if someone is trying to thwart my plans. It started small—a burst pipe, a mix-up in reservations—but now I have some major concerns. Our primary focus, and income source, is our team-building program. With the death of two patrons, and several other incidents, I have lost liability coverage and am on notice of losing all my insurance. This all may be a run of very bad luck as I can't put my finger on any particular pattern, but I could use another set of eyes. Please be discreet.

Roy

Insurance statements, letters from guests, a timeline of events, employee information, and reservations for the resort rounded out the packet. I could probably knock this out in a few hours, do some casual interviews, then grab the next horse and wagon back to town. Yee-haw.

My irritation with Scott dissolved. I might even enjoy this.

Under all the paperwork was some bubble wrap enclosing a plastic sandwich bag with three small rocks inside and a note. I unfolded the note.

Darby,

I wanted to give this to you in person before you left but was called away. As per our tradition with all residents of Clan Firinn when they leave for the first time, I'm giving you two Bible verses and a small gift. The first verse is for the challenges of the present. It's from Joshua 1:9. "This is my command—be strong and courageous! Do not be afraid or discouraged. For the Lord your God is with you wherever you go." The second you will need to look up— Jeremiah 29:11. This will help with your future. The gift is in the plastic bag. Memorize the verses and reflect on them. Carry the gift with you. When the time comes, you'll know what to do with both.

Scott Thomas

I hadn't packed the Bible they gave me when I arrived at Clan Firinn. Although daily chapel was a part of the Clan Firinn program, I'd left my faith five years ago.

Maverick stood, then walked over and sat in front of me, but well out of reach.

"What?"

He blinked.

"Are you hungry? Thirsty?"

He cocked his head but remained seated. He was so large, even seated, that his head was higher than mine.

"Need to go to the bathroom? Eat a treat? Discuss whether you cried more over *Marley and Me* or *Old Yeller*?"

His gaze went to the note still in my hand.

"Do you want to know what it said?" I read it to him, then held up the rocks. "Got any ideas for these?" *I'm talking to a dog.*

He yawned.

"Yeah, well, you're not exactly a sparkling conversationalist yourself. Come to think of it, your previous owner was Shadow Woman. Probably not much for rousing debate.

Am I a step up or a step down?" *Not only am I talking to the dog, I'm waiting for an answer.*

The chamomile tea didn't make me sleepy. Or maybe the thought of another visit from my nightmare kept me on edge. Whatever the case, I was restlessly awake.

What now? Art class wouldn't start for several more hours. Darkness lurked outside. No internet to surf or television to watch. But I was alone . . . wasn't that something I sought?

I casually looked at the paperwork Roy had sent to Clan Firinn, focusing on the employee information. As I'd already figured out, Wyatt had been in prison on an assault charge, but that was when he was much younger. Cookie's real name was Irma Dankworth. No wonder she didn't mind Cookie.

I checked out several magazines on the end table. *Outdoor Idaho* had an interesting story on livestock guardian dogs. Pictured were Great Pyrenees, Akbash, and an Anatolian Shepherd. I folded a corner down and left the magazine on the top of the stack. I didn't feel like reading.

The fire was burning down. I pulled out another small log and added it, stirring the coals to freshen the blaze. A small door behind the stacked logs allowed someone to restock the fuel from outside without hauling the logs through the cabin. They'd thought of every detail.

I slipped out of my iWALK, curled up, and watched the fire.

Barking jerked me awake. Maverick was on his feet and

Holly had leaped off the bed. I didn't have to wait long for the earthquake. This one was short, almost an earth shiver.

What had Grace, the retired teacher, said about the number of earthquakes? *One possible sign that the volcano is waking up is an increase in seismic activity. More earthquakes.*

After tugging on my iWALK, I slowly stood. Was God really going to take me out with a supervolcano? He could have simply let me die.

But I didn't believe in God.

"Stop it!" I said out loud. Both dogs gave me a questioning look. The light seeping in around the curtains told me it was daybreak. Finally. I opened the door and let the dogs out for their run.

As always, the night before I'd rolled down the outer sleeve of my prosthetic leg, removed the liner, washed it, and hung it up to dry. I'd washed my residual limb, then put on a compression sock for the night, which helped reduce phantom pain. In the morning I reversed these steps, took a shower, and downed several cups of coffee.

I got as far as the door before returning to put on my glasses, then dropped the three rocks into my back pocket. They tugged my pants down. I shifted them to a front pocket where they did the same. *What was Scott thinking?* He could have given me three hankies. Three dollars. Three platinum credit cards. *Now we're talking.* I finally put one rock per pocket. If I was going to have floppy pants and lumpy hips and rear, at least I'd have a fairly even sag.

A high-pitched buzzing and rank odor greeted me outside. I followed the sound and smell to the next cabin. Both dogs were fixated on something above them.

A very dead raccoon was wedged between the end logs of the cabin.

My stomach tightened, a jolt of acid burned the back of my throat, and my neck itched as if a thousand mosquitos had bitten me.

There was no way that critter could have ended up there on its own.

And if it hadn't crawled up between the logs, then someone put it there.

Maybe. Raccoons were notoriously inquisitive creatures. And they were known for being host to many diseases, such as rabies and distemper.

My neck continued to itch.

———

Bram spent the night on the top bunk in the seasonal staff building. His roomies were a maintenance man from West Yellowstone, a dishwasher from St. Anthony, and an assistant horse wrangler from Cheyenne. The only name he could remember belonged to the dishwasher, whom they called Spuds. St. Anthony was in the middle of potato country.

The building had a shared living area in the middle, with the women's quarters on the other side. Wyatt, Angela, and Cookie had their own private quarters in a separate building. Roy lived above the lodge.

Bram woke with Darby on his mind. What was it about her that stayed in his thoughts? *Maybe because she's the first attractive and interesting woman I've met in a long while.* After finishing high school and graduating from the Citadel, the Military College of South Carolina, he'd done a stint in the navy, then sought out and been hired by the Fremont County Sheriff's Department. Unfortunately, the number of available females in the county was limited. Extremely limited.

And his time was equally limited.

He'd finally looked into internet dating services and met Rachel. Perfect in almost every way—beautiful, slender, intelligent—but with the morals of an alley cat. The divorce came six months after the wedding when he found her in bed with his best friend.

Once bitten, twice shy, as his grandmother used to say.

Sitting up, he swung his legs over the bed and jumped down. The other male staff members had already left to start their chores. The sheriff would expect him to head back at daybreak, and he'd slept in.

He rolled up his jeans and shirt as well as yesterday's uniform shirt and placed them into a laundry bag. He'd arranged some months ago for one of the staff to wash and iron his clothes and have them ready whenever he was here. He hated the smell, and feel, of stale clothing. After a long shower, and longer battle with his hair, he dressed in a fresh uniform shirt and headed to the kitchen for a cup or two of coffee before harnessing the horse for the trip to town.

———

The dogs trailed me to the lodge and selected a patch of grass on the right of the building to observe any activity.

An early morning jogger passed through the trees in the distance. I admired the discipline it took to run daily when no one was chasing you.

A fire blazed in the oversized fireplace, but none of the guests had arrived at the lobby. The sign outside the dining room stated breakfast would be ready in a half hour, and the building was filled with the mouthwatering aromas of bacon, cinnamon, and baking bread.

Next to the map of Mule Shoe on the wall hung a photograph that looked like it was taken for a Christmas card. Snow blanketed the ground, with cobalt-blue shadows under the trees. Sam's big Belgium, covered with bells, was hitched to his wagon that had been decked out in red bows and pine boughs. Sam and Cookie were on the spring seat, waving at the photographer. In the back, Wyatt, Roy, and the rest of the staff, all wearing red Santa hats and ugly sweaters, were laughing. Underneath, written in ink, was *Have a Merry Christmas, from our family to yours.*

I turned away quickly. The nearest thing to a family I had now were two dogs, one of which wouldn't even come near me. "Next thing I'll need is pâté and crackers with my whine," I whispered.

The gift shop, on the opposite side, was open, although no one was staffing it at the moment. I sorted through racks of expensive western wear and read the back-cover copy on a few books before moving to the jewelry case. Mounted gemstone earrings and necklaces were arranged by color in their black-velvet cases.

Without thinking, I rubbed the ring finger of my left hand, then quickly turned away, crashing into Roy.

"Looking for someone to show you some jewelry?"

"I—"

"Idaho's nickname is the Gem State." He moved to the opposite side of the display and opened it with a key.

"Really? I need to tell you—"

"This dark red stone is a star garnet." He pulled out a pendant and held it under a light to show a six-rayed star. "Northern Idaho is the only place you can find it in the United States." He touched the next piece. "This rare pink opal is also from Idaho, as well as this amethyst and topaz."

"Interesting. But I want to—"

"Only a few gemstones aren't found here. Diamonds, of course. Rubies. And emeralds."

Emeralds. I broke out in a sweat and touched my ring finger. *Great.* Was jewelry joining darkness and guns as PTSD triggers?

Roy didn't seem to notice. He placed a pair of rich,

cornflower-blue faceted stone earrings on the counter. "And these beauties are Yogo sapphires from Montana."

"And they have my name on them." An immaculately dressed woman with a soft southern drawl appeared beside me. "Sorry, my dear, but I've no willpower when it comes to cut stones."

She wasn't kidding. She positively glittered, from her diamond studs to the rock on her finger. Quite the art class—*Golden Girl* Grace and Dee Dee Denim was joined by Madam Sparkles. With my lumpy rocks in my pockets, that would make me Dumpy Darby.

My moment to talk to Roy about the dead raccoon had passed. "The sapphires are all yours."

"Done." Roy beamed at Madam Sparkles as he slid the earrings across the counter to her.

I'd had a chance to see the price tag. The earrings cost more than my car. I wanted to mentally *tut-tut* her spending habits, but having just invested in an almost eight-hundred-dollar bag of dog food and two stray dogs, I was hardly a model of frugality.

Roy pulled out a small book and turned it so I could see. "This is from the International Gem Society and tells you about colored gemstones as well as their value. You'll learn to appreciate the rare Yogo. You can borrow it. Now, over there"—he pointed with pride to a wall display behind me—"is my collection of raw minerals, and—"

"Breakfast is served." Wyatt had entered. While I'd been

in the gift shop, the lobby had filled with guests who were now filing into the dining area.

Roy grinned at me. "I do get carried away. Come, my dear, let me see you to your table."

Taking the book, I followed everyone toward the dining room. On the way, I was finally able to tell Roy about the raccoon.

"Oh dear. I hope you didn't touch it. Raccoons are notorious for carrying rabies."

"No, I didn't touch it, but you need to look at it. I'm wondering if the raccoon was, maybe, placed there."

"That seems far-fetched." We'd reached the table and Roy patted me on the hand. "We'll talk later," he whispered.

This time I was seated with the couple and their teenage son. The young man stared at the table as if he could make a cell phone appear by sheer will. I was surprised his fingers didn't automatically scroll down his napkin.

The father looked like he worked out daily. His neck was as wide as his face and his shoulder muscles strained at his shirt. His olive complexion was a richer brown from a deep tan.

On impulse I asked him, "Were you out jogging earlier?"

He nodded at me. "I was. Allow me to introduce myself. I am Teodoro Rinaldi. This is my wife, Nona, and my son, Riccardo."

"Nice to meet you, Mr. and Mrs. Rinaldi. I'm Darby Graham."

"Please, call me Teddy." He had a slight accent.

The waitress brought around coffee and small menus with several breakfast choices. After we'd chosen our meals, Teddy turned to his son and whispered, *"Sei ancora punito per essere sgattaiolato fuori la scorsa notte. Rimarrai in la stanza fino al termine della lezione. Ora siediti e smetti di mettermi in imbarazzo."*

He'd just said to his son, *You are still being punished for sneaking out last night. You will remain in the cabin until we finish class. Now sit up and stop embarrassing me.*

An awkward silence followed. My neck tingled with an uneasy itch. I really wanted to ask what on earth the young man hoped to find at night in the middle of an Idaho wilderness. Instead, I concentrated on stirring cream into my coffee so he wouldn't realize I understood Italian. And I could take this opportunity to start interviewing people.

"Teddy, is this your first visit to Mule Shoe?"

"Yes, but I'd heard about it, of course . . ." Now it was his turn to stir his coffee.

Of course? Perhaps something there. He'd abruptly stopped speaking. *Interesting.*

"Have you been studying watercolor painting for long?" Nona asked me after first shooting a deadly glance at both her husband and son.

"First time." Breakfast came and ended further conversation.

Halfway through the meal I caught a glimpse of Bram heading down the road driving the wagon. My quick inhale of air made Teddy look up. I made a point of staring out into the lobby.

Angie, the art instructor, was crossing the lobby heading toward the dining room. I was about to look away but noticed her lips were pressed tightly together and her hands balled into fists. I surreptitiously watched her as I sipped my coffee. No one else seemed aware of her presence. She arrived at the door, looked around the room, then caught Roy's attention. He stood and moved toward her. She didn't wait for him but spun and stalked away.

"Excuse me." I placed my napkin on the table, picked up the book, and stood. "I need to use the powder room."

Teddy politely rose slightly in his chair, and Nona gave me a half smile. "See you in class."

I slipped from the room. Neither Roy nor Angie were in the lobby, but I could hear voices coming from the art room. I quietly followed the sound.

"Who would *do* such a thing?" Angie's high-pitched voice conveyed outrage. "I can't start class. I don't even know where to start!"

The art room door stood open. From my position in the hall, I could easily see the upended tables, overturned easels, paper-strewn floor, and tubes of paint and brushes strewn across the front table.

CHAPTER 5

Roy spotted me. "Darby, you were here when I got in. Did you see anyone around? Hear anything?"

I thought about the sullen Riccardo roaming around last night. "I saw Mr. Rinaldi jogging in the distance. No one was around the lodge when I got here and I didn't hear anyone in here. You might, however, talk to Riccardo."

Roy walked closer. "I . . . we'd appreciate it if you don't mention this or the dead raccoon to the other guests."

"Of course."

"Angie," Roy said in a soothing voice, "why don't you grab up some sketchbooks and take a short hike to the pond. Do some of that . . . what's the word?"

"Plein air."

"Yeah, that's it. I'll get the room cleaned up. No one any wiser. We'll look into the vandal while you're gone. And we'll keep this room locked up from now on."

"Thank you, Roy." Angie ran a hand through her hair. "This is just all so . . . upsetting. You need to catch the man who did this."

"Or the woman," Roy said. "I'll go make an announcement."

I turned to leave.

"Darby?" Angie bellowed. "Could you help me find the sketchbooks and drawing supplies?" Apparently she didn't have a volume control on her voice.

"Of course."

She picked up a black wire-bound book and held it so I could see it. "The sketchpads look like this." Another quick glance around the room and she lifted a metal tin beside an overturned chair. "Pencil set."

Lifting a nearby chair, I found two more sketchpads.

"Roy tells me you're in law enforcement."

I turned so she couldn't see my expression. "No."

"Oh. I wonder why he thought that."

I shrugged.

"He could use a good investigator." She stopped searching for art supplies for a moment. "Wait. Are you a *private* investigator?"

"No."

"Oh well, just asking. I'm concerned about Roy. He's had a lot of bad luck lately. Or what may seem like bad luck."

"Really?" I would need to pursue several topics Angie had brought up, such as why she believed me to be an undercover investigator and what she meant by "bad luck," but before I could ask, she started for the door.

"Thanks. There are ten in the class, so this should be

enough for everyone." She took one last look around the trashed room. "Let's find the group and head out. At least this day won't be a complete waste."

———

Bram arrived in Targhee Falls, where Sam met him outside the store. "Thanks for the horse and wagon, Sam. Do you want me to unhitch him?"

"Nah. I got it. The sheriff left word for you to call her when you got here."

It must be important or the sheriff would have waited for him to call on the radio or when he got into cell-service range. Bram headed toward the store but paused at the parking lot. All the Mule Shoe guests had parked in the lot. On impulse, he jotted down the license plates. His interest in Darby was pushing him into borderline-unprofessional behavior. Even when he'd tried to track down his family history, he'd been scrupulous not to use confidential documents.

On entering the store, he spotted Julia flirting with Liam, the deliveryman. She noticed him and sashayed over. "Hello, Bram."

He nodded at her. "I need to use the phone."

She frowned, pointed to the office, then stalked over to Liam and draped one arm around his shoulder. Her gaze shot to him to see if he was paying attention.

If jealousy was what she intended, she was wasting her

time. Liam was a far easier target for her amorous advances than he was. She was hardly in Bram's pool of potentials for marriage bliss. She'd been married three times already. Or was it four?

Liam's eyes opened wide, then he grinned and put his hand on her waist.

If Liam was looking for a girlfriend, Bram wasn't about to get in the way. Liam's mother was Bram's boss, the sheriff.

He sat behind Sam's desk and dialed. "You wanted me to call."

"Yes. I didn't want this to be overheard on the radio."

"I got the message from the fire marshal—"

"Oh? Why did he call you?"

"He couldn't get hold of you. He asked me to secure the barn and he'll go ahead and do the investigation."

"He should have waited to get my go-ahead. We have protocols—"

"I think the insurance company asked him. Anyway, I'll run over—"

"I need you to do a welfare check." She gave him the address.

"Not a problem. I'll go right after I secure the barn. Did a note arrive?" The arsonist had written taunting notes to the sheriff after each fire, a fact the department had withheld from the public.

"Yes, and it's being processed, as usual. I need you to do the welfare check first. I can send someone else out on the arson. Again, that's not why I wanted to talk to you. Sam told me what happened with the dogs you were sent to take care of."

Bram shifted and cleared his throat. "I . . . um—"

"Next time I send you out to do something, just do it. Don't get involved in conflict resolution. You could have put the sheriff's department in a lot of hot water. Do you even know if those dogs are vaccinated against rabies? What if they bite that woman . . ."

He made a point of loosening the tight grip he had on the phone receiver as his boss continued her rant. She finally finished and hung up.

Bram stayed seated. He knew his face would reflect the tongue-lashing he'd just received and he didn't want the sheriff's son to report the reaction to his mom.

He picked up the local paper lying on the edge of the desk. A photo of the latest arson was splashed across the front page. The last paragraph of the story snagged his attention. Someone had started a recall petition for the sheriff due to her lack of progress in solving the case. *Whoa.* No wonder she was in such a black mood. He refolded the paper, stood, and headed for his parked patrol SUV.

"Bram." Liam caught his attention as he strolled through the store. "Hey, did you hear the news?"

Bram sighed and glanced at Julia. The woman was pointedly straightening boxes of macaroni.

He really didn't have time to listen to Liam's gossip, but he didn't want to give his boss another reason to chew him out by ignoring what she called "potential informa-tion sources." Especially if the source was her only child.

"What news?"

Liam grinned and moved closer. "About the recall peti-tion for my mom."

"I just saw it in the paper." Bram started to leave.

"She's already looking for a new job. No way we're stay-ing here." Liam looked around as if someone might overhear them, then said quietly, "San Francisco or Denver. Some-place big. We're getting out of this podunk town and state."

"I take it you would move with her?"

"Yeah. Get me a job that really pays, you know? Get my own place."

Julia gave up her pretense of work. "You rat! I thought we'd . . ." She stomped into the restroom and slammed the door.

Bram bit back a smile. "And I would guess Julia's not going to be joining you."

"No way! You got that right."

———

Roy was just finishing up his announcement as I entered the dining room.

". . . you'll return here for lunch. And be sure you fill up those water bottles you received in your welcome bags. As refreshing as the ponds and streams look, you can't drink the water. Beavers live in the pond and the water is full of giardia, a parasite. We'll assemble outside in"—he glanced at his watch—"twenty minutes."

Everyone rose and funneled out to head to their cabins.

The raccoon had been removed, and the dogs were sprawled across my cabin's small porch. Maverick took up most of the space, with Holly staking out a spot in the corner. The dogs stood at my arrival and trailed me into the room. I dropped off the book, found the water bottle and filled it, then attached it to my belt by the carabiner. Grabbing a lightweight jacket, I looked around the room. My neck tingled slightly. I didn't like the idea of leaving my things in an unlocked cabin and going for a long hike. Roy may have felt everyone was honest at the ranch, but the condition of the art room proved him wrong. That room, at least, would now be locked.

I tucked my wallet and the letters from Scott Thomas and Roy inside my Mule Shoe bag. Shadow Woman's drawings were still there.

I checked my watch. Still time to do a little work. Opening a notebook, I started a new page on what I'd learned and seen, along with questions I needed to follow up on. It seemed strange to use a pen and paper rather than my laptop. Once again I went over the materials from Roy—insurance statements, letters from guests, a timeline of events, employee information, and resort reservations. The problems seemed to start in the spring with a wrongful-death lawsuit over a hiking accident. Insurance claims for water damage, electrical problems in the staff building, and injuries from a horseback riding incident followed. A letter from the insurance carrier noted they would no longer cover the team-building activities, and any more claims would result in their dropping Mule Shoe entirely. The final set of papers were various offers, dating back to the first of the year, to purchase Mule Shoe. The offers came from a variety of real estate agencies and appeared to be generous at first, but considerably lower after the lawsuit and accidents. That did raise the possibility of deliberate sabotage, in which case I'd need to find out who wanted to buy the resort.

I closed the notebook, removed Shadow Woman's drawings from my bag, moved to the table, and spread out the artwork. There were eight drawings, all well rendered and dated.

The drawings the clerk had placed into the old phone book were a portrait of Sam and a rather odd sketch of two men standing on what looked like a cloud with two lines coming out at the bottom.

Sam's image wasn't particularly flattering. No wonder the clerk hid this one from her boss.

In addition to Sam's sketch, there was one of Roy, a woman I didn't recognize, and a fourth, probably a self-portrait—a face mostly hidden in darkness. All of the portraits were off somehow, capturing enough of the likeness to be identifiable, but not totally accurate when it came to the faces I knew.

The remaining drawings were of her dogs beside a stream, and two landscapes. Underneath all the sketches were a check and note. The check was from Gem Mountain Bank and had a full name and address—Mae Haas, PO Box 12, Targhee Falls, Idaho. *Account closed* was stamped across the check. Mae Haas. Shadow Woman.

The typewritten note was equally unhelpful.

Sam, Im moved to Pocatello. Heres what i owe you.

Returning the drawings, check, and note to their folder, I added them to the bag. I grabbed up my camera, called the dogs to follow, and tramped back to the lodge. No one had arrived yet. Wandering into the as-yet unlocked art room, I looked for a place to store my things.

All the locker doors had been opened, and many of the Mule Shoe backpacks tossed to the floor. My locker was untouched. I stuffed my things into the backpack and stepped back to see the results. The backpack still looked empty. *Perfect.* Hiding in plain sight.

I took one last look around. Something was bothering me, but I couldn't put my finger on it.

Returning outside, I found Dee Dee Denim and *Golden Girl* Grace in deep conversation with Teddy and Nona. No sign of Riccardo. I wondered if he would stay in their cabin as his dad demanded. Somehow that seemed unlikely. Hiding my wallet and other things in the soon-to-be-locked art room had been a good decision.

We were joined by Madam Sparkles and a distinguished-looking older gentleman, both looking like they had stepped out of an REI catalog. Several other class members wandered over.

Cookie joined us and handed out sheets of paper. "After your class, you can take advantage of some of our other activities. This is a list. Look it over and if something appeals to you, mark it, write your name on the paper, and give it to me. I'll get it all set up for you."

I read my copy. The first item made my hand sweaty. Horseback riding. *I'm not ready for that yet.* Gold panning. Nature hike. Target practice. Star gazing. Now I was shaking. Two PTSD triggers on a single sheet of paper. I quietly folded the list and stuffed it in my pocket.

Angie arrived and began handing out sketchpads and pencil tins. "Ready, everyone?" She didn't wait for a response but set out at a brisk pace along a marked path to the right of the lodge.

I thought the dogs would accompany me, but they opted to investigate the park-like grounds. Maverick marked every tree to stake out their new territory.

The sky was a rich, ultramarine blue, the crisp autumn air filled with the aroma of pine needles, and the landscape worthy of an Ansel Adams photograph. We moved toward the cedar grove on the left side of the lodge. Beyond the fern-like needles, a log triplex appeared. Angie pointed. "Cookie, Wyatt, and I stay there if you ever need to find someone after hours. The rest of the staff are in the bunkhouse behind the lodge."

The trail dipped slightly downward, then paralleled a

burbling stream. The eight-thousand-foot elevation left us all gasping for breath, even at our leisurely pace.

Farther up the trail we arrived at a small waterfall gushing around mossy granite rocks and forming an amber-and-emerald-colored pool. We paused to admire the scene, and I took a couple of photos. The rest of the guests watched me with envy. Their ability to take photos had vanished with their cell phones. We climbed a short distance. The stream originated from a small lake, with cattails at the far side and a pebble beach on ours. Log benches on the beach formed a semicircle, allowing us to sit and admire the view. To my left was a small shelter that probably served as a blind for photographing wildlife. I could have stayed there all day.

Madam Sparkles and the well-dressed man sat next to me. "We haven't formally met yet. I'm Stacy, and this is ma husband, Peter. Isn't this the most beautiful place in the world?"

If you don't count the numerous earthquakes and potential for a massive volcano eruption . . . I nodded. "I'm Darby and, yes, it's paradise."

"Miss Darby," Peter said. "Pleasure to make your acquaintance."

Stacy had replaced her diamond studs with the Yogo sapphires. They matched her deep blue eyes.

"Is this your first visit to Mule Shoe?" I asked.

"Yes, but it will definitely not be our last." Stacy touched her husband's arm. "Right, my dear?"

Peter nodded.

Angie walked in front of the impromptu classroom. "After I finish the lesson, feel free to spread out and sketch." I suspected Roy could hear her back at the lodge. "For those of you new to plein air sketching, keep your drawing loose. Capture the essence of the landscape and don't be bogged down by details. Think about the whole range of values—"

Stacy raised her hand. "I'm so new to this. What do you mean by *range of values*?"

"The term *value* in art means light or darkness and is usually referred to as relative value. For example, if I put my hand on my pants"—she placed her hand on the ample thigh of her dark blue jeans—"my hand is lighter than my jeans." She rested her hand on her white T-shirt. "But my hand is darker than my shirt. In a successful drawing, you'll want the full range of values, from lightest light—your white paper—to the darkest dark your pencil will create. This will bring dimension to your work."

The slight breeze, smelling of boggy plant life, cooled the air around me, making me grateful for my light coat as Angie gave us further instructions. Another puff of wind brought the whiff of fish. I glanced around, but no one else was reacting. The scent came again. Not just any fish. Sardines.

I had to be imagining the smell. I was pretty sure the fish in this pond didn't reek of canned sardines.

"Okay." Angie waved her arms. "Find a good spot and start drawing. I need to grab a jacket, but when I return, I'll be wandering around to help you."

Everyone stood and wandered around, looking for the perfect angle and view. I opted to locate the source of the smell. I moved to a rocky outcropping near the water. The tang of wet dog replaced the sardine scent.

I stopped and stared at the woods. The dense pines showed only black between the branches, with snowberry shrubs around the trunks. The wet-dog odor grew more pungent, now joined by a scratching sound. Looking around, I checked to see if anyone nearby noticed the sound and smell. The closest to me were Dee Dee and Grace. Both were seated on a log at some distance and intent on their sketches.

Several branches moved and I caught a glimpse of something brown.

I took a step backward.

A massive muzzle poked through the underbrush, followed by two beady eyes peering from an immense brown head. *Grizzly.*

CHAPTER 6

Adrenaline flooded my body. I was rooted to the ground, unable to move, to think.

The bear sniffed the air, huffing slightly.

The sound shot through me. *Do I run? Play dead? Climb a tree?* I couldn't remember. Couldn't focus. Couldn't unstick my limbs.

A woman screamed, the shriek ripping up my spine.

The bear reared. He towered over six feet tall.

I spun away. *Too fast. Too fast!* My prosthetic leg didn't react fast enough. I fell.

The two women raced away down the path toward the resort. I pushed against the ground to rise, glancing over my shoulder.

The bear had dropped to all fours.

Scrambling upward, I faced the charging grizzly.

Branches snapped. His huffing grew closer, his body larger. I was going to die. Again.

A blur of brown and black flew past me.

I turned.

Maverick, hackles raised, flew directly at the bear with

a flurry of snarls and teeth. Holly flanked him, barking wildly.

The bear roared at the dogs, then took a swipe at Maverick. The huge dog dodged the paw and continued his barrage.

Holly got close enough to nip his leg.

He spun and swatted at her, allowing Maverick to get in a bite of his own.

The grizzly had enough. He turned and loped into the trees.

Holly stopped barking and trotted over to me. I hugged her. "Oh, you beautiful girl! You brave, beautiful girl."

Maverick continued to bark, albeit more intermittently, as if to be sure the bear got the message.

"Are you okay? Are you hurt?" Wyatt arrived, rifle in hand.

Behind him was Angie, panting from the run, face pale. "Dee Dee and Grace told us about the bear."

"I'm fine." I continued to pat Holly. "Let's just say if I had the hiccups, they're gone now."

"We usually don't have a problem with black bears." Wyatt swung his rifle over his shoulder by its sling. "We're very careful with food and garbage."

"I don't think it was a black bear. It was brown—"

"Black bears come in brown, cinnamon, tan, and a variety of other colors." Wyatt smiled and waved me toward the resort. "He was probably just warning you off. We should have sent everyone out with bear bells."

Or a loaded rifle. That wasn't a black bear. I wasn't going to argue with them, but I recognized that distinctive hump over the shoulder, broad head, and size. Only a grizzly has that body structure. When I used to trail ride my horse, I had to know the difference. Black bear = run fast. Grizzly = run for your life. I turned away from them and patted my leg to get Maverick to come closer. I felt the three rocks Scott had given me. I should have thrown them at the bear. *Ha!* That would have just made the grizzly mad.

I called Maverick's name. The dog remained at a distance but stopped barking.

Angie started walking down the trail with Holly and me behind. Wyatt brought up the rear. Maverick slowly followed.

After a step, I heard it. My prosthesis had a tiny squeak. *Great.* Just what I needed. Maybe no one would notice.

Squeak.

Holly perked up and sniffed my leg.

Squeak.

I winced. *There goes my career as a cat burglar.* I hoped a small amount of plumber's tape on the pin would help. I wouldn't be able to get it adjusted until I returned to civilization.

Maybe I could ask for that bear bell and wear it to hide the sound? Come to think of it, a bear bell would have been handy during our outing. Wyatt mentioned how careful they were with garbage. If bears had been a problem in the past, we *would* have been given bells, or someone would have been armed to warn them off.

The lack of concern for bears was possible evidence that *this* bear had been deliberately lured close. Why?

Don't assume the worst. When a bear needed to be live-trapped for relocation, the strong odor of sardines or tuna was the perfect bait. "Would the Department of Fish and Game be live-trapping a rogue bear?"

Angie stopped and turned. "Why would you think that?"

I shrugged and feigned indifference. "Just a thought." A thought that sent a chill down my arms. What if it wasn't the Rinaldis' son who trashed the art room? What if someone did that to make sure we'd go to the pond, where a can of sardines lured in a bear?

That didn't make sense. Roy had suggested we go up to the pond. Why would he be trying to frighten or hurt his guests? And just leaving out a can of sardines didn't mean a bear would wander by. *Right.* Then why was my neck itching?

———

Bram pulled out of the parking lot and headed over to secure the fire scene for the fire marshal. His boss may have wanted that welfare check first, but he was close to the ranch and securing the scene wouldn't take long.

From the county road, the burned-out shell of the barn

was easy enough to spot. A quick interview with the owners made it clear they hadn't seen or heard anything, and the livestock that had been in the building got out safely. The barn itself was falling down, and insurance would pay for a new structure. The owners seemed almost grateful for the fire.

As he surrounded the building with crime scene tape, he thought about that. Could the arsonist be up for hire—get rid of old buildings for the insurance money? Not particularly original, but possible.

The fire marshal arrived by the time he was done stringing the tape. This was a new guy. "Hey there." He held out his hand. "Deputy Bram White, thanks for being so prompt."

"Deputy. I'm Tom Meyer." The young man shook Bram's hand.

"Could I ask you a few questions about our pyromaniac?"

"Sure, but I don't think you have a pyromaniac. That's extremely rare."

Bram let go and waited for the other man to continue.

"Pyromania is a mental illness. Most fires are set deliberately as a criminal act. The arson might be motivated by insurance, or some cause, or anger or vengeance. Possibly even impaired judgment. Or it might be a cover-up."

Bram nodded. "The FBI profiler said as much but didn't correct me on the pyromania. The way the owners reacted made me wonder if the arsonist isn't someone up for hire."

"Possible, but it's not as if you can advertise your services."

Bram chewed on the fire marshal's words.

Tom cleared his throat. "I'm surprised you haven't made more progress on this investigation."

Bram's face grew warm. "I seem to run into a lot of resistance."

"From the locals?"

From the sheriff. "Something like that."

———

The resort was a flurry of activity by the time we returned from the pond. "What's going on?" I asked Wyatt.

"I'm sure it's nothing." He spotted Roy and angled in that direction. I casually followed.

Roy was repeatedly running a hand through his white hair. He didn't see me at first. "Wyatt, there you are. I take it no one was hurt?" Without waiting for an answer, he continued, "More guests are leaving. One said the bear frightened her and her daughter out of her wits. The other was in the cabin that had the dead raccoon. All three will catch a ride with Liam when he brings in supplies."

"Did they—"

"Ask for a full refund? Of course. We do guarantee our guests will have the perfect vacation." He spotted me behind Wyatt. His face flushed and he hurried over to me. "There you are, my dear. I hope this little adventure didn't upset you too much." He took my arm. "Let's go into the gift shop and let me give you a little something to brighten your day."

"That's not necessary." I really didn't want a T-shirt or trinket from China, but Roy seemed insistent on moving me into the main building. He didn't seem to notice my squeak.

"Some jewelry? Earrings for your lovely ears?" He moved behind the counter.

"Really, I'm fine. Maybe a bone for the dogs—"

"Not so much for jewelry? Maybe a collectable mineral from my collection? I have many fine specimens." He pointed to a glass case displaying various rocks, all neatly labeled, at the back of the shop. "It's the least I can do to make this right for you."

I wanted to say the bear wasn't his fault, that someone at the Mule Shoe might be luring bears to come closer, but I couldn't be sure. Instead I held my tongue and made an effort to study the rocks. Most were labeled from Idaho and Montana. *Keep him talking. Come up with something brilliant to say about rocks.* "Um, what made you become a rock hound?" *That's the best you could do?*

"At first guests would show me the rocks they'd found on their hikes and leave a few." He joined me at the display. "I didn't know anything about them, but several years ago we had a geologist guest. She identified the various stones and minerals for me. She owned a mining company and came back every year with her employees for our team-building course."

"I've heard that mentioned. Is that stuff like you write something encouraging about someone and put it into an envelope, then open them and share?"

Roy smiled. "Not quite. Here at Mule Shoe we put together programs that address real workplace issues, like reliance on others during violent events, as well as self-reliance in deeply challenging situations. Here are some brochures." He offered me a handful and I stuck them in my pocket. "Our geologist friend always wanted some kind of rock or mineral component. Before she left every year, she'd always add to my collection and look over the newest crop of rocks." He unlocked a drawer under the case. Inside were a number of stones—some bland, some with embedded colored crystals. "She was in a terrible hiking accident recently—"

"She wasn't, by any chance, the one who fell near the Devil's Keyhole?"

"Unfortunately, yes." Roy's brows had furrowed and lips thinned.

"I'm so sorry." I quickly picked up a small, sparkling yellow rock. "Gold?"

"Fool's gold. Iron pyrite." His face brightened and he pointed at the different rocks. "I think this is jade, petrified wood, topaz, beryl, agate, and maybe tourmaline."

"You know, G—" I almost said *Golden Girl*. "Um, I think Grace is a former science teacher. Maybe she can help you identify these."

Roy smiled. "Why yes, that would be wonderful. I'll ask

her after lunch." He pivoted to leave, then turned back. "Oh, and she's more than a science teacher. Have you ever heard of Taborcrest Prep School?"

"Near Seattle? The most expensive . . . oh, *that* Grace Tabor. Doesn't she also own the Tabor Inns and Suites, Tabor Foods, and Tabor Publishing?"

He nodded. "Her husband did, and when he passed, she inherited it all. She could buy this place in a heartbeat just for conservation purposes. And maybe she will." He waved toward the dining room. "Lunch should be ready soon."

Wyatt stepped into the gift shop and signaled Roy.

"If you'll excuse me?" Roy quickly locked up the collection and followed Wyatt from the shop.

That was weird. I sensed his reason for offering me something from the store was to occupy me. He never asked me if I'd read Scott's packet or investigated anything. It was almost as if he didn't want to find out.

CHAPTER 7

B ram finished up at the arson scene and performed the welfare check before heading to the sheriff's department in St. Anthony. The route took him from the high mountains of the Caribou-Targhee National Forest to eastern Idaho's rolling fields and grazing land. The town perched on the Henrys Fork of the Snake River with a population around 3,500. The farming community held both sinners and saints, with thirteen churches juxtaposed against the largest state-run juvenile correctional facility and a correctional work center. Over 65 percent of the town's population was Mormon.

He never told anyone he'd moved to St. Anthony and later taken a job there to be near his brother, incarcerated at the prison work camp. He thought he'd help his wayward sibling by staying close by. His plan was derailed when his brother committed suicide shortly after his release. His grandmother's voice rang in his ears every time he thought of his brother. *Don't be like your worthless mother or brother, Bram. It's up to you. Choose the right road. Make sure you do something perfectly or don't bother . . .*

A copy of the arsonist's latest taunting note was in a plastic sleeve on his immaculate desk. He pulled the case file and added the note to the others. No fingerprints so far, according to the chief. DNA would take a great deal longer to process.

After entering his reports on the welfare check and barn fire, including the fire marshal's comments, he flipped through his phone messages. Nothing that couldn't wait. Returning to the fire marshal's comments, he thought for a moment, then typed some notes to himself.

- Arson for insurance? Different families but maybe for hire? How contact?
- Arson for a cause? No claim, and letters would reflect this.
- Criminal cover-up? No evidence.
- Impaired judgment? Too controlled a scene.
- Anger or vengeance? Against whom?

Early in the investigation, the sheriff had asked an FBI profiler for help. The profile hadn't added much to what they already knew. He said the criminal was likely a white male twenty-five to thirty-five years old who had a low-paying job or was not employed. Ninety percent of Idaho was white, and the median age was thirty-five. Everyone had low-paying jobs.

Bram returned to the notes from the arsonist and reread them, even though he knew them by heart. Could the content of the letters be useful? The words themselves? The Unabomber had been identified by his manifesto. And Roy had said Darby's job had something to do with language and deception.

Or maybe Bram was just devising some way to see her again.

Sheriff Turner wouldn't let him head back out to Mule Shoe unless he could convince her Darby might prove useful to the arson case.

He'd start with her name, job title, and work. He typed in what he knew about her.

The results were immediate. No Darby Graham lived in Washington state.

Maybe she recently moved there. He typed in the name of the company she said she worked for, Clan Firinn. A short article appeared.

Clan Firinn, located outside of Pullman, Washington, offers hope and rehabilitation to law enforcement and first responders suffering from various forms of PTSD and other disorders arising from their work. It is privately owned and funded. Clan Firinn does not accept general applicants but reviews referrals on an individual basis. While participating in the program, members experience therapeutic work, educational opportunities, physical training, a structured schedule, personalized feedback, nutritious meals, and spiritual guidance. Graduates are assisted with career counseling, job referrals, and relocation.

PTSD? Bram sat up straighter. That might explain her reticence. And possibly her limp.

He tried a nationwide search on her name with no useful results. Next he typed in the license plates for the two Washington state vehicles in the parking lot beside Sam's Mercantile. One came back with a Teodoro Rinaldi of Bellevue. The second was for a Darby Carson, in care of Firinn Farm, Rural Route 3, LaCrosse, Washington.

Carson? She'd been introduced as Graham. Divorced?

His fingers hesitated over the keyboard. He was just following a lead about who might help him with this case. *Right.* He was snooping, maybe even stalking. This wasn't healthy. The notes had nothing to do with deception.

He squeezed his hands into fists, then typed *Darby* + "*Washington state.*" Three thousand two hundred seventy-seven hits. He randomly clicked on a few before finding a photo that looked familiar. It showed a younger, much longer-haired Darby. She was dressed in a one-piece red outfit and was posed on the side of a galloping horse with only one hand holding the saddle horn and a leg through a loop.

Snohomish County News

Darby G. Bell, a youth champion rider, will be one of the celebrity judges at the upcoming Western Horseback Games Alliance's O-Mok-See and Trick Riding event...

O-Mok-See. He looked up the term.

O-Mok-See: The western term derived from the Blackfoot Indians' description of a style of riding called "oh-mak-see passkan," meaning "riding big dance." Most of these youth events are set up to show tight horse-and-rider teamwork, precise actions, and a variety of skills performed at a high rate of speed.

Trick riding: Performing stunts, usually on a galloping horse, such as spritz stand, layout fender (also known as the Indian Hideaway)...

When she'd mentioned she was perfectly capable of riding a horse, she wasn't kidding. She'd competed in timed horseback riding events since she was a child.

The next article was from the *Seattle Post Times.*

Skagit County, North Cascades

Several people are dead or seriously wounded in a shootout outside a north Skagit County home on Saturday afternoon, according to the Skagit County Sheriff's Department.

The incident happened around 2:45 p.m. Saturday on Pine Creek Road.

A Skagit sheriff's deputy said the homeowner, later identified as Franklin Olsen, killed two members of the county forensic unit who were conducting a follow-up investigation on Kirt Walter Daday, dubbed the Butcher of Sedro-Woolley...

Bram clicked on another article written a couple of days later. Darby Carson was described as a forensic linguist working for the state crime lab and had been with the lead detective on the day of the shooting.

He jotted down *forensic linguist*. He'd never heard of it.

The second article mentioned the incident wasn't discovered until a motorist driving down the road near midnight stopped to check out what appeared to be an abandoned vehicle.

The next series of essays was brutal. Mistaken identity, careless investigation, real serial killer free to murder a final time before shootout.

Harsh finger-pointing came next, including accusations about Darby's work on the case that had bungled the correct identification. Apparently Franklin Olsen, the real Butcher of Sedro-Woolley, had asked Daday to write the notes for him as Olsen was functionally illiterate. The word choice and phrasing came from Daday, half brother to Olsen, and had led to Daday's mistaken identity.

Bram leaned back in his chair. Darby wasn't to blame if anyone really thought about it, but she'd been smeared just the same. He'd just caught a glimpse of Darby's nightmare.

———

After leaving the gift shop, I strolled outside toward the kitchen's exterior door, hoping to score some bones for the dogs. A variety of delicious aromas escaped the screen door, and the low hum of a generator came from a fenced-in area behind the building. Cookie answered my knock. "Miz Graham! Welcome."

"Please, call me Darby. I hope I'm not interrupting."

"Come in, Darby. Nope. Just working out the menu and schedules." Her grin made her long, thin face quite attractive. The kitchen was far from primitive. All the latest commercial-grade appliances gleamed with polished perfection.

"I thought there wasn't any electricity," I said.

"For the guests. Way too crazy to try and cook five-star meals on a cookstove. So let me guess why you're here. Perhaps for bones for two hero dogs?"

"So you heard about the bear."

"Yup. And the dead raccoon." Cookie turned and waved at one of the kitchen helpers. "Would you pull a couple of beef bones out, Maja?"

The woman nodded and opened a walk-in cooler.

"Gossip, rumors, and small talk are an art form around here," Cookie said. "We've even started a betting pool as to who will get enough nerve to ask you on a date first: Bram or Wyatt."

My face burned. "Oh no. That's ... what ... I'm not ..."

Cookie patted my arm with a callused hand. "Now, sweetie, don't get upset."

"Why would you all even *think* that?"

"Wyatt actually attempted to polish his cowboy boots, and he's *never* escorted anyone to their cabin. And Bram's horse-drawn taxi service to bring you here didn't go un-noticed. In either case, those are two hunky men—"

Maja returned with two large bones in a plastic bag and handed them to me.

"Would you go see if the tables are ready?" Cookie said to the woman. When we were alone again, she said to me, "Don't worry, Darby. I know all about you. I'm a graduate of Clan Firinn myself. Scott Thomas wanted to be sure you had someone you could turn to on your first job after going through the program."

I almost dropped the bag of bones. "How long—"

"Since I left? Ten years. How long was I there? Two years. About the same as you. How long did I battle PTSD? I still have my moments. I didn't lose part of my leg, like you did, but I did lose a lot."

I nodded mutely.

"Scott told me you were a rodeo star."

"No. I competed as a kid in O-Mok-See competitions. Did a little barrel racing, team roping, trick riding, but . . . not since . . ."

"Feel free to talk to me anytime, but please keep our conversations confidential. Like you, I don't like to share my personal information."

"Of course. I would like to talk to you about Mule Shoe."

"That would be a good idea. Maybe later when I have a break and your class is over for the day. Now, why do you suppose a bear wandered so close to the resort?"

I blinked at her change of topic. "I think it was lured here by sardines."

Cookie's eyes narrowed and she said in a low voice, "I was afraid of that. You need to be very careful—"

Maja returned to the kitchen. "Tables are all ready."

"I hope your dogs enjoy their treats." Cookie's voice was back to normal. She gave me a long look, then turned to the kitchen.

Very careful? I smoothed the scratchy feeling on my neck, then left, heading for my cabin. So much for reading a few statements, asking a couple of questions, and enjoying my stay. What had I gotten myself into here?

———

Bram typed *forensic linguist* into the search engine. More than three hundred thousand hits showed up.

He rolled his lips. He'd never heard of the profession, but it seemed both recognized and established in law enforcement. The field encompassed legal language in court, foreign languages, as well as deception and evidence. Any kind of threatening communication, such as extortion demands, could be examined by a forensic linguist. He read that linguists had been consulted in two well-known cases—the manifesto of the Unabomber and the note from the JonBenét Ramsey murder case.

He stood, grabbed up the notes from the arsonist, then paused. Sheriff Turner might be over her earlier rampage about the dogs, but he couldn't gauge her present mood. He took a deep breath and tapped on her office door. "Got a minute?"

The older woman looked up from a stack of paperwork. "Yes, Bram?"

"I think I might have an idea for a new angle on the arson case." He held up the copies of the notes. "I know we've been focusing on fingerprints and bio evidence, but what about the notes themselves? I believe a forensic linguist could—"

"Forensic linguist?"

"A specialist in clues through language. Law enforcement used one with the Unabomber."

"Do you know where you can find a forensic linguist? I know the state doesn't have one, and I have no budget left to pay an expert for something that could prove to be a long shot. I need results, especially . . ."

He waited a moment. "I . . . heard about the petition. I'm sorry."

She looked out the window, eyes unfocused. "Maybe it's for the best," she said under her breath.

He frowned at her. "Excuse me?"

She shook her head as if waking from a daze, waved him away, and returned to her paperwork.

Bram slowly walked back to his cubicle. *Maybe it's for the best?* Sheriff Turner was a good-enough chief, but something was off about this whole arson ordeal. Maybe it was the magnitude of the case. Before scoring the job as sheriff in Fremont County, she'd been deputy sheriff in neighboring Clark County, population 852. With a population of over thirteen thousand, Fremont County had been a dramatic step up for her.

He was about to return the notes to the case file but paused. Sheriff Turner hadn't exactly said no to the idea of showing the letters to Darby. He stepped over to the copier and made several duplicate sets, then placed two sets into a file. With all the problems at the Mule Shoe, it was only a matter of time before he'd be called in and could see Darby.

CHAPTER 8

My walk back to my cabin took me past the horse pasture. Several stopped grazing and gave me a curious look. They appeared to be mostly Quarter Horse crosses with a few Appaloosas and a couple of mules.

The events described in Roy's letter seemed random and not particularly unusual, but the destruction of the art room and the possibility that the bear had been deliberately lured convinced me something was wrong at the resort. Unfortunately, I'd only smelled the fish, and Roy had cleaned up the art room, so I didn't have tangible evidence. The raccoon incident was up in the air. None of the events I'd witnessed targeted a specific individual.

One of the mules sauntered over to see if I had a treat. I stroked his velvety nose. "What do you think? Should I just hop on your back and find out if I'm ready to ride again?" He puffed into my hair and wandered away.

I continued to my cabin. The dogs were calmly lying on the small porch. When she spotted the bone I held out, Holly leaped up, grabbed it, and trotted to a nearby tree.

Maverick simply stared at me.

"Come on, big guy. You deserve this treat." I held out the bone. "You saved me from certain death, or at least a nasty mauling."

The Anatolian was unmoved by my words.

I placed the bone on the porch, then moved to the other side and sat in a willow armchair.

Maverick, gaze never leaving me, stood and retrieved the bone. I stayed seated. He lay down and began gnawing on it.

"You know, Maverick, everyone is betrayed at least once in a lifetime. Everyone has wounds and scars. Maybe if I knew where yours came from, you'd learn to trust me even a tiny bit." I took the three pebbles from my pockets, rolled them around in my fingers, then put them back. "I don't know why Shadow Woman would leave the two of you to starve. I'm trying to find out more. Maybe once I know your background better, I can find a way to reach you."

Maverick continued to chew on his bone.

I still had the brochures Roy gave me. I opened the one on team building.

CORPORATE TEAM BUILDING

Whether you want to bring together new employees or reenergize the creative working spirit in long-time staff, we are poised to customize the perfect program for you. Our exercises are designed to challenge and sharpen your skills, refine objectives, and develop reliance and trust.

Consider our wilderness scavenger hunt, where participants are placed in a remote location with only a few tools and must live off the land while recovering specific items.

Our most popular challenge, and most useful in today's difficult environment, is active-shooter and workplace-violence response . . .

I stepped inside and dropped most of the brochures on the counter. I placed the one on team building in my notebook. The insurance carrier had dropped their coverage on team building. How big a hit did Roy's pocketbook take for that? I'd need to talk to him.

The creaking and rattling of a wagon accompanied by the *clop, clop, clop* of a horse announced the arrival of the supplies. Liam drove Sam's wagon around to the side of the lodge, then began unloading it into the kitchen. *Perfectly timed delivery for Liam to stay for lunch.*

Dee Dee Denim and *Golden Girl* Grace were standing under a ponderosa in deep discussion with Angie. I could have easily heard Angie's powerful voice, but Grace did the talking. Were they discussing the bear or reviewing the deeper meaning of relative values? Or something more sinister? *Now I'm getting paranoid.* I wandered closer to eavesdrop.

"Yellowstone's incredibly fragile geothermal pools and

geysers," Grace said, "can be destroyed or altered by man. For example, people routinely throw pennies, garbage, even soap into geysers and pools. This can change the direction of a geyser or . . ."

Grace seemed to relish the subject of natural disasters. I caught a glimpse of someone near the barn before the figure dodged out of sight. Returning to my cabin, I kept an eye on the barn. When I reached the porch, I had a good view of an opening where two windows lined up. This time I saw him.

Riccardo Rinaldi, the teenage son of Teddy and Nona. The one who'd been restricted to his cabin for sneaking out last night. Obviously he'd decided to ignore his punishment.

"Well," I said to Maverick. "You already know what I'm going to say."

Maverick paused midchew and squinted at me.

"Right. It's none of my business to get involved with teen discipline."

A horse whinnied in the barn.

Maverick glanced at the barn, then at me.

"No. He wouldn't be so foolish as to try to leave. I doubt he even knows how to bridle a horse, let alone cinch a saddle."

Both Maverick and Holly jumped to their feet and faced the barn.

"I suppose . . . I *could* interview him, although I doubt I'd get him to say he trashed the art room."

Holly whined.

"You're laying it on pretty thick." I stood. "You save me from a bear, I check on a wayward teen. Is that it?" I sauntered toward the barn, muttering, "Who'd have figured my two dogs were the cruise directors for a guilt trip?"

The nearest door of the barn opened to the milking stanchions, all spotless. The rich odor of hay filled the air, and light streaming in from the window highlighted a ginger-colored cat sprawled in the warmth.

Thump!

It sounded like a bale of hay had been dropped from the overhead loft. A half door opened to a hallway, with a ladder attached to the wall in front of me leading to an overhead trapdoor. The feed trough for the stanchions lined one side. The hall continued to my right, dimly lit. At the far end was a small pile of hay and something blue. I moved in that direction. Slowly the image became clearer. A second ladder to the loft was open at this end, allowing a shaft of light to illuminate the hay. The blue turned out to be jeans.

My vision narrowed to a single focus. I slowed and shuffled through the carpet of loose straw. I didn't want to see but couldn't look away.

A foot extended from one denim-clad leg. The pants disappeared into the pile of motionless hay.

Reaching forward with a trembling hand, I brushed the dried grass from where I figured his face would be.

Riccardo Rinaldi. The young man's white face was in stark contrast to the blood around his lips. I knelt beside him and touched his neck, feeling for a pulse I didn't believe would be there.

He opened his eyes, then closed them.

I started to stand and go for help, but the light from the loft glinted on something. I stared at it, trying to figure out what I was looking at. *Two pieces of metal. Pointed. Bloody. From the center of his chest.*

Bile rose in my throat. *Oh no.*

Riccardo had landed on a pitchfork.

I jumped to my feet and ran, not stopping until I was out of the barn. I slid to a halt, frantically searching for help. Next to the lodge, Wyatt was unloading the last of the supplies from the wagon. I raced to him, gasping for breath. "Barn. Riccardo. Fell. Pitchfork—"

He dropped the box of fresh vegetables and grabbed my arms. "How bad?"

"Bad."

"Go find Roy. He should be in the dining room. Tell him to get on the radio and get a medivac chopper here immediately." He turned me toward the lodge and shoved, then took off running to the barn.

I found Roy just entering the dining room. I was still sucking in air but made an effort this time to make cohesive sense.

Roy blanched as I described what happened. Without a word, he ran from the room.

I turned and found myself face-to-face with Teddy and Nona. Heat rushed to my face.

"Miss Graham, have you seen our—" Teddy peered at my expression. "Where?"

I opened and closed my mouth before I could squeak out, "Barn."

They rushed past me.

Turning to stop them, I found they'd already crossed the distance to the barn. I should have kept my mouth shut. *I've probably made things worse—*

They entered the barn. Shortly after, Nona let out a guttural scream.

The anguish in her cry cut through me, leaving me dizzy. *I should go help her, help someone, do something.* I couldn't move.

The sound drew the others, who gathered around me.

"What's going on?"

"Who screamed?"

"Is it another bear?"

"What's happening?"

The questions flew at me like small darts. Their pressing nearness threatened a panic attack.

Someone grabbed my arm and pulled me from the group. Cookie. Her lips were pulled down and a vein pounded in her forehead. "Folks, please head into the lodge. We'll update you shortly. You come with me, Miz Graham." She towed me to the kitchen and poured a glass of water. "Tell me what happened."

After taking a gulp, I explained, trying to control my voice.

Cookie sucked in air, making a hissing sound. "Nasty business." She looked at her watch. "The chopper will be here soon. You stay here while I—"

"I'm okay now. I want to help. I need to help."

Cookie nodded. "Very well then. I'll give you some things to take over to the barn. I'll get Liam to finish unloading the wagon so we can use it. I'm sure Riccardo's folks want to be with him, but the chopper can only evacuate one adult plus the patient. We'll need the wagon to get any others to town." Without waiting for me to respond, she bustled off, returning shortly with a clean sheet and blanket. "See if they can use these. I'll try and calm the rest of the guests."

I took the items and trotted to the barn.

Riccardo was already covered with a blanket. Roy and Wyatt were huddled over him while Nona was sitting cross-legged next to him holding his hand. Teddy stood behind her, hands on her shoulders.

Wyatt took the items from me and used the second blanket to slightly elevate Riccardo's legs.

I shifted my weight from leg to leg. What should I do now?

You know.

My mind shifted to a symposium I'd attended years before on mass-disaster and crime-scene reconstruction. The presenters told of horrific experiences—Pan Am Flight 103 that crashed in Lockerbie, Scotland. The *Challenger* space shuttle disaster. The Hyatt Regency walkway collapse in

Kansas City. In each case the presenters told what happened, what they did right, and what they did wrong. Again and again they shared how, out of compassion, first responders didn't do their jobs. They wanted to help but often just got in the way.

I couldn't help Riccardo right now. I had very little medical knowledge beyond basic first aid. But I did know about potential crime scenes.

I gazed up at the opening to the hayloft. How could Riccardo have fallen through that opening? It was over three feet square.

I backed away and walked to the other end of the hall, where the second access to the loft was located. Grabbing the ladder, I stopped. At that same symposium they talked about the effects of PTSD, which wasn't well understood at the time. First responders were told they could get counseling, but if they did, it would be viewed as weakness and lack of professionalism. Marriages collapsed, families fell apart, careers ended, and suicides resulted.

Mental health had come a long way since then.

I rested my head against the ladder rung. *What's it going to be?* Use my knowledge to look into his fall, or scamper off, tail between my legs, and whimper about having a PTSD moment? I hadn't signed up for this. I was here to examine some documents. Interview a few people. Find either a pattern or a run of bad luck.

Not investigate potentially lethal accidents.

I scrambled up the ladder to the loft. The center of the

barn was filled with hay bales neatly stacked and bound with orange baling twine. The air was rich with the mingled scents of hay, straw, alfalfa, and oats.

On the far side was a matching loft holding bales of the distinctly green timothy hay.

This loft had no bales, only a thick mat of loose hay. From where I stood, I couldn't see the opening over Riccardo. I slowly walked forward, looking around for anything out of the ordinary.

I stopped when I reached the place where Riccardo had fallen, then knelt and inspected the area.

Below me, Riccardo's parents were praying over their son.

Several new-looking nails had been hammered into the wood around the opening. Caught on one nail were several strands of orange baling twine.

Rocking back on my heels, I put a possible scenario together. Someone could have created a wolf pit type of trap. If baling twine was looped around the nails to form a base, then the loose hay spread over the top, the opening would disappear. Anyone could bait the trap by placing something on the far side. If Riccardo was the intended victim, most any electronic device would work. He'd head straight for the device. The twine wouldn't hold any weight, and the victim would crash through, fall backward, and land on the conveniently placed pitchfork.

Cleanup would involve pulling any remaining twine and removing the bait.

I shook my head. Of course, all of this was speculation.

Riccardo might have been exploring without looking where he was going.

When I was working for law enforcement, I could run my observations past my coworkers to be sure I was being objective. But here? I ran into a bear and thought it had been lured to that spot. A young man fell through a hayloft and I thought it was attempted murder. The therapist at Clan Firinn warned me that PTSD could warp how I viewed life and events.

The distant thumping of a helicopter announced help was on the way. The much closer barking of the dogs revealed an impending earthquake. The barn seemed to sigh and a cloud of dust rose with the mild quake.

Nona let out a short scream below me, and Riccardo moaned.

A lump formed in my throat. *I hope he can get to a hospital in time.*

I rose and moved toward the other end of the loft. By the time I climbed down the ladder and left the barn, I'd decided that whether it was imagination or reality, I needed to photograph the twine, then bag it as evidence.

And I had a whole lot more work to do to get to the truth.

CHAPTER 9

R oy was outside waving to the arriving helicopter. I stayed next to the barn until the copter landed.

Bram was the first to exit the chopper. He was out of uniform but had a holstered gun and carried a leather messenger bag.

My heart thumped a bit harder. Unbidden, Cookie's comments rose in my mind. *We've even started a betting pool as to who will get enough nerve to ask you on a date first: Bram or Wyatt.* I squeezed my hands into fists. Silly and pointless speculation in the midst of a crisis.

I stepped out of his line of sight. I needed to stay focused on the events, not complicate anything by adding a layer of . . . *Go ahead, admit it. Attraction.*

If I had a phone, I would call Scott Thomas, my counselor, or *caraid*, as we called them—Scottish Gaelic for "friend." I'd ask him for advice. My nightmares were back. I was having panic attacks. I wasn't sure how well my brain was working. And I wanted to run and hide.

I *could* talk to Cookie. She'd been through something

pretty horrific if she'd ended up on the farm. Clan Firinn didn't rehabilitate only first responders and law enforcement. They took people who'd reached rock bottom, who'd destroyed their families and careers and were on the verge of ending their lives.

The three stones in my pockets pressed against my legs. *Maybe while I'm talking to her I can ask what I'm supposed to do with the rocks.*

The medical group from the chopper had entered the barn, so I trotted over to the lodge, my prosthetic leg squeaking with each step.

All the guests and a few staff were seated in the main lodge. Everyone stopped speaking and stared at me as I entered.

Low profile. I did an about-face to leave when Roy came in behind me, blocking my exit. "There you are. I just went looking for you." Roy turned to the group. "The medivac will take Riccardo and his mother, and Mr. Rinaldi has arranged for a second helicopter to pick him up and take him to the hospital in Idaho Falls. Mrs. Eason, you indicated you wanted to leave with your daughter, Lauryn, as did you, Mrs. Kendig. Mr. Rinaldi has offered seats in his helicopter to all of you. You'll have to arrange to get your cars from Targhee Falls. Or you can go with Liam"—he pointed to the young man—"who will be taking the supply wagon back to town."

The *chuff, chuff, chuff* of the helicopter taking off made speaking difficult for a few moments. When the sound retreated, Roy continued, "We'll be serving lunch soon, and the art class will resume after that."

The staff got up and moved to the kitchen.

Someone touched my shoulder.

I spun, almost falling. My leg let out a protesting squeak.

Bram caught my arm and steadied me. "I'm sorry, I didn't mean to startle you. Do you have a minute?"

My face grew warm. "I . . . um, yes." I was acutely aware of his hand on my arm.

He glanced around the room, seemingly aware of the sideways glances and grins coming from the people around us. "How about the picnic table outside?" He guided me to the grassy area under the pines. Once I sat down, he let go of my arm and moved to the other side of the table. I could still feel the impression of his warm hand.

"Are you here investigating Riccardo's fall?" I asked.

"Is there something to investigate?" Bram leaned forward. "I spoke to both Roy and Wyatt. It seems it was just a terrible accident."

My neck tingled.

He straightened. "Is there something I need to know?"

I told him about the raccoon, the trashed art room, the bear, the baling twine caught on new-looking nails.

"Are you here on assignment from Clan Firinn?" he asked.

I was silent for a moment. "Why do you ask that?" *Answering a question with a question after a significant pause is a sign of possible deception.* I hoped Bram wasn't an expert in the field. Just because I could recognize deception didn't mean I was any good at lying.

"From your answer, I would guess you *are* here to investigate the incidents."

Flapperdoodle. "Please don't mention this to anyone. I'm supposed to be checking things out. I do need to interview you on what you've uncovered."

He smiled, showing those perfect teeth, and placed his hand over mine. "Then we need to work together."

Double flapperdoodle. My brain went blank. The air grew thinner, the day suddenly hotter, my vision much narrower. "Um . . ." I cleared my throat. "What did you need to speak to me about?"

"Your work as a forensic linguist."

I scratched my neck. "You've been investigating *me.*"

"Don't take this the wrong way, Darby. I'm not stalking you. I just need your help."

I gently extracted my hand. It was too hard to think when he was touching me. "We have a deal. Me first. I was about to get my camera and photograph that baling twine caught on the nails, then bag it for evidence. I was also going to bag any twine found on the floor under Riccardo. Now that you're here, could you do that?"

"Sure."

"And tell me if, in the past, you've been out here investigating . . . anything."

Bram stared off into the distance. Birds chirped and twittered, and a chipmunk lectured us from a nearby tree.

The slight breeze brought the scent of dried grasses. He finally said, "Here? Not really." He rubbed his chin. "I mentioned the hikers who fell at Devil's Pass."

"Yes. Roy said they were guests."

"Right. Roy had one of the most popular, and I'm sure most expensive, team-building experiences in the country. Rock climbing, rappelling, wilderness camping, you name it."

"I was reading a brochure on it. It's one of the angles I want to look into."

"Good. Anyway, even though the two hikers started out here, they were supposed to be hiking to the east, toward Yellowstone Park, not in Devil's Pass. The maps found on them showed they had strayed miles from where they were supposed to be. The court acquitted Roy and the Mule Shoe of all liability, but it really shook him."

"I read his insurance carrier withdrew coverage and he had to drop the program."

"He took a big hit, that's for sure. He's scrambling to set up less dangerous programs this summer, hence the art class this week."

"I hear a *but* in what you just said."

He sharpened his gaze on me. "You *are* good. Does anything get past you?"

"A lot. I don't usually listen that carefully unless I need to."

"Roy also started thinking about selling the place and retiring. But"—he frowned—"he seemed to run into more . . . glitches."

"Now these so-called glitches have taken a nasty, if not possibly fatal, turn." I adjusted my glasses. "Thank you. Now it's your turn. How can I help you?"

He opened the messenger bag, pulled out a file folder, and set it on the table. "As you surmised, we do have a serial arsonist. Counting yesterday, eight fires. The fire six months ago killed two men."

"So it's more than arson. It's murder."

"Probably—"

"Probably? What do you mean by that?"

"We assume the two men died in the fire."

"Assume?" I pulled my glasses down and stared over the rim at him. "An autopsy would show—"

"There wasn't an autopsy."

"Why not?"

"The sheriff can't order one in this county, although if she asked, I'm sure there would have been one. Anyway, it was clear the two men died when a hot water tank exploded and started the fire."

I cleared my throat and tried to marshal my thoughts. "If the fire started from an exploding hot water tank, how can that be arson?"

"Someone rigged the tank to explode." He shifted in his seat. "Anyway . . . the arsonist has sent a series of taunting notes to the sheriff's office. With your background, I was hoping you could look at the notes and maybe give me some insight."

"No."

"But we don't have any leads—"

"No."

"Look, I realize you took a trouncing with the Butcher of Sedro-Woolley case, but you were right."

The name caused my heart to hammer in my brain. I opened and closed my mouth, but didn't have enough breath to speak.

"You correctly identified the man who physically wrote the notes, Daday. It wasn't your fault that the author of the notes was writing down what the butcher said to him."

I wanted to jump up and run, but my muscles wouldn't respond.

"I also have some idea of all that you went through, but—"

"Do you?" My voice shook. *Five years.* I'd spent five years battling demons. Learning how to walk again. Discovering my new normal, my new identity. I shouldn't have been so shaken over Bram's request.

His eyes had widened at my reaction.

I couldn't leave him with the idea that I was a wack job. *Why not?* Did I want to admit that I liked him?

Taking a deep breath, I folded my hands in my lap and looked down. What verse had Scott Thomas sent? *This is my command—be strong and courageous! Do not be afraid or discouraged. For the Lord your God is with you wherever you go.*

I finally looked up. "In your obvious research on my background, you must have read about Clan Firinn."

He shifted in his seat, then nodded. "A place for law enforcement to recover from their work-related PTSD."

"That's how they phrase it, but working in law enforcement today leaves most with emotional and often physical damage, as you well know."

"Yes," he said quietly.

"Sometimes . . . there's an issue with . . . reputation. For different reasons. I'll never be able to work in my field again—at least not on any case going to court."

"Voir dire."

"Right. As soon as I tried to qualify as an expert, cross-examination would expose my past. I know it wasn't my fault that the wrong person was identified, but all any attorney needs to do with any expert witness is create doubt."

Bram picked up the file folder and tapped it on the table. "So you're not here at Mule Shoe to investigate. More to . . . observe and advise?"

"Right. If I think there's more going on—and I do—I'll step away and let the authorities take over. That's why it's better if you collect the evidence and record it. As soon as I write up my findings and get them to Clan Firinn, I'm out of the picture."

"In that case, would you consider looking over the notes and just . . . advising me?"

"You're persistent, Bram White."

"When it's something I want, yes."

I couldn't meet his gaze. I didn't want my own thoughts to show. "No promises." I took the file and headed to my cabin. Once there, I leaned against the door. *This is my command—be strong and courageous! Do not be afraid or discouraged. For the Lord your God is with you wherever you go.*

The verse was helping. Maybe I could leave the God part out of it.

As I set the file on the copper-top table, Maverick and Holly's salvo of barking heralded another earthquake. This time only the overhead lantern swayed slightly.

Opening the door, I found the dogs pacing on the porch. "I know what would soothe your nerves. Kibble." I returned to the cabin, grabbed a scoop of dog food, and dumped it into their bowls. As I expected, they inhaled the food.

"Okay, dogs. We are not going to be afraid." Neither dog looked up. "Yeah, jury is still out on that one. So . . . let's just look at the facts. You know that earthquake? We could be at ground zero of a supervolcano." Holly wagged her tail but didn't look up from her food dish. "You do seem pleased by news of a potential existential disaster." Hearing my own voice helped steady me. Maverick was too busy chasing the last nugget around his food dish to even look up. He captured and loudly crunched it.

I sighed and stepped back inside the cabin. The cleaning staff had freshened the room while I'd been out, replacing the throw pillows on the bed and putting away the coffee cup I'd left on the dish rack.

My closet door was open a crack. I strolled over and opened it. My suitcase was lying on its side.

My stomach tightened. I was sure I'd left it standing up.

After closing the door, I slowly moved around the room. Nothing else was disturbed. I rubbed, then itched my neck. *Keep looking.*

My wallet was in the Mule Shoe bag and currently locked in the art room. If someone was looking for money, they would have gone away empty-handed.

I tried to picture the room as I'd left it. *No, that isn't all that useful.* Housekeeping had cleaned my room. What would the cleaning staff *not* disturb, but someone searching inadvertently rearrange? Like my suitcase.

Once more I circled the room.

This time I saw it. The magazines on the lower shelf of the end table were in a different order than I'd left them. I'd been reading about livestock-guarding breeds the night before. Now *Rock & Gem* magazine was on top.

At some point, maybe when I'd gone out to draw by the pond or been in the lodge, someone had searched my room. Who? Roy had dragged me into the lodge to look at rocks, then released me when Wyatt appeared and nodded at him. Was that the signal the search was completed?

Or was I seeing things that didn't exist? Believing things that didn't happen? The cleaning staff could have easily and unknowingly moved a few things around.

I needed to talk to someone before my paranoia mounted.

I strolled to the door and opened it. Both dogs trooped in and sniffed around the room, paying particular attention to the bed, sink area, closet, and magazines. *Inconclusive.* Both sat and stared at me.

"Right. I called this meeting to discuss some recent events . . ." *Do you "discuss" when the conversation is one-sided?* "Correction. Review, not discuss."

Holly lay down.

"I won't be that long. Here's the deal. I'm pretty sure something is dangerously wrong here at the Mule Shoe. I don't know if I'm being targeted or maybe just paranoid. If I'm losing my mind, I suppose someone will eventually notice that I'm sitting around with tinfoil on my head."

Maverick yawned.

"Don't be so cavalier, Maverick. You'll be wearing a tinfoil hoodie as well."

He blinked.

"That's better. So, bottom line is I need some solid evidence to report to Clan Firinn. Hopefully the twine will be just that. Agreed?"

Holly rolled onto her back and wagged her tail.

"I'm going to take that as a four-paws yes vote to continue. Maverick, are you abstaining?"

The dog yawned again.

"Four yes, one abstain, and I vote yes as well, so we'll continue our investigation. I would advise you to keep this meeting and vote a secret for now. Are there any questions?" *I probably need that tinfoil hat.* "I'm going to lunch. You two are on guard duty." When I opened the door, both dogs bolted outside.

Everyone was seated when I arrived and the servers were busy delivering bowls of soup or plates of salad. The one open seat was at the table with Dee Dee Denim, *Golden Girl* Grace, and Angie Burton. All three acknowledged my presence with nods, but Angie continued to address the other two. "Art is more than the subject, medium, or application of paint. The artist might be conveying a message, a feeling, a story, maybe their philosophy."

"Would that be a deliberate message?" Grace asked.

"Maybe." Angie broke some saltines into her soup.

A waitress moved next to me. "Soup or salad?"

"Salad."

"Are you saying I need to think about not just what I'm trying to draw or paint," Dee Dee asked Angie, "but what I feel about it? I'm overwhelmed with just painting something recognizable."

Angie smiled. "Don't worry about it. For many artists, your thoughts go into your work without conscious effort. If you know this, however, it makes it fascinating to study art." She looked at me. "I hope you're recovered from the bear incident. And I understand you were the one to find poor Riccardo. You've had quite a morning."

"I'm fine." *As long as they don't find out about the dog meeting.* "How long have you worked here, Angie?"

"This is my first summer."

The waitress delivered my salad and I casually placed my napkin in my lap. "I suppose this has been the craziest day so far."

Angie nodded. "Outside of a broken pipe in one of the cabins that made a mess, yes."

Broken pipe. Dead raccoon. Ransacked art room. Fishy sardines. Pitchfork trap. "Mmm." I took a bite of salad.

"I, for one, will look on the bright side," Dee Dee said. "I love Angie and look forward to more one-on-one instruction. The class will be a lot smaller after today." She looked at each of us as if to challenge us to say anything.

"I would normally agree with you, Dee Dee." Angie had two bright spots of red on her cheeks. "But I'm paid per student. Roy offers a full refund if anyone isn't satisfied. The couple with the broken pipe, along with their daughter, the Rinaldis, Mrs. Eason and her daughter, Mrs. Kendig, and another four people who had their reservations screwed up means I'm down eleven people. That's a chunk of change."

Now it was Dee Dee's turn to blush. "I'm . . . I'm sorry, Angie. No offense intended. I just . . ."

The waitresses brought our main course, breaking up the awkward moment.

I did a quick calculation in my head. If eleven people were no longer coming, that amounted to eleven thousand–plus dollars a day that the Mule Shoe wasn't receiving. Roy still had to maintain the staff and other costs.

Was financial ruin the saboteur's goal? Why? And where else did I need to look?

CHAPTER 10

Bram watched Darby walk off to her cabin. He'd hoped for expert help but understood the line she had to walk. He drummed his fingers on the picnic table. She hadn't looked at him when he confirmed he was persistent. He hoped she hadn't noticed his double meaning.

What if she had? What if . . .

He slammed his hand down on the table, then stood. He had a job to do on the arson fires and no time for idle thoughts and useless speculation.

He didn't need to wait for the supply wagon to head to town. Roy had mentioned a second helicopter would be taking one of the parents to Idaho Falls. He'd ask them to drop him in St. Anthony.

Roy stepped out of the barn.

Bram waved to him, rose, and trotted over. "Would it be okay if I take a look at where the accident occurred?"

"Sure. Are you thinking it could be anything other than a terrible accident?"

"Just being thorough."

"I'd appreciate it. What bothers me is I know my staff. None of them would be careless enough to leave a pitchfork on the ground."

"You've already asked them?"

"All the ones who would have reason to be in the barn."

"All right. Can you make out a list of your staff? And what about your guests?"

"Of course, although I can't see any of them messing around in the barn—"

"Riccardo was."

"So he was," Roy muttered. "I'll get you that list. Let me show you where it happened." In the barn, he led the way to the end of the hall. Bloody hay, medical packaging, and a pair of blankets lay underneath an open trapdoor to the loft. A pitchfork, missing three tines, leaned against the wall.

Squatting down, he shifted the hay, looking for lengths of baling twine. If any had been there, they were gone now.

"Do you think he could have slipped backward off the ladder?" Roy asked.

Bram stood, stepped over the blankets and other debris, grabbed a rung, and climbed to the loft. "The wood has been worn smooth and could possibly be slippery." He looked down at Roy. "But he would have had to step over the pitchfork and know it was there." He surveyed the landing area and hall. "There's a lot more hay directly below here, which makes me think he fell through this opening rather than off the ladder."

He climbed up another rung and looked for the nails

and baling twine thread. The nails were there, but no orange fibers. He took out his phone and snapped a few photographs anyway.

"What are you looking for?" Roy asked.

"At this point, just looking." He climbed down. "Who handled the pitchfork?"

"The medical staff, of course, when they cut the tines. Wyatt. Um . . . me. Probably all the outside staff at one time or another."

Interesting. Roy didn't ask him why he wanted to know.

The older man dry washed his face. "I did it, finally. Took the offer."

"Offer?"

"To buy the place. Today was the final straw. I think the new owner will keep the staff on. I hope so. I haven't told anyone so far. I don't want them to be angry or get their hopes up."

"Who bought it?"

"I don't know. Quite frankly, I signed all the paperwork a month ago and left it with the real estate agent. The money's in escrow. I just had to give the final yes. I just kept hoping things would change, get back to . . . well, you know."

Bram patted the man on the arm. "You should have a tidy nest egg to retire on."

"Yeah. Right. Nest egg. More like retire before this place kills me."

———

The art room had been neatly placed back into order. A swift look at the backpack in my locker showed my wallet and Shadow Woman's drawings undisturbed. Five sets of supplies mutely spoke of the absence of the Rinaldis, Mrs. Kendig, and the Easons.

I took my place at a long table.

Angie held up a plastic tub. "You'll need water, so fill your tub three-quarters full. Be sure the water is cool, not hot. Hot water isn't good on your brushes." She pointed to the side of the room where a wide shelf ran underneath the windows. "Speaking of water, remember to stay hydrated. It helps prevent altitude sickness. Those carafes hold decaf, coffee, and hot water for tea. Cold drinking water is in the pitcher."

Everyone lined up at either the sink to fill buckets or the ledge to get refreshments. I poured a glass of water and started to take a drink.

The water smelled of boggy plant life.

I moved the glass away from my face and sniffed the room. A hint of turpentine mixed with a pine cleaner. I smelled the drinking water again. It reeked of the pond, filled with the parasite giardia.

"Stop!" I shouted.

Angie sloshed the bucket of water she'd been carrying to her table. "What is it, Darby? You scared me to death!"

"Don't drink the water in the pitcher. I think it's from the beaver pond."

Grace dropped her glass, shattering it on the floor. Dee

Dee raced to the sink and vomited. Angie dashed to the pitcher and sniffed. Color drained from her face.

I wasn't crazy. This was deliberate. Again.

—

Bram took his place with the other passengers awaiting the chartered helicopter. The *chuff, chuff, chuff* of the whirling blades drowned out any conversation with Mr. Rinaldi or Mrs. Eason. Bram turned his head to keep the flying debris out of his eyes. When the copter-driven wind slowed, he looked back at his ride. The pilot nodded at him and the copilot gave a salute.

Darby burst from the lodge, waving her arms frantically.

He ran toward her. Conversation was impossible over the noise. He pointed to the lodge. Once inside, he asked, "Change your mind?"

"No. I think someone tried to poison the guests."

Bram's chest tightened. "What happened?"

"Come with me." She led him to the art room. Angie was rubbing Dee Dee's back as she bent dry heaving over the sink. Grace was frozen over a mess of shattered glass. The remaining two members of the class, Peter and Stacy, were seated at their table holding hands. Darby pointed. "Someone put water from the beaver pond into the drinking pitcher."

The clatter of the copter blades increased.

I need to ask them to wait. Bram bolted from the room

but was too late to catch the pilot's attention. He returned shortly.

"I'm sorry," Darby said. "I made you miss your ride, but I thought this was important."

"I'll catch the supply wagon. What makes you think it's not fresh drinking water?"

"Smell it."

Bram picked up the pitcher, held it to the light, then sniffed. It did smell like a stagnant pond. He turned to Angie. "Do you have a sterile jar or container of some kind?"

She nodded and left the room, returning with a jar and lid. "Will this work?"

Bram grimly nodded, then poured some water into the jar. "I'll take this with me for testing. I'd like to speak with each of you individually, starting with you, Angie. The rest of you should remain here."

Darby caught his gaze and mouthed, *Twine?*

He shook his head, then turned toward Dee Dee. "Did you drink the water?"

She nodded.

"The good news is giardia is pretty easy to treat. Did any of the rest of you take a drink?"

No one spoke.

"Okay. I'll find Roy, update him, and see if I can borrow his office."

A search of the lodge turned up cleaning staff at work and Cookie. He debated telling her but decided to wait until he'd spoken to Roy. He finally found Roy standing next to Wyatt at the fenced field.

Roy's face was pinched and he was compulsively opening and closing his hands.

"What's wrong?"

"Looks like the helicopters must have spooked the horses. They pushed through the gate. A couple of us are going to go after them."

"Including the Belgian that pulls the supply wagon?"

"No. He was in the barn. I thought you were leaving with the second copter."

"Something came up."

Roy turned to leave, then stopped. "What do you mean, 'something came up'? What now?"

CHAPTER 11

As soon as Bram left to find Roy, Angie began pacing and gnawing on a fingernail.

"Please sit down, Angie," I said.

"I can't sit. First my art room is trashed, then the bear, now this! Someone is out to get me."

I wanted to point out that the bear was out to get *me*, but she didn't look in any mood to be corrected. Her agitated movements were upsetting the others even more. Dee Dee seemed loath to leave the sink, Grace still hadn't moved from where she'd dropped the glass, and Stacy had buried her head in her husband's shoulder.

I wasn't here as a first responder, but if I didn't calm them down, I'd never be able to get any evidence or information from them. *Address their needs.* They needed to feel safe, to express their emotions, and to know what would come next.

Angie stopped pacing for a moment. A fat tear ran down her face.

"As Bram said," I began in a low, soft voice, "even if you did take a sip, you'll be fine. It's normal to be upset and frightened, but Bram will find out how it happened. For now, let's take a few deep breaths." I demonstrated.

Everyone followed suit.

Change the focus, ground them in the present. Pull out pencils and get everyone to start drawing? *Angie's a basket case.* Suggest a hike? *Bear.* Okay, something that would engage all their minds for a time. What about . . . art, drawing, paintings . . . An idea struck me.

I moved to my locker and removed Shadow Woman's drawings. "Angie, maybe you can help me. You mentioned at lunch that people may put a message, feeling, or story into their art. These drawings are by a woman named Mae, the original owner of the dogs. Some people called her Shadow Woman. What do you see?"

Angie had stopped pacing with the breathing exercise. She approached the drawings, which I'd spread out on an empty table. Dee Dee released her death grip on the sink and joined her, as did Stacy and Peter. Grace found a dust pan and broom and began sweeping up the glass.

"Very nice." Angie arranged the drawings on the table by date, then selected one of the landscapes. "These are dated pretty close together, so not much difference in the way of artistic development, but she does use the full range of values, good texture, interesting composition." She picked up the second landscape. "This looks like the same location. See this tree snag?"

I hadn't noticed, but Angie was right. Both landscapes had the same distinctive tree, although in one drawing the tree was in the distance while the other featured the tree in the foreground. "I think I see people in this one." I handed it back to Angie.

"Maybe . . . Yes, you're right." Angie gave the drawing to Stacy.

"I think they're hikin'." Stacy returned the sketch to the table, pointing. "Those could be backpacks."

Grace finished her cleanup and joined us. "That drawing looks like two men running in a fog."

"Or a cloud." Dee Dee nodded. "Maybe angels? Running to help?"

"Could be." Angie tapped the sketch with her finger. "But what are these two lines? A path? Road?"

Stacy grinned. "I'd say that's an unfinished sketch of Jacob's ladder. You'd just need lines going across the two lines." She looked at us, then shook her head. "Y'all know. From Genesis. Angels in the clouds."

"'Behold a ladder set upon the earth, and the top of it reached to heaven: and behold the angels of God ascending and descending on it.'" Dee Dee grinned back at Stacy. "That's good. Really creative."

"The whole thing could be an allegory," Angie said. "I'd love to hear what the artist was thinking."

"What about the portraits?" I asked. "I think this one might be a self-portrait. But they all seem . . . off. Well, at least the ones I recognize—Sam and Roy—aren't perfect likenesses."

Angie studied the four portraits. "Fascinating."

"What do you see, Angie?" Grace asked.

"You all know that the two sides of your face don't match, right? If you were to photograph your face, split the image down the middle, mirror one side and then the other, your face would look very different."

We all nodded.

"There's more about the face that I find interesting. Studies have shown that true emotion is reflected on both sides of your face equally. Conflicting emotion will come out on just one side. So let's say you were both angry and frightened. One side of your face will show anger, the other will reflect your fear. Generally, we tend to look at the right side of the face more than the left, and the right side will reflect the 'public' emotion." She reached behind her and picked up a blank piece of paper, then placed it so the right side of Roy's face was exposed. "His public face." His eyes crinkled and lips pulled back into a smile. She slid the paper over, now showing the other side of his face. "This is the emotion he is hiding."

On that side his eye was sunken, skin sagged, and mouth drooped. He looked utterly defeated.

"Oh!" Grace said. "He looks so sad."

"What about Sam?" Dee Dee asked.

I had a pretty good idea what his face would reveal. Sure enough, his right side was friendly and engaging. The left side sent a chill up the small of my back. His skin was rough, eye open wide, and lip shiny.

"That's creepy," Stacy said.

"Schadenfreude." The word slipped out before I could stop it. Everyone stared at me. I cleared my throat. *Might as well finish the thought.* "Or the English word *epicaricacy*. The German word comes from *schaden*, which means 'harm' or 'misfortune' combined with *freude*, 'joy.' It means taking pleasure from someone else's suffering."

In the silence that followed, Bram entered the room. He stopped when he saw us gathered around the table. "What's going on?"

Angie caught him up on the drawings.

He moved until he could see the sketches.

"Do you know anything about these drawings?" Angie asked. "We believe this is Shadow Woman's self-portrait. You knew her—"

"No, never met her, but I can tell you about some of the other drawings." His hand touched each sketch as he spoke. "These landscapes look like they were drawn near Beryl Creek, east of here. Of course, you all recognize her dogs. Sam, Roy, and . . ." His eyes opened wider. "My boss, the sheriff." He pointed to the fourth portrait.

"Shadow Woman knew the sheriff?" Stacy drawled.

"Apparently." Bram's eyebrows drew together.

Angie covered the public side of the sheriff's face, exposing only her private emotions—an eye narrowed, slight furrow in her brow, tension in the jaw, mouth tightened. "To me, she looks worried."

"Upset. Unhappy." Grace nodded. "What do you see, Bram? You know her."

"All I can say is she's in the middle of a serial-arsonist case, you know," Bram said. "So I'm actually not surprised."

I frowned at Bram. *All I can say* meant there was more to be said. *You know* meant a sensitive topic. *Actually* was an unnecessary word, usually for comparing two or more items. What was he holding back?

No one else seemed to notice Bram's evasion of the question.

Angie indicated the drawing of the older woman. "So we still don't know if this is Shadow Woman's self-portrait, but it seems like a good guess."

I lifted the sketch. Julia, the clerk at the store, had said something was wrong with Mae's face. This drawing showed a woman in deep shadow, with a small chin, short nose, thin upper lip, and flattened midface. I passed the sketch to Grace.

"Whoever this is, she looks like she has fetal alcohol spectrum disorder." Grace gave the drawing to Dee Dee. "That might explain her lifestyle. And her nickname of Shadow Woman. FASD can cause a whole range of difficulties throughout life. Antisocial behavior, mood swings, poor judgment are just a few of the problems."

"Julia mentioned her anger issues," I said slowly. "She left her dogs and mule to fend for themselves, then wrote a check that bounced."

Dee Dee took the sketch from me and placed it on the table, then covered the public side of her face with her hand, displaying her private emotions. Shadow Woman's eyes twinkled and the corner of her mouth curved slightly upward. "I see happiness. A sense of humor."

"Why would she hide that?" Grace said.

We silently contemplated the question.

"She would have been looking in a mirror when she drew herself. This side is what she is concealing." I placed my hand over the other side. The woman's iris looked small in the white of her eye. Her mouth was slightly open, the skin taut against her cheek. It was the look of absolute terror.

CHAPTER 12

The drawing of Sheriff Turner bothered Bram more than he wanted to say. She'd never mentioned a word about knowing Shadow Woman when she'd ordered him to shoot her dogs. And neither Sam nor his chief had asked him to look into her bounced check. Under Idaho law, if Shadow Woman were convicted of false pretenses, she could spend up to three years in prison and be fined as much as fifty thousand dollars.

The dogs yipped, followed immediately by the earth trembling.

Bram checked the time. The supply wagon would be leaving soon and he needed to get the water sample to the lab. He could delay Liam for a little bit, but if he waited too long, the road wouldn't be safe. "Angie, would you wait for me in Roy's office? I'll be right there."

She nodded.

He headed for the kitchen, where he figured he'd find Liam mooching. He was right. Liam had a bowl of ice cream and was leering at one of the waitresses.

"Liam, I need you to delay leaving for a bit."

Liam pointed his spoon at Bram. "I thought you left in the last helicopter."

"Obviously I didn't."

Liam gave the waitress a slow smile. "No way do I mind at all. Take all the time you need."

Bram shook his head. Liam must be working on having a woman at every stop. He grabbed a cup of coffee, then made his way to Roy's office.

Angie was pacing as he entered. "Please sit down, Angie."

She sat, but her leg bounced rapidly. "This has been a disaster! The room trashed, the bear, the Rinaldis' son, now the contaminated water. I think someone hates me." Her voice filled the room.

Or Roy. Or anyone who drank the water. Or even the Rinaldis. He decided not to mention the horses currently racing loose. After sitting behind Roy's cluttered desk and placing his messenger bag on the floor, he pulled out a small notepad. "Who usually fills the water and coffee in the art room?"

"I have no idea. One of the waitstaff. Sometimes Roy himself if the others are busy."

"Is the art room secure?"

"Locked? Didn't used to be, but after this morning, we did lock it."

"Who has a key?"

"Well, that's the thing. Only the office, gift shop, and art room can even be locked. The keys are on a panel in the hall that leads to here. They're labeled, but you do have to know where to look."

Bram tapped his pen against the notepad. "Who knows about the keys?"

"Everyone. Everyone on the staff, that is."

Someone tapped on the door.

"Come in," Bram said.

Roy entered with a sheet of paper. "The list of staff and guests." He placed it in front of Bram.

"Thank you." Bram looked at Angie. "You can go now. Would you send Darby in next?"

Angie rose and hurried from the room.

Bram reached for the list of names but paused. A small pile of unopened mail rested on the edge of the blotter. The top one had a red stamp across it saying *Final Notice*. He glanced at Roy.

The older man snatched up the mail and dropped it into the trash container. "It's nothin'. At least I'll be able to pay everyone off now," he muttered.

Bram picked up the list of names. "I see you've listed Liam Turner as staff."

Roy let out deep breath. "Yeah, um, he fills in part-time when I need extra help. Corporate retreats with team-building exercises, for example, take extra staffing. I've even hired townspeople like Sam at times. At one time he was military."

"Do you have employee records I can look at?"

Roy moved over to a file drawer and began pulling files.

While Roy's back was to him, Bram took the opportunity to look at the pile of papers on the desk. Several were overdue bills. "How goes the roundup?" he asked casually.

Roy stacked the files in front of Bram. "We caught a few. Wyatt's going out with the assistant wrangler and handyman to round up the rest."

—

Angie signaled to me. "Bram wants to interview you. He's in Roy's office. Go through the gift shop, through the door on the far side, down the short hall to the room at the end."

I paused at the door.

"How goes the roundup?" Bram was asking Roy.

"We caught a few. Wyatt's going out with the assistant wrangler and handyman to round up the rest," Roy said.

I nudged the door wider. "What's going on with your remuda?"

"We think the helicopters spooked them." Roy gave me a tight-lipped smile. "Though they should have been used to the sound by now. Don't worry about it. I have my wranglers out rounding them up. Wait, weren't you a champion rodeo rider?"

My hands became sweaty. "More like O-Mok-See games and trick riding, and I'm rusty."

Roy's gaze had drifted to my left leg. "Never mind. I don't really need an extra wrangler to catch the horses. I understand."

I wanted to say I'd try—that I wasn't the disabled has-been he thought me to be. I could handle it. Instead, I just shrugged.

"Darby," Bram said. "What can you tell me about the contaminated water?"

"Not much to tell. I didn't see anyone deliver the water. I just recognized the boggy smell."

"Okay," Bram said to Roy. "Who assigns the various tasks?"

"Me. Or Cookie. Sometimes Wyatt. We maintain a whiteboard in the kitchen with job assignments. We'll put a name next to who's doing the work."

Bram stood. "Let's go see—"

"Already did. There's a check next to 'Take coffee, hot water, fresh water to art room. 12:45.' That means someone did it. Doesn't say who."

Bram slapped his hand on the stack of files. "Let's start in a new direction. Roy, who could have gone up to the pond this morning to get water? Was everyone accounted for?"

"I'm afraid that won't help you," Roy said. "The lodge and cabins are on a gravity-fed well system. We pipe the pond water to the outside faucets to irrigate the lawns. All of them are labeled non-potable water, of course."

"Would your waitresses know that?" I asked. "English isn't their first language. It could be just a mistake."

"We make the water situation very clear to all our staff," Roy said stiffly.

"At this point," Bram said, "I've gotten about as far as I can here. I need the computer and internet back at my office. If you'll let me take the employee records with me, I'll do a background check and get the water over to the lab."

Roy nodded.

Bram placed the records in his messenger bag and stood.

Wyatt poked his head through the doorway. "Cookie said you'd be here. I've rounded up most of the horses. I'm going out after the three I haven't found. The gate's been repaired."

Roy turned to Bram. "Let me see if anyone else wants to go to town with you. Dee Dee may want to be checked for giardia by a doctor." He walked to the door, his shoulders slumped, and left.

Before Wyatt followed him, he gave me a wink and tipped his cowboy hat.

My face grew warm. I charged from the room before Bram could see me blush, again wishing Cookie hadn't mentioned Bram's and Wyatt's interest.

Roy aimed toward the art room and Wyatt sauntered to the lobby. I followed Roy.

"Ladies and gentlemen," Roy said to Angie and the art students. "The supply wagon will be heading to Targhee Falls within the hour. If any of you would like to leave today, let me know and we'll bring your luggage over." His voice trembled slightly.

I slowly walked to the lobby. The air was pungent with lemon wax cleaner. One of the female staffers was just leaving the room with a plastic bin of cleaning supplies. Sunlight streamed in the windows on one side, and the ginger tabby cat had moved from the barn and now sprawled in the sunbeam lighting the floor. The distant clatter of dishes came from the closed dining room.

I stopped. Everything seemed so ordinary and calm. It was hard to believe that not long ago, a young man clinging to life had to be airlifted out. Things could have been going wrong here for months, and the remote beauty of the place would have lured people to doubt their conclusions.

With the contaminated water, I now had actual physical evidence that someone was actively working against Roy. Or it could have been Riccardo's plan to head home. I wished Bram had been able to recover something from the barn.

Maybe it was time to head back to town and make my report to Clan Firinn.

I still had to dig into the paperwork in the packet. At this point, did it matter?

I was scheduled to be here for five days, and it was hard to believe less than twenty-four hours had passed. If I stayed, maybe I'd see Bram again. *Maybe* . . . "Shut up!"

"Are you okay, Darby?" Cookie had entered the room, a handful of stamped envelopes in her hand.

"Sorry, Cookie. I didn't realize I spoke out loud." I walked over to her, still making the slight squeak. *Flapperdoodle.* Yet another problem. "I'm thinking about heading to Targhee Falls, but maybe I could ask you something."

"Sure, ask away."

"What can you tell me about the rocks?"

She turned and placed the envelopes neatly on a nearby table. "What did you want to know?"

I pulled them from my pocket and held them up. "What did your counselor say to do with them? Or maybe more precisely, what did you do with yours?"

She approached and stared at the three pebbles in my hand. "You remember I left a long time ago. All I can tell you is at that time they didn't give us rocks or other types of gifts."

"Funny gift. They just make my pants sag." I slipped the rocks back into my pocket.

She studied my face for a long moment. "I take it your PTSD is rearing its ugly head and that's why you want to leave. I can't say I blame you." She held her hands out in front of her. They shook slightly. "Look at me. Shaking like a leaf and I've been away from Clan Firinn for over ten years."

"You said you're still having PTSD moments. What do you do to get through them?"

"I have a dear brother I can talk to. How about you? Family?"

An unexpected lump formed in the back of my throat. "Um, well, I just adopted a couple of four-legged dependents. They seem to be good listeners. As long as they don't start to drink out of the toilet, we'll get along famously."

Cookie grinned. "That's good. So you're heading home?"

"I'm not sure I'm leaving for good. I just want to report in and see what Clan Firinn wants me to do next."

"Whatever you feel is best. You'll be taking today's supply wagon to Targhee Falls then?"

"Yes."

She patted my arm. "The next wagon won't be back until tomorrow, so you might take your things with you. That way, if your PTSD gets too overwhelming and you change your mind about returning, you're set. Your cabin will remain yours until you let us know."

"Good idea. And thank you."

The dogs spotted me as soon as I emerged from the lodge. Holly flew at me as if I'd been gone for years, circling me with a wiggling, tail-wagging, openmouthed greeting. Maverick stood still, and for a moment his tail waved gently. I grinned. Silver lining?

I'd stuck all the rocks in a single pocket, and they now poked me in the hip. I pulled the stones out. Cookie didn't know what they were for either. Why three? Ugly, lumpy, heavy . . . I should just throw them away. Instead I again put one in each pocket.

It didn't take long to pack up my bag. I decided to leave Roy's packet in the cabin and just take my handwritten notes with me. If I returned, I wouldn't have to ask for them again, and if I decided to head to Clan Firinn, Roy would have his materials. When I picked up my purse, I realized I'd left my wallet and Shadow Woman's drawings in the art room. I grabbed my suitcase and duffel and placed them on the porch next to the dog dishes, then walked over to the lodge. For now I'd leave the dried fruit still in the basket and the dog food.

Liam was leading the harnessed Belgian from the barn to hitch up to the wagon. He waved at me.

I waved back. "Hi, Liam. I'll be going with you. Could you see that my bags and the dogs' dishes are loaded?"

He grinned. "You betcha, Miss Darby. You can ride up front with me."

In a pig's eye I'll ride up front with you. "Thank you, Liam. I believe Dee Dee will be coming. I'd bet she'd like to sit with you. She loves classical music. Maybe you could introduce her to bro-country."

He gave me a sour look and stalked away with the horse.

The lobby was empty and silent as I made my way to the art room. After retrieving my wallet and Scott Thomas's note from the backpack, I moved to where I'd left the sketches.

They were gone.

CHAPTER 13

Angie must have picked up the drawings. I checked her desk, then around the room. The drawings were definitely missing. Returning to her desk, I started pulling out drawers.

"Excuse me? What are you doing?" Angie stood in the doorway. Her voice was louder than ever.

My face burned. "Um . . . looking for my drawings . . . technically Shadow Woman's sketches. I'm going to Targhee Falls on the supply wagon and wanted them. Where did you put them?"

"I didn't. They were still there when I returned from Roy's office. Everyone left right after you did—Dee Dee to pack, Peter and Stacy for a walk. I went back to my room."

"Did you lock the art room?"

"No. But I can't imagine why someone would take them."

My neck tingled. "Maybe because they revealed a bit too much about some people?"

Angie folded her arms and leaned against the doorjamb. "Admittedly Sam's sketch wasn't very flattering, but

he's not here. Come to think of it, didn't you buy those drawings from Sam in the first place? He could have destroyed
the drawing when he had it."

"He never saw it. The clerk hid it in a phone book."

Angie straightened. "So we have a mystery! And you're
an investigator!"

"You said that before. I'm not. I'm just missing my
drawings."

"I don't believe you, you know, when you deny being in
law enforcement. My dad and brothers are all in the field,
and I can spot an officer a mile away." She squinted at me.
"Not patrol or dispatch, more like a crime expert of some
kind."

I took a deep breath. "I'm a forensic linguist."

"I knew it. I *knew* it! That's like analyzing ransom notes,
lies in what people write, stuff like that?"

"I examine words people use. What they write. What
they say."

Angie moved from the door and pulled out a chair.
"Give me an example."

"I really can't talk about actual cases."

"Come on, Darby. Something!"

I sighed and thought for a moment. "Okay, the easiest
part of what I do is related to lying and deception."

"Aren't those the same thing?"

"No. Most people don't lie, but they do deceive. A lie
is false information. The reason most people don't lie is
they can't remember what they said. People commonly

do deceive. They'll stick to the truth as much as possible, just concealing one thing. So if you have, say, a case where an employee took some money from the boss's desk, the employee will keep to the real events and just leave out the theft."

"And you can tell that how?"

"The truth will be full of detail—where they were, how they were feeling, what was going on around them. When they get to the deception, the story will be lean, little detail, and full of certain phrases like 'the next thing I knew,' or 'later on.' You want to listen to exactly what people say. You don't add to it or subtract from it."

Angie picked up a pencil and twirled it. "Go on."

"Deception happens all the time in advertising. For example, marketers claim a supplement works because it was clinically tested."

"So?"

"*Clinically tested* doesn't mean the same as *clinically proven*. They're not saying it works, only that it was tested. Sometimes they can't even say that, so they'll say that it's the bestselling supplement, implying that if a bunch of people buy it, it must work."

"Oh, that's good. Who are the best liars?"

"The best liars," I said slowly, "and the most devastating lies, come from the people you'd never believe would lie to you."

Clang, clang, clang. Someone rang a triangle outside the lodge.

"That's the signal that the supply wagon's leaving in half an hour." Angie stood. "I'll keep looking for those drawings and let you know when I find them."

Just before I exited, she put her arm out and stopped me. "I believe you were sent here to find out what's rotten at Mule Shoe." She moved her arm. "Go ahead and make your report in Targhee Falls to whomever you work for, then get back here before something even worse happens."

I hurried away, Angie's words bouncing in my brain. Cookie, Roy, Angie . . . how many other people knew why I was here, and how did that figure into what was going on?

I had a few minutes before I had to leave—time to write a few notes. Moving to the front porch of the lodge where I could watch for the departing wagon, I selected a seat and opened my notebook.

Angie was the last person I saw, so I wrote down her name. *Think about the art room.* I paused. Although the room had been ransacked, nothing, really, had been destroyed. The pencil sets were intact, nothing had been broken. Could Angie . . .

The ground shifted. Holly and Maverick, resting in the shade in front of me, leaped to their feet and began barking.

"Ha! One got past you."

Cookie charged out the door and looked at her watch. "What the . . ."

The ground continued to tremble. Both dogs looked left and kept barking.

The rumbling grew louder, turning into a thunder of

hoofbeats. The entire herd of horses burst into sight, raising a cloud of dust.

"Not again!" Cookie put her hand over her mouth.

The horses were followed by Wyatt on foot. He spotted us and walked over. "Between the helicopters and that last earthquake, the horses are all on edge. They found a spot in the fence to push through. Don't worry, the main gate is closed, so they'll just circle around and head back—especially if I rattle a bucket of oats. But I gotta tell you, I'm tired of chasing horses. Never did catch Shadow Woman's old mule, and one other horse is gone." He stomped off, muttering.

I turned to Cookie. "You said 'not again.' I know the horses got out earlier today. Has this happened before?"

"It happens. Barbed wire would keep them in better, but they can injure themselves on it. When they break out like this, it's just best to get out of the way and let them run. They'll return to their pasture soon enough."

Almost before she'd finished speaking, the horses had swung around the outside of the cabins and were galloping toward the barn.

The ground shook again. The dogs hadn't stopped barking. I couldn't tell if it was another earthquake or the racing horses, but my neck was on full-scale fire.

—

Liam stuck his head into Roy's office. "Getting late and a storm's comin'. Can you help me?"

Bram glanced at his watch. It *was* getting late. He didn't want to be anywhere near the Devil's Keyhole at dusk. He trotted from the office and helped Liam hitch up the horse, then they circled around to the cabins collecting luggage. Returning to the front of the lodge, Bram jumped down and rang the triangle. Liam guided the Belgian to the side of the building to collect any last-minute mail and packages.

Clouds had been gathering over the past few hours, and the temperature had dipped. The helicopter taking the guests to Idaho Falls should have been ahead of the storm. In fact, they should have landed by now. He hoped any rain would hold off until they reached town. The wagon was charming and rustic when the weather was nice, but plenty miserable when the elements changed.

As he strolled around the lodge, something nagged at the back of his brain, but he couldn't pull it out. What was he forgetting? He had the contaminated water. Was it something else? Weather? Idaho Falls? Supply wagon? Mule Shoe?

A small earthquake was followed by the barking dogs at the front of the lodge. Shortly after came the sound of a stampede.

"Grab the horse's head," he yelled at Liam. The young man took hold of the Belgian's bridle on one side while Bram held on to the other. The big guy stomped and tossed his head as the herd raced through the center of the resort, kicking up a dust cloud. By the time the cloud settled, the horses had reached the perimeter fence and turned back toward the barn.

"Glad we had him hitched up," Liam said. "No way would he have been able to pull the wagon if he'd been running with the herd. Too jacked up."

Still holding the bridle, both men walked the horse and wagon to the front of the lodge.

Dee Dee, Grace, and Darby were waiting. The two dogs circled Darby but remained some distance from the others. The suitcases were stacked behind the spring seat, and a thick mattress covered the remaining area. Cookie bustled from the lodge with several blankets. "You might get cold at the top of the pass. If, heaven forbid, it should start raining, there's a tarp under the spring seat." She pulled Darby aside and spoke quietly, but Bram could hear her. "I hope you'll return after making your report, and I hope whoever or whatever is behind all this is caught and punished. This is too glorious a place on earth to lose it now. Be safe."

I hope she returns too. Bram busied himself by placing a box on the ground to serve as a step, then helped Dee Dee to the wagon bed. When Darby placed her hand in his for help, it felt like downy feathers tickled his palm. She made a point of not looking at him, but two red patches appeared on her cheeks.

Bram jumped up onto the seat next to Liam, who frowned his displeasure. "Let's go."

Roy wandered out and watched them leave. He looked like he'd aged twenty years.

Grace waved good-bye to her friend. "I'll call you when I get back to town."

Everyone's mood seemed to match the gathering dark clouds. Dee Dee leaned against one side of the wagon bed, opposite Darby. The women spread the blankets over their outstretched legs. Without encouragement, the two dogs followed, neither letting Darby out of sight. The air held the earthy scent of rain.

Bram thought about Shadow Woman's drawing of the sheriff. "Liam, did your mom meet Shadow Woman at some point?"

Liam thought for a few moments. "Nooo . . . wait, yeah. Around the time of the fire that killed those two guys. Everyone went to see the burned-down house. Mom was really upset, but I . . ." He clicked at the horse.

"But you what?"

"Nothin'."

Bram waited, but Liam just focused on the road.

Halfway up the mountain, the rain struck. Dee Dee snatched out the tarp, but before she could completely open it, the full deluge hit. Both Bram and Liam hunkered down but were almost immediately soaked. All Bram could see in the back of the wagon was the blue tarp covering a pair of moving lumps.

He looked around for his messenger bag before realizing he'd left it in Roy's office. That was what he'd forgotten. *At least nothing will get wet.* He made sure his pistol stayed dry.

A blast of wind lifted the edge of the tarp, then ripped it from the women's grip and sent it sailing over the edge of the mountain. Dee Dee let loose with a colorful string of cuss words, while Darby ducked farther under the swiftly soaked blankets.

Liam pulled up his collar. "What else can go wrong? I told Roy if he was going to keep up this ridiculous 'primitive' theme, he needed a backup plan." He continued to gripe, swear, and whine until Bram had enough.

"Liam, just drive the wagon and keep your mouth shut."

The rain ceased as quickly as it had begun, and the clouds parted enough for tepid sunlight to add a sheen to the puddles. The previously crisp *clop, clop, clop* of the big horse became muted in the mud.

They'd reached the point where the road narrowed, with a rocky cliff on one side and steep drop on the other. Around the next corner was the top of the pass and the Devil's Keyhole. The sun dipped behind a cloud, further chilling the air. He'd be glad when this trip ended.

They moved around the bend and stopped.

The road ended at a mountain of rocks, uprooted trees, and dirt.

—

I couldn't decide if I'd be less miserable with or without the soaked blanket covering me. Dee Dee's shivering matched mine. I was about to put the blanket issue to a vote when the wagon stopped.

Bram turned and looked at us. "Ladies, it looks like we'll have to go back to Mule Shoe. A landslide has blocked our leaving."

Dee Dee groaned, then snapped, "Let's get to it. I'm chilled to the bone."

"No way," Liam said. "It's too dangerous to back down, and it's too narrow here to turn around. We'll have to un-hitch the horse, then use him to pull the wagon so it's facing the other way."

Bram jumped down. "I'm going to get a rock to put behind the wheel. Darby, if you could hold the horse's head while Liam unhitches him. Dee Dee, get up on the driver's seat and hold on to the brake lever."

Before Bram could help me, I'd hopped off the back, walked to the horse's head, and taken hold of the bridle. Bram grabbed a good-sized rock from the side of the road. As he moved toward the wheel, Liam unsnapped the har-ness from the wagon.

Crack!

At the sound of splintering wood the horse tossed his head, pulling me off my feet. I clung to his bridle until I regained my footing, then looked around to see what had made the sound.

Dee Dee was holding the shattered end of the brake lever.

The wagon lurched backward, gaining speed, aiming straight for the cliff edge.

"Jump!" Bram yelled.

"Dee Dee, jump!" I screamed.

Dee Dee leaped from the driver's seat, hit the road, and rolled. The wagon flew off the road and out of sight.

I held my breath. *Please, Lord...*

Dee Dee grabbed at grasses and dirt to stop her momentum.

A loud crash echoed across the mountains as the wagon hit the bottom of the ravine.

Bram raced toward the frantically thrashing woman.

Dee Dee screamed once just before she disappeared over the precipice.

I became light-headed. My vision blurred. If I hadn't been clinging so hard to the horse's bridle, I would have collapsed.

Bram stumbled to the edge of the cliff and looked over, then spun away. "Oh, my sweet Lord." His face was ashen.

Liam moved next to Bram, glanced down, then turned and vomited.

This time I did crumple to the ground. The enormity of Dee Dee gone in an instant washed over me.

Holly reached my side, sat, and rested her head on my shoulder.

Without a word, Liam turned and started trotting back to Mule Shoe.

Bram reached over and picked up the broken handle of the brake.

The Belgian sniffed my hair, then shuffled restlessly.

His enormous feet were inches from my leg. As I started to get to my feet, Bram came over and held out his hand. I gratefully took it. He pulled me up, then into his arms. I clung to him, shivering, feeling his warmth.

We stood there for a long moment. His arms wrapped around me, cradling me, felt so good, so right . . . *Just wait until he finds out.*

I straightened and shifted away from him. "We . . . need to get back to Mule Shoe and call it in . . . get a recovery team . . . it's getting late."

Slowly Bram released me. "Rain check, then."

I ducked my head so he couldn't see my expression, afraid it would be one of pathetic longing.

He held out the brake handle for me to see. Part of it was ragged slivers of wood. Half was a neat cut.

"How long ago do you think someone sabotaged the brake handle?" I asked him.

"It's fresh. Yet another 'accident.'" He made quote marks in the air.

"And this time someone is dead."

He nodded, took the reins from me, and pulled me around until I faced the right side of the horse. Like most of his breed, the Belgian towered over me at over eighteen hands—over six feet at the withers. "Use the harness and grab on. I'll give you a leg up."

Without thinking, I bent my leg. Bram boosted me up to the equine's massive back.

I clutched the mane and stared down at him.

He stood motionless, staring at my left leg. Slowly he reached forward and tugged my jeans up, exposing the metal rod of my prosthesis.

A gust of wind hit the ponderosas in the ridge above us, filling the silence with creaking branches and murmuring needles. The dogs, restlessly pacing the road, paused and looked at us.

I took a deep breath and blinked rapidly to clear my vision. "It was only a matter of time before you learned the truth. I'm not ashamed. This is my new reality."

"When were you going to tell me?" he asked quietly.

"What's to tell?" I swallowed, grateful my voice remained steady. I wasn't going to tell him I was a coward as well. My amputation should be enough to kill any interest.

The horse shifted and Bram patted him on the neck. Silence again stretched between us. With every particle of my body, I wished that he'd say it didn't matter, that he'd look past all my flaws. Then he'd leap on the back of the horse, put his arms around me, and we'd ride off together into the sunset. Ending credits would roll. Happily ever after.

Without a word, he turned, tugged on the reins, and started leading the big Belgian toward the Mule Shoe.

I tangled my fingers through the horse's mane and stared sightlessly at the horizon. *I will not cry. Not anymore.*

CHAPTER 14

Bram couldn't marshal his thoughts. They flew through his brain like the flurry in a snow globe. *She's disabled.* But he'd never seen more than a slight limp. *She lied.* No, she just never told him. *She led me on.* Or had he pursued her?

He risked a glance at her face. Skin pale. Eyes . . . He looked away quickly and walked faster.

He *had* pursued her in his mind. He'd allowed himself to picture being with her, getting to know her better. *Face it, Bram. She's not perfect.*

Don't be like your worthless mother or brother, Bram. It's up to you. Choose the right road. Make sure you do something perfectly or don't bother . . . His grandmother's warning slammed into his brain. He'd fallen head-over-heels in love and married a woman who was perfect on the outside and amoral inside. His plan to help his brother had failed. He'd stayed on at a dead-end job because he didn't have the courage to seek work elsewhere. For crying out loud, he had a master's degree in project management. He could get a job anywhere. His grandmother's voice was a chant in his head. *Make sure you do something perfectly or don't bother . . .*

He shook his head and gripped the horse's bridle tighter. *Just get back to Mule Shoe.*

The two dogs kept close to them, not stopping to check out any trees or interesting smells.

It was nearly dark and they hadn't caught up with Liam before the resort came into sight. As they passed through the gate, the dogs took off toward one of the cabins.

Shortly, Holly yipped.

"Something's wrong," Darby said.

Bram let go of the reins and ran toward the sound.

Both dogs were circling around a dark object. It looked like someone had dropped a jacket or pile of clothing. The object took form as he approached.

A body. The assistant wrangler.

Bram didn't need to feel for a pulse. The man's sightless eyes stared upward.

Darby was right behind him, still mounted. She expertly turned the big horse sideways to see. "Is he—"

"Yes."

"How?" She slid from the horse's back, landing lightly on the ground.

He lifted the man slightly and looked underneath, then gently lowered him. "There's a rock with blood on it there." He pointed. "And blood on the back of his shirt. I'd say stabbed, maybe shot, but I'm not a medical examiner." He looked around. The ranch was quiet. There should have been guests moving around, staff working on evening chores, the sound of food preparation in the kitchen.

"What is it?" She was scratching her neck and staring intently at his expression.

He reached for his holstered pistol. "Darby, I have no idea what's going on, but I want you to stay close to me, okay?" He kept his gaze on the surroundings and felt, more than saw, her nod.

The wind bent the tops of the pines, sounding like distant traffic. The rapping of a woodpecker was followed by the scratchy *rac-rac-rac* of a Steller's jay.

The big draft horse sidestepped away from the smell of blood. "Bram—"

"Shhhhh."

"Look at the dogs."

Both Maverick and Holly were running back and forth, sniffing the ground. Then they took off toward the barn.

He waved her behind him, then led the way. They entered the side door open to the horse pasture. Inside, Bram held up his hand and listened. He couldn't hear the dogs. He helped Darby with the straps and buckles on the Belgian's harness, then removed the heavy collar. He left her to unbridle and turn the horse loose in the pasture while he examined each stall. At the last one, he stopped.

"Here's another one."

Darby joined him. "Who is it?"

"One of the workers, a maintenance man from West Yellowstone. I never caught his name." He moved over to the man and checked for signs of life. "Looks like he was struck on the head, just like the wrangler, then stabbed or maybe shot as well." When he straightened, he expected to see Darby on the verge of collapse. Instead her jaw had tightened and her eyes narrowed.

"How many people were here when we left?" she asked.

Bram placed the broken brake handle inside his belt to free his hands. "The staff, maybe four or five of them. Roy, Wyatt, Angie, Cookie . . . the remaining art students . . ."

"Grace, Stacy, and Peter. And where did Liam go? We'd better find them." Without a word, she headed out of the barn.

Bram ran to catch up with her. "We need to stay together. Whoever did this could be out there . . . waiting."

—

My heart slammed against my chest, my stomach twisted, and sweat chilled me. The familiar PTSD symptoms swarmed me like hornets defending their nest. I reached into my pocket and felt the rocks Scott Thomas had sent me, then squeezed them until they hurt my fingers. *Not this time.* I wasn't going to give in. Two people had been murdered, and several others were missing, Dee Dee was dead, and I needed to keep my head. I turned and started toward the barn door.

Bram ran up behind me. "We need to stay together. Whoever did this could be out there . . . waiting."

I jerked to a stop. "It'll be dark soon. Shouldn't we split up? We could cover more ground."

"No. We need to stay in sight of each other. Those two men were attacked from behind."

"Right." I took off my glasses and tossed them aside.

Holly let out an excited yip.

"That came from over near the staff housing." Bram motioned for me to follow, scanned the area, then raced toward the rear of the lodge. I kept up the best I could, my leg squeaking with every step. As we cleared the corner of the lodge, the next body came into sight.

Cookie.

Bile rose in my throat. Had she survived whatever horrible event took her to Clan Firinn only to be murdered here?

Holly circled her, giving anxious yips.

As with the two men, a bloody rock was next to her body. Bram leaned over her and placed his fingers on her neck to check for a pulse. "She's alive!"

I awkwardly knelt beside her. Freckles I'd never noticed stood out against her pale skin, and her chest rose and fell with shallow breathing. I found the knot where the rock had smashed her skull behind her ear. "Do we dare move her?"

"We'll have to. We can't leave her here. Can you carry her legs?"

"Yes."

He offered his hand to help me up.

I ignored it and stood.

He cleared his throat. "You know, I—"

"It's not necessary—"

We both stopped. "Let's just get her inside." He holstered his pistol, then lifted her to a seated position.

I grabbed her legs, trying not to grunt at her weight. As soon as we lifted her, it was apparent she had been stabbed as well. Blood stained the back of her shirt. We shuffled her to a door leading to the lobby. Once inside, we moved her to the sofa facing the unlit fireplace.

Liam entered, drinking a can of beer. "Where is every— Whoa, what happened?"

"Someone's murdered two people and attacked Cookie."

Liam dropped the beer. "No way!"

Bram ignored him. "I'd really like to take her someplace where we could lock the door, but for now . . . at least we can see anyone coming. Liam, don't just stand there. Get a fire going. I'm going to get on the two-way radio and call for help. Darby, can you see how badly she's been hurt?"

Liam slowly moved toward the fireplace.

Bram hesitated a moment before leaving. "I guess I don't have to say watch your back." He pulled out his pistol, then sprinted from the room.

I carefully rolled Cookie onto her side and lifted her blouse. The injury was a nasty-looking slice below the ribs. It looked painful, but fortunately not deep. "Liam, do you know where I can find a first-aid kit?"

"Kitchen. I'll get it." He left, returning shortly with a

respectably large kit. Inside I found bandages and tape, which I used to bind up her injury. After covering her with the throw from the back of the sofa, I trotted to the door we'd just come through, opened it, and called the dogs. I wasn't sure how much aggression they'd show a knife- and rock-wielding killer, but they would react. Holly entered without further encouragement, but Maverick stayed outside at a cautious distance.

"Okay, Holly," I whispered to the wiggling canine. "If you see a bad guy, lick him to death." By the time I returned to the fireplace, Liam had a decent fire going.

Bram returned, his lips compressed into a straight line, carrying a messenger bag. Behind him was Roy.

"Did you get through on the radio, Bram?" I asked.

"Someone destroyed it," Roy answered before Bram could speak. "How's Cookie?"

"She was stabbed, but the bleeding has stopped. I was just about to get ice for her head." I sent a questioning glance at Bram.

"I'll come with you to the kitchen." Bram pulled the brake handle from his belt, placed it into the bag, then dropped the bag next to the sofa. I followed him toward the dining room. Once we were out of earshot, he said, "I found Roy in his office. He said Cookie came by and said no one had shown up to start dinner prep. She was going to look around and see why the staff was AWOL. He went to his office and found the radio destroyed. He thought he heard something, so he jammed a chair against the door."

"I see some holes in his story." We entered the kitchen. Everything looked chillingly normal. "When Cookie didn't return, why didn't he go looking for her?" I picked up a dish towel, opened the oversized freezer, and filled the towel with ice.

"Agreed."

"Then again"—I closed the freezer and walked toward the door—"why would Roy go on a murderous rampage on his own ranch?"

"We can't assume anything, but if he is the killer, we just left one of his victims alone with him."

We both rushed back into the resort lobby, then jerked to a halt.

Wyatt stood at the front door with a rifle aimed at Roy and Liam. He immediately shifted his attention, and his aim, to us. "Drop the pistol, Bram."

Bram shook his head. "You don't want to do this, Wyatt."

My focus narrowed. A high buzzing started in my head. I reached for a nearby wall to keep from falling. The world was moving in slow motion.

Wyatt's face was flushed. "Don't move. Drop the pistol. Don't make me have to shoot."

"Why did you do it, Wyatt?" Roy asked.

"I didn't do anything." Wyatt moved so he could keep the rifle on all of us. "I just got back from trying to find that last horse and mule and found the body in the barn."

I clung to the wall.

"How do we know you didn't kill him?" Bram asked.

"And how do I know *you* aren't the killer?" Wyatt shot back.

Cookie moaned.

Her voice shook me out of my stupor. I walked on unsteady legs to the prone woman. "Go ahead and shoot me, but don't let Cookie suffer." I reached her and placed the ice on the lump behind her ear. "Wyatt, I've been with Bram and Liam this whole time."

"Not quite," Bram said. "You were with me the whole time. Liam walked back to Mule Shoe by himself."

I nodded. "Right. Anyway, there was an accident . . . or at least we thought it was an accident." I told the others about the landslide, the wagon, Dee Dee, the brake handle, and then finding the wrangler's body behind the cabin and the man in the barn.

Wyatt slowly lowered his rifle. "The radio—"

"Destroyed," Roy said.

Wyatt returned to the front door and shut it. "So we're effectively cut off from the world with a badly injured woman and a homicidal maniac on the loose."

CHAPTER 15

The sun dropped low. Roy sat hunched in a chair, bent over, head in his hands. Bram and Wyatt kept their weapons out and stared at each other. Liam mopped up his spilled beer, found another can of brew, then settled near the dining room. I stayed next to Cookie, pressing the ice pack to her head. Her color looked better, and her breathing was less labored.

My neck itched like crazy, but I held off scratching, knowing once I started, I wouldn't be able to stop.

Wyatt relaxed slightly. "There's still four members of the regular staff unaccounted for, plus Angie and the three guests. And we need to move those bodies. Bear, wolves, cougars—"

"We get the drift." Bram looked at me.

My chest tightened and heat flushed my face. Bram saw me as a delicate invalid. Even without knowing I was a coward, he'd discovered my prosthesis, seen the PTSD episodes.

I just wanted to get back to Clan Firinn. Back to safety.

Bram glanced out the window. "We'll need to locate everyone one way or the other. They could be injured, like Cookie. And we need to secure an area for the night. We don't know if this person is armed, and there are too many ways to get into this room."

A log popped in the fireplace.

I jerked, then listened. Only the slight crackle of the fire. "Do you hear that?"

"I don't hear anything," Bram said.

"Right. The hum of the generator is gone."

Roy shook himself slightly and looked up. "It's probably out of fuel. Unless we can get to the generator, the fresh food won't keep."

"And no way will the beer stay cold." Liam stood and headed for the kitchen.

Cookie stirred and opened her eyes. "Darby? I . . . I thought you left."

"I'm here now." I gave her a reassuring pat on the shoulder. "Do you remember what happened to you?"

Her eyebrows knitted together for a moment. "I couldn't find my staff. Told Roy, then started for the staff housing . . . I heard a horse walking on the road . . . someone behind me, I turned . . . then nothing."

"The horse on the road would have been us," Bram said. "So the killer took off before he could . . . finish with Cookie."

I caught Bram's attention. "How long do you think those two men had been dead?" I whispered.

"Not long. Why?"

Liam sauntered into the dining room, fresh can of beer in hand.

I looked at Liam, then back at Bram.

He nodded. "Maybe."

Wyatt shifted his rifle from hand to hand. "We gotta get out of here. We're sitting ducks, just waiting."

"Roy, how many firearms do you have?" Bram asked.

"Several rifles, a shotgun, two pistols . . ."

"Where are they?" Bram asked.

"Oh." If possible, Roy's face had gone paler.

"Oh, what?" Bram moved to the older man and sat in a chair next to him. "What?"

"I didn't register this earlier. I can't concentrate—"

I reached over and squeezed the man's arm. "What is it, Roy?" I said softly.

"The guns were shut up in my office with the radio. They're gone."

———

Bram didn't think things could get any worse, but the news of the missing firearms was the final blow. He figured the killer had knocked out his victims, then used a knife so as not to alert others. But the killer had enough firepower to take out all of them.

Bram rubbed his face. "The way I see it—"

"Who put you in charge?" Wyatt faced him.

"I'm law enforcement. We have three homicides and an attempted homicide, plus missing individuals." Bram stood. "I'm taking over."

"Yeah, well, you don't know this ranch. I should be in charge."

"Wyatt, you're nothing but a broken-down cowboy."

"And you're nothing but a Barney Fife wannabe!"

Darby stood, moved to the door, and opened it. Her face flamed red.

Bram ran after her and caught her arm. "Where are you going?"

"To find the missing people. You two can stay here and decide who gets to be the boss, but someone's got to take action."

"Come back inside." Bram could feel his own face getting warm as he gently pulled her away from the door and closed it. He looked at Wyatt. "You're right. You know the ranch. But before we leave here, let's make sure the lodge has been searched. Darby and I were in the dining room and kitchen, so those rooms are cleared."

"Roy's quarters are upstairs," Wyatt said, "and there's the art room and gift shop." He strolled toward the hall leading to the art room. Bram followed.

Once there, it took only a moment to see the room was empty. Without a word, Wyatt left, opening a door halfway down the hall. A narrow set of dark and dusty stairs led upward.

Bram patted the door opposite. "What's in here?"

Wyatt opened it to a storage area, clearly void of human occupants.

Bram pulled out a small flashlight. Wyatt stepped away and let Bram lead. At the top of the stairwell, a simple bathroom was on the left. He played his light over the area on his right. A wood-burning stove sat in the corner with a threadbare wingback chair facing it. A single bed with a quilted bedspread and a small bureau bracketed the fireplace. The closet door stood open.

"Seen enough?" Wyatt pivoted and clumped down the stairs.

Bram flashed his light around the room one more time, his flashlight lingering on a pair of worn slippers next to the chair.

"Wyatt." Bram caught up to the other man at the bottom of the stairs. "How much do you know about what's going on at Mule Shoe?"

"You mean like the murders?"

Bram turned off his flashlight. "You know what I mean."

"He's my boss. It's none of my business."

"It is now. Roy told me he sold Mule Shoe."

Wyatt smoothed his mustache. "Yeah. He told me today. Did he tell you who bought it? And what they're going to do with it?"

"He didn't know." Bram looked toward the lobby. "Maybe someone wasn't happy with the sale. Guess one way to cool any interest is to turn this place into a death camp."

"Who? And why?"

"Don't know. Just saying." He turned and ambled toward the lobby.

While they'd been searching the lodge, Cookie had shifted to a semiseated position, though she still held the towel of ice to her head. Her color was normal. She opened her mouth when she saw them, then closed it.

"Cookie," Wyatt said. "You were heading to the staff housing. I take it you didn't get a chance to go inside?"

She shook her head, then winced.

"We'll start there. But we can't leave the four of you here unarmed."

"Give Darby your rifle," Bram said.

"Why don't you give her your Glock?"

"Ah . . ." Darby had grown pale. "Give the gun to Roy."

Bram clenched his jaw and handed his pistol to Roy. "Do you know how to use—"

"Yes." He took the pistol, pulled back the slide, chambered a bullet, then gave Bram a jerk of his head.

"Let's secure the lodge as much as possible." Bram glanced around the room, then retrieved a chair, which he wedged under the front doorknob. "Wyatt, see if you can block the kitchen door. Darby, we'll go out the back. I want you to do the same to that door if you can."

She narrowed her eyes, tightened her mouth, and looked like she was about to punch him.

"Um . . . be careful." He picked up a chair and headed to the back door. Darby followed. Wyatt soon joined them.

"You're not wearing your glasses," Wyatt said to Darby. "Looks good."

Bram clenched his fist and bit back his reply. "Let's go."

Outside, they waited until they heard the bump of Darby wedging the chair under the knob. The sun was dipping behind the mountains and the air was cool and sharp. The staff building matched the rustic log structure of the lodge and was about two hundred feet from the main building.

Wyatt took the lead while Bram kept watch from the rear. They entered the shared living area, a comfortable room with well-worn furniture and smelling faintly of cigarette smoke. The men's bunk room was on the left, women's on the right. Swiftly they checked the men's side. Empty. Returning to the living area, Bram leading this time, they opened the door to the women's side. Also empty.

The long shadows and dense pines formed perfect locations for sniper's nests. "We need to keep moving." Bram nodded toward his right. "Darby and I were in the barn, but we didn't look beyond the body in the stall. How well did you check the rest of the stalls, loft, and tack room?"

"It's clear. Cabins?"

"Let's go. When we get to the cabin where the wrangler's body is, we'll move it inside for now. Keep low and don't run in a straight line." Both men dashed for the line of cabins. Half an hour later the sun had set and they'd uncovered only empty rooms, cleaned and waiting for guests. They moved the body of the wrangler before heading to the final cabin. Here the knob turned, but the door remained closed.

Bram rattled the knob, then banged on the door. "Anyone here? It's Deputy White."

A *thump*, then the door opened.

All three of the female staff members were in the room. They appeared to have been crying. "Wh-wh-what happened to Gary?" the oldest of the three asked.

"Gary?"

"The man, the horse man." The woman spoke with a strong Polish accent. "Zofia found him." She nodded at a short blond woman. "She said . . . someone kill him."

"I'm afraid so. What happened here after the supply wagon left?" Bram asked.

"We started cleaning." Zofia waved at the other two. "I saw the men bringing some horses when I finish cabin five. I keep working to here. That's where I found Gary. I scream and Maja and Alicja ran over. We decided not safe out there. We . . ." She paused to search for a word.

"Shove." Maja made a motion as if pushing a chair. "Blocked the door. We wait."

"Did you see any of the guests?" Bram asked.

"I think some were going to pond." Zofia looked at her watch. "But that was long time ago. Maybe they now dead—"

"Let's not get ahead of ourselves." Wyatt looked at Bram. "We'll run the three women to the lodge, then search the pond area?"

Bram nodded. He figured they both had the same thought. If no one had returned from their hike, they'd most likely be recovering bodies, not rescuing guests.

CHAPTER 16

After jamming the chair under the door, I moved around the room, closing the wooden shutters against the encroaching darkness. I felt less exposed, but not any safer.

Roy stood and began lighting the lamps, his movements robotic. I approached him to help, but he wordlessly waved me away.

I moved to the fireplace and added another log to the fire before sitting. "How are you feeling, Cookie?"

"Pretty rotten." She nudged Bram's messenger bag. "What's this?"

I took it from her and opened it. Inside were files with employee names on the tabs plus one labeled Arson Notes. "Looks like Bram's bag. I'm guessing he left it in Roy's office when he was interviewing us. That was probably a good thing. If he'd had it in the wagon . . ." I sucked in some air. *Don't go there.*

Cookie leaned back and closed her eyes.

"Can I get you an aspirin?" I asked.

"That would be nice. There's some in the kitchen, above the sink."

I stood. On impulse, I grabbed up the bag and took it with me. Chances were that Bram's notes on the interviews he held on the giardia water were inside, along with other case information. I'd hold on to it and give it to Bram personally. *At least I don't have to worry about what he might think about me. He made that perfectly clear.*

After placing the bag on one of the dining room tables, I continued to the kitchen. Roy had left one lamp burning, but there were too many shadows. I quickly found the aspirin and a glass of water, then returned to Cookie. "Here you go. Can I get you anything else?"

"Thank you, Darby. This will help." She took the proffered items, then glanced toward the door, eyebrows furrowed. "I wonder what's keeping them."

Someone tapped at the front door.

No one moved.

The tapping came again. "Darby, open up. It's Bram."

I ran to the door, pulled the chair out of the way, and opened it. Bram, Wyatt, and the three women who worked at the resort pushed in. Behind them were Grace, Stacy, and Peter.

"We found the staff in cabin one," Bram said quietly to me. "Grace, Stacy, and Peter were returning from a hike to the pond. Or so they say."

"Do they know . . . ?" I asked.

"You can update them while we finish searching. We're still missing one staff member, a guy called Spuds, and Angie." He lowered his voice still more. "We don't know who's been doing what, so just listen carefully."

I nodded. "Be careful."

———

Wyatt and Bram stepped from the lodge and waited for Darby to secure the door. "All we have left to search is the building where Cookie, Angie, and I are housed," Wyatt said.

"Okay. I've never actually been there."

"Let's hope our killer hasn't either." Wyatt peeked into the darkness. "No flashlights?"

Bram's gut tightened. "No flashlights, but warn me if there's something on the path."

The half-moon provided just enough light to see the path but kept the shadows in ebony darkness. The temperature had dropped again, and Bram could see his breath.

Wyatt plunged into a row of trees and disappeared.

Bram paused. The breeze tossed the pines, making them look like they were waving him away. His hand dropped to his empty holster, then grabbed his flashlight. It wasn't much of a weapon, but he could blind someone, and it was made of metal. Pushing through the branches, he almost collided with Wyatt.

"Stay close," the other man muttered, then moved forward.

He followed Wyatt, feeling more than seeing the path. The log triplex reared up before them suddenly.

"Cookie's quarters are on the right, Angela's are on the left," Wyatt muttered. "Mine are in the middle."

"Normally I'd say let's just check out yours and Angela's side since Cookie is accounted for, but we're still missing Spuds—"

"Kevin. His name is Kevin."

"Kevin and Angela. Let's do a quick sweep of your place first, then Cookie's, just to be sure, then Angela's."

Wyatt grunted his acknowledgment.

Like the rest of the buildings at Mule Shoe, Wyatt's door was unlocked. Wyatt flicked on the lights as they entered. Unlike the rest of the resort, the living room–kitchen combination was far from primitive. A refrigerator hummed and a small red light glowed from the flat-screen television. The room looked lived in, with a jacket thrown over a chair, boots by the door, and a couple of glasses half full of liquid on the kitchen counter. The bed was unmade in the corner. Wyatt took a quick glance into the bathroom and a closet. "Nothing."

They moved to Cookie's place. As at Wyatt's, the same comforts were present—modern kitchen, flat-screen television, and on a nearby desk was a MacBook Pro. A computer printer sat beside it.

"We're in business," Bram said. "We can contact—"

"No internet connection." Wyatt opened a nearby door, peeked in, then shut it and glanced over at Bram. "Sorry."

"You both have television. How do you get—"

"Television reception? We don't. I don't turn mine on. Cookie's a movie buff. When all the guests have left, she has us all over for movie night." He opened another door, revealing a wall of DVDs.

A quick glance at the titles proved Cookie's taste ran to documentaries and regional outdoor shows with a few popular titles tucked in. Bram suddenly felt grubby for snooping. "Let's go," he said gruffly.

After switching off the lights, they left Cookie's side and entered Angie's apartment. The light switch didn't work, so Bram turned on his flashlight. The illumination lit up the artist lying in a pool of blood.

His stomach twisted. *Not another one.* He raced to her side and checked for a pulse.

Wyatt joined him. "How bad?"

"Bad. She's lost a lot of blood." Bram glanced around the room. "She can't stay here. We can't secure two locations. We have to get her to the lodge—"

Before he could finish, Wyatt scooped up the injured woman and headed to the door. Bram followed. He knew the flashlight he held would be a beacon for the killer, but he didn't want Wyatt to trip and further injure Angie. His spine prickled, anticipating a bullet between his shoulder blades. Sweat dampened his shirt. The trees seemed closer together, the trail longer, the night darker.

Once they cleared the forest, the pale moon illuminated their path. Wyatt broke into a trot. Bram shut off his flashlight and raced to the lodge door. "Open up, quickly!"

It seemed to take forever. As soon as the knob started to turn, Bram grabbed it and flung the door, bursting into the lobby.

"Angie's been stabbed." Wyatt tore over to the sofa and gently placed Angie on it.

Cookie slowly rose to her feet, swayed a moment, then said, "We have to get this bleeding stopped."

The three women staff members rushed to help. Roy seemed to have shaken some of his lethargy and covered the prone woman with the sofa throw.

Bram caught Wyatt's attention and jerked his head toward the dining room. When both men were out of earshot, he said, "We have to get word to the outside. Angie's in rough shape, and Cookie isn't much better. How long before someone notices the supply wagon hasn't returned?"

"Good question." Wyatt smoothed his mustache. "It's Sam's horse and wagon, but Sam isn't around his store every day, and Liam takes care of deliveries here. Cookie or Roy place orders over the radio when they need to. It isn't necessarily a daily trip." He frowned and looked down, then at Bram. "How long before the sheriff will miss her son . . . or you for that matter?"

"She knows I'm working on the arson fires and gives me a lot of leeway." Now it was Bram's turn to study the floor.

Roy joined them. "Did you find Kevin?"

Bram shook his head.

Darby approached, lips tightly pressed. "Angie needs professional help."

"That's what we're working on." Bram looked up. "How often did you check in with Sam on the two-way?" he asked Roy.

"Only for supplies or emergencies," Roy said. "Nothing regular. You're sure the road's blocked? We can't get a horse and rider out?"

"I'm sure," Bram said. "Not on that route at any rate. Is there another way out of here? Besides the Devil's Keyhole?"

Wordlessly Roy moved to a framed map of the Mule Shoe and pointed. "We're here. Roughly fifteen miles east is Old Faithful in Yellowstone. There are a number of hotels, a visitor center, lots of people." He moved his finger north. "The town of West Yellowstone, in Montana, is roughly eighteen miles north. Both routes cover some extremely rough terrain."

"What about here?" Wyatt traced a route south, then east.

Roy studied the map for a moment. "Yeesss, that would get you to Targhee Falls. You'd be basically riding around the back side of the Devil's Pass. It's farther than the other two options, but the route would be passable with the right horses and riders."

"We can't wait for someone to notice something is wrong." Wyatt's gaze had drifted to Angie's still form.

"If we hadn't surrendered our phones in Targhee Falls, we'd just have to find a place with cell service," Darby muttered. "I bet you wish you'd caught that helicopter ride earlier today."

Bram froze. *Helicopter.* He closed his eyes. *What about the copter?* He pictured it landing. The blades slowing. The pilot had nodded at him and the copilot had given a salute. Bram shook his head. *Focus.* He had been ready to climb aboard when Darby caught his attention. He'd gone into the lodge to the art room. He'd heard the rotors ramping up and he'd run to catch his ride, arriving outside just as the copter flew away.

What was so critical? He went over the events again. The third time he tried going through the events backward. The copter flew away . . . he'd caught a glimpse of the pilot, looking the other way.

No copilot.

A jolt went through him. "Did anyone watch the second copter leave?"

"I was in the barn," Roy said. "Then Wyatt found me and we walked to the pasture."

"That was about the time the horses broke through the fence," Wyatt said. "Why are you asking?"

"Because someone got off. Someone we haven't seen since."

CHAPTER 17

I found myself holding my breath and staring at Bram. "Do you think that's who's out there? Not the missing staffer, who suddenly went postal?"

"It could be both." Bram rubbed his chin, now sprouting a five o'clock shadow. "I don't know."

"Why would someone fly out here just to murder a bunch of innocent people?" I asked.

Bram turned to Roy. "So I have to ask, do you have any enemies? Anyone that would want to hurt you or destroy the Mule Shoe?"

Roy was silent for a moment. "No. And really, it's not about me now."

"What do you mean?" I asked.

"He sold Mule Shoe." Bram kept his eyes on the older man. "Roy, you said no one knows about the sale outside of the buyer and agent. We have to assume this *is* about you. So my question still stands."

Roy shook his head. "I don't have any enemies that I know of. I just know a crazy person is out there." He pivoted and stalked to the lobby.

"Now what?" I asked Bram. "We need to get help."

"Not tonight, though," Bram said. "There are more than a million and a half acres of wilderness between us and help. We can't afford to get lost. We'll head out at dawn."

Liam sauntered into the room with yet another beer. When he noticed me staring at him, he shrugged. "No way I'm going to let these beers go to waste. Gotta drink 'em when they're cold."

Bram moved to the middle of the lobby. "Listen, folks, we're going to ride out to get help—"

"You're not leaving me—"

"There's a killer out—"

"What are we supposed to do—"

"Who's leaving—"

Bram threw up his hands to stem the flurry of words. "Please, please calm down, all of you. We're working on the details, but we can't leave before first light."

"I'm going with you." Peter's face was flushed. "My wife, Stacy, and I are going with you."

"I am too." Grace's hands were squeezed into fists.

Bram looked at Roy, Wyatt, and finally me. "We won't force anyone to go, or to stay, but someone has to stay here with Angie and Cookie. And for those who go, this will be extremely difficult, not a casual trail ride. Think about it, and try to get a little sleep."

"Be sure you're not near a window," Wyatt said.

People moved around, looking for comfortable chairs, throws, pillows, or cushions. Roy turned the lamps down so the room had a soft golden glow. Liam aimed for the kitchen, undoubtedly for another beer.

Bram came to Wyatt and me. "We need to take turns standing guard."

"I'll take the first watch," Bram said. "Roy, I'll need my Glock."

Roy handed Bram the pistol.

Holly started barking. Outside, Maverick let out a howl.

I drew in a sharp breath.

The earthquake was short. Just a slight roll of the earth that left the hanging lamps swaying.

Holly flew to my side and I bent down to comfort her, then stood and looked for a place to sleep, though I felt restless and jumpy. My missing limb ached with phantom pain, and my PTSD made me irritable and on edge. I'd worn my prosthesis for more time than usual, and my residual limb was sore.

After pacing around the dining room, I pulled up a chair and sat at one of the tables. I tried rubbing my leg and tried not to scratch my neck. I could feel Bram's gaze on me. *I need a distraction, something to focus on.*

I stood to pace when Bram walked over. "What's wrong, Darby?"

Resisting the urge to bite his head off, I said, "Nothing. I'm peachy. Life is grand. What could possibly be wrong—"

"Okay, okay, you don't have to bite my head off."

So much for resisting urges. "Sorry."

His shoulders drooped.

A weight dropped into my stomach. "Look, I really am sorry." I waved my hand as if to wipe away my nasty comments, then turned and strolled to the map. Vast tracks of wilderness surrounded Mule Shoe. Nobody knew we needed help. And one person or maybe two were bent on killing us.

And Bram . . . well, I knew my life would be like this. Single, simple, sane.

I spun and searched for something, anything, to break this chain of thinking. I finally slapped my hand. Hard. That hurt.

Bram's head jerked up. "Darby?"

"Um . . . mosquito." I flicked the imaginary bug's carcass off my hand. *That certainly broke my chain of thinking.*

Bram, still watching me with a puzzled expression, moved to another table and spread out the files from his messenger bag. He bent over the paperwork.

There *was* something I could do.

He glanced up as I approached him. "Do you need someone to bounce ideas off of?"

He pointed to a chair. "I was just going over all the events, trying to figure out who was where, what someone's motive might be for the murders, who has alibis, and so on." He'd written the names of everyone at the Mule Shoe on Post-it notes—orange for staff, yellow for guests. Index cards had the events—the murders of the two staff members were on blue cards, and Cookie's and Angie's attacks on pink. He tugged the collar of his shirt. "Yeah, I know, on television the police place the clues on a wall, neatly color coded, and with a map and studio photographs. This is the best I could do."

"Looks pretty color coded to me. And you used two different pens—"

"Ran out of ink."

"Oh."

"Whoever got off the second helicopter is likely our perpetrator. If Spuds—uh, Kevin, is involved, then the two of them are out there. It makes sense that someone who knows Mule Shoe would be involved—someone who knew where the guns and radio were, and probably with a grudge against Roy."

"That doesn't make sense." I spread out his notes.

Bram reached out to straighten them, paused, and shuffled the index cards into a neat pile.

"As soon as we can get out of here and call for help, we can identify the extra passenger on the helicopter." He started to rearrange the notes into his original order.

I touched his hand to stop him.

He jerked it away as if burned.

Flying solo. "Um . . . what if the plan is for no one to get out of here alive?"

"That's a pleasant thought. If that's the case, we're stuck with *why*? And the pilot could still ID the passenger."

I stared off into space. Holly's barking brought me back. The earthquake rattled dishes and caused a few sleepers to grumble.

A gem of an idea formed in the back of my brain. "Let me try a few what-ifs."

"Okay."

"First a question. Would the helicopter from Idaho Falls fly over Devil's Pass?"

"Maybe."

I nodded. A few puzzle parts dropped into place. "So now a non sequitur. We just had two earthquakes fairly close together."

"If you're starting with the eruption of the Yellowstone caldera . . ."

"No. I mean, it may blow, but I was thinking more about my two dogs barking every time an earthquake is about to start."

Bram placed his elbows on the table and raised his eyebrows.

Cookie entered the dining room heading for the kitchen. "Sorry," she whispered. "I need another aspirin and a drink of water."

"I'm sorry, Cookie. I should have thought of that. Do you need help?" I asked.

"I'm fine. Ignore me." She wiggled her fingers at us before leaving the room.

"You were talking about barking dogs," Bram prompted me.

"Right. Once, though, the dogs barked *after* the ground shook. After the second helicopter left, the ground trembled."

"You're going somewhere with all this?"

"Now I come to the what-ifs. What if that 'earthquake'"—I made quotation marks in the air—"was the slide at the Devil's Keyhole?"

Bram's gaze became unfocused and he absently rubbed his chin. "The slide was large, possibly big enough to be felt here. And if it happened after the helicopter flew over that spot, no one would see we were cut off, but if the pilot saw the slide, he could send help. Can we take that chance that help is on the way?" He thought for a moment. "There's still the issue of the identification of the unknown passenger."

Now it was my turn to stare off into space. "I can think of several prospects. One is that the person sitting in the copilot's seat merely took another seat in the copter for the return trip. Or you were wrong—"

"I know what I saw."

"I'd rather you were wrong. The other possibilities are that the helicopter didn't make it to Idaho Falls, or whoever got off doesn't care if they're identified. He, or she, doesn't plan on getting out of here alive."

Bram frowned. "Those are pretty grim thoughts."

"Four people were attacked. Two of them are dead, and a fifth person is missing. That's grim."

We were silent for a few moments. Soft snoring came from the other room.

"We haven't explored the idea that the passenger could have a good reason for being here," I said.

"Who could that be? And why wouldn't he make himself known? And why didn't anyone see him—or her?"

"Maybe they did," I said slowly. "Do you have something I could write on?"

"Full sheet, Post-it note, index card? Any particular color?"

"Five-by-seven mint-green index card, unlined."

Bram pulled up his messenger bag, opened it, and began searching. "I'm not sure I have—"

"Bram, I'm kidding."

"Oh." He pulled a piece of blank paper from his bag and handed it to me.

The window nearest the kitchen shattered as a barrage of gunfire erupted.

Adrenaline shot through my body. I dove to the floor.

Bram grabbed the table and flipped it on its side, creating a barrier, then yanked me behind it.

Screams came from the lobby as everyone took cover.

I curled up, covering my head with my arms. My brain became a pulsing strobe of thoughts: *Run! No! Wrong! Help me! Blackness.* I was moving, shaking. A sharp pain on my cheek.

I opened my eyes. Bram was shaking me. "Darby, stop! Look at me."

He'd slapped me.

I slapped him back.

He let go, then grinned. "I guess you're better. It's over. The shooting stopped."

"Sorry," I muttered. "PTSD trigger. Nobody's ever slapped me before. Except me."

"Yeah, well, I'm sorry about that. I've never hit a woman before, either. You were screaming. I probably should have done this." He kissed me.

The burning on my cheek spread to my whole body.

He let go and turned toward the lobby. "Everyone okay?"

Wyatt answered. "No one was hit."

"Good. Stay low," Bram said. "Roy, do you have a hammer and long nails here in the lodge? We can use a table to board up this window." Roy, Bram, and Wyatt soon had the table hammered across the shattered window.

I remembered Cookie had gone into the kitchen for water. The room at first appeared empty except for a broken glass and spilled water on the floor. I soon found her in a corner crouched under a table. "It's safe now. Come into the other room."

The two of us joined the three men gathered in the lobby. "Ladies." Bram had to speak up to be heard over the panicked voices and crying. "Please, be calm. There is only one person out there." He glanced at me quickly, clearly wanting to keep the possibility of two a secret for now. "The shooter doesn't know how many armed people are in here, so he isn't going to try to get in."

"We have team-building exercises," Roy said, "to teach companies what to do in an active-shooter situation. We are implementing these steps to keep you safe."

"What we need you all to do," Wyatt said, "is spread out

even more and stay as far away from windows as possible. We want you to adopt the survival mindset. You *will* get out of this."

Bram indicated the fireplace. "We'll only have Angie and Cookie by the fire with one of the staff members. Wyatt, you'll need to cover the back of the lodge. Got it?" The men nodded.

To stop shivering from the combination of a PTSD incident and Bram's kiss, I returned to the dining room, then crawled across the floor picking up the notes we'd been working on. By the time I'd collected them all, everyone had settled down, or at least settled down as much as they could knowing a killer was outside. And knowing we had far fewer tables than windows.

CHAPTER 18

Bram went from window to window, checking locks and making sure drapes or blinds were closed. While he was doing the security check, I arranged the case notes on a table away from any windows. I found a blank piece of paper and drew a rough layout of the Mule Shoe. By the time he returned, my brain fog from the PTSD trigger had lifted enough to make intelligent conversation. Unfortunately, his nearness formed a different kind of muddled thinking.

"Everybody settled?" I asked.

"Not really. Stacy is really shook up and her husband is trying to calm her. One of the Polish ladies can't stop crying. Grace helped herself to a stiff drink and seems to be less upset. Speaking of which, can I bring you a brandy or . . ."

I didn't think this would be a good time to bring up my drinking and pill-popping that landed me in jail after my injury. "No thanks. I cope best by changing my focus. I have an idea I'd like to run past you. Unless the missing staff member just shot up the lodge, it's a pretty good confirmation that a stranger got off the helicopter . . ."

"Agreed."

"Okay, now let's look at everyone else. Mrs. Eason, her daughter, Mrs. Kendig, and Mr. Rinaldi boarded the copter. You'd gone into the art room because of the giardia incident. Also present there were Angie, Grace, Dee Dee, Peter, Stacy, and me." I placed seven circles in the art room with names on them.

"The copter left." Bram sat down and took the pen from me. "I ran outside to try to keep it here but was too late. Then I went looking for Roy. I found Cookie and the three female staff members in different parts of the lodge, working." He drew four circles inside the lodge. "We've accounted for eleven, twelve counting me, who were occupied when the stranger got here. Roy and Wyatt were here." He drew two circles next to the pasture. "The horses had broken out. Wyatt, the assistant wrangler, and a maintenance worker were going out after them."

I tapped the paper. "You mentioned the assistant wrangler and maintenance worker—did you actually see them?"

"No."

"And those were the two men we found dead."

"Riiight."

"Then what happened?"

"I asked to use Roy's office to interview you and Angie about the contaminated water. Before I went there, I located Liam in the kitchen eating ice cream and told him I'd be going back with him and to slightly delay the departure of the supply wagon."

I nodded. "In other words, everyone who *could* have

seen someone get off the copter wasn't physically able to do so—except three people: the three male staff members, two of whom are dead and one missing."

The room seemed darker, the pools of light more isolated. The air had grown chilly from the broken window and smelled faintly of spilled beer. The heat from the fireplace barely penetrated the dining area.

"You know," Bram said, "it was critical that a copter bring someone here. Who could guarantee that would happen unless the pitchfork accident was actually a murder attempt?"

"But how would someone know Riccardo—"

"Exactly. Maybe the trap was for someone who actually should have been in the barn, someone who believed that trapdoor would be shut because it always is closed?"

"Yet another complication."

Bram seemed deep in thought. "It was Roy who said that Wyatt was going out with the assistant wrangler and handyman to round up the rest of the horses."

"I know. I came in as he was saying that. But later, Wyatt said that *he* had caught the horses and that *he* was going after the missing few."

"Looks like we need to ask Wyatt about the last time he saw the two victims."

Pulling the small scraps of paper to me, I arranged the events Bram had been studying. "Got another piece of paper?"

Bram grinned at me before handing me a sheet. I tore

it into small pieces and wrote on each piece. *Riccardo's fall/ pitchfork/orange fibers, giardia, bear/sardines, contaminated water, vandalism of art room, full refund, Angie paid per head, broken brake handle, busted pipe? mix-up in registration?* I thought for a moment, then wrote, *slide at Devil's Keyhole?*

"What's all this?" Bram asked.

"It just occurred to me that Roy isn't the only person affected by these events. Angie also suffered financially."

"And she was attacked. But who would want to injure or kill her? And why was Cookie attacked? And why did you write about the slide?"

I let out a sigh of frustration. "I don't know about Angie or Cookie. The slide just seemed to be awfully . . . convenient and coincidental."

"That doesn't make any sense either. Someone causes the slide to . . . what? Isolate the people here? So the killer can pick them off, one at a time? To what end? Motive, Darby—there's no motive!"

The lodge wheezed and sighed around us as the logs shifted. Bram pushed away from the table, strolled into the lobby, and added a couple more logs to the waning fire. I turned Bram's list toward me. Even if the killer was the person who got off the helicopter, other events happened before that arrival. Kevin, our missing staffer?

Maybe.

Bram returned and sat down. "Any further ideas?"

I handed him the list of incidents. "I keep thinking we

have to look at all this from a number of directions. We've been lumping all the events together. If we separate the murders and just look at the two conclusive events—"

"The destruction of the art room and the contaminated water."

"Right. Both were clearly deliberate acts. I suppose, technically, Riccardo could have done both. He wanted very badly to leave. He had the most motive."

"Then we could just examine the motive for the murders and attacks."

Cookie walked in from the lobby. "I couldn't sleep. Or maybe I'm afraid to sleep. What are you doing?"

I waved my hand over the notes and torn pieces of paper. "At this point, we're just trying to figure out what's going on. Bram saw someone get off the helicopter—"

"So that's who's out there. The killer!" Cookie said.

"Possibly. Probably." Bram looked at her. "Are you sure you didn't see the person who attacked you?"

Cookie closed her eyes for a few moments. "Mmm. I left Roy in his office . . . caught a glimpse of Gary, the assistant wrangler, leaving the staff housing . . . heard the horse on the road—"

"That's it!" I held up the map I'd drawn. "Are you sure it was Gary?"

"I figured it was. I don't know, now that you mention it. Why?"

Bram's face was tight. "We found Gary's body shortly after we got back to the ranch. There's no way he could have been at the staff quarters, then shown up dead out by the cabins. He probably was the first person killed. The body in the barn would have been next, and we now know why you were attacked. You saw the killer."

Cookie shook her head. "The irony is I didn't recognize him. What's the motive for killing, outside of preventing identification?"

My missing limb twinged with more phantom pain. "The most common reasons for murder are financial gain or greed, some kind of sexual gratification, or the desire for power or control. And of course the ever-popular cuckoo-for-Cocoa-Puffs crazy."

"And we don't have enough information to know which it could be," Bram said.

I stood and stalked to the map, traced the three routes out of Mule Shoe, then turned to Bram and Cookie. "Regardless of the motive or reason, this has been a systematic attack, deliberate and lethal. We're going to have to outmaneuver the enemy."

"And how do you propose we do that?" Cookie asked.

"We don't send just one rider or even a small group in just one direction. We already know he's out there and can pick them off at his leisure. We'll send three parties." I pointed to the three routes. "It's the only chance that at least someone will make it to civilization and get help."

Bram held up his Glock. "We only have two weapons and three people that will need them."

"We need four. The three groups going out on horseback

and the one staying here with Angie and Cookie. It's the only chance we've got."

I could see Bram formulating our chance of survival. Returning to my seat, I said, "Think about it. Sending one rider to get us rescued could result in his or her death, and we'd be in the same situation. Staying put and hoping someone will eventually miss us would guarantee Angie's death . . ." *And possibly Cookie's.* The words formed in my brain. "Plus, the killer could flush us out by setting the lodge on fire, then pick us off at his leisure, or just keep shooting out the windows until we're out of ways to block them. With this plan, we might have two chances out of three that a rider could get help."

"Who would leave? And who would stay?" Bram finally asked.

"Cookie, you and Angie would stay," I said. "Someone would have to stay with you."

Cookie took in a sharp breath as if to say something, then rolled her lips.

"Cookie?" I asked.

She just shook her head.

"I think you and Wyatt should be riders," I said to Bram.

"What about the third?" Cookie asked.

I sat still, but my thoughts were racing. The three women from Poland were unlikely to know the area and even less likely to be expert horsewomen. I didn't trust Liam. For a time after he returned to Mule Shoe, he could have been running around with a rock and a knife. Even if he was innocent, he was full of beer. Would he be in any condition to make the difficult journey? I didn't even know if he could ride a horse. Maybe he only knew how to drive a wagon. Roy was easily in his eighties, although tough as nails, but I had my doubts about him as well. That left the art students. They wanted to leave, but that didn't mean they'd want to become targets for a killer.

So. Me. At one time I could ride any horse anywhere—but I'd also had two legs. I could feel the horse, grip it with my leg muscles, guide it with my heels. I could hang off a galloping horse's side and grab things off the ground. I was fearless. If I got thrown, I'd get back up.

But I hadn't been on a horse's back until I'd ridden the Belgian earlier today—which was like sitting on a kitchen table—and we'd walked down off the mountain.

I reached into my pocket and took out the three small stones.

No one would think poorly of me if I stayed. In fact, Bram and Roy would expect it. I was, after all, racked with PTSD and partially disabled. And I didn't want to get shot. *Coward.*

I placed the stones in a line on the table. Scott had given me three rocks. Ugly, lumpy, heavy. Weighing me down.

Cookie studied my face, then quietly stood and moved back to the lobby.

Bram picked one up. "What are these?"

"My graduation present from Clan Firinn. I'm pretty sure they represent the final burdens I carry. Or maybe my David's ammunition against the Goliath hurdles I still have." I'd so glibly suggested Bram and Wyatt sacrifice themselves by going for help while I was thinking about staying here. The words swarmed in my brain. *Be strong and courageous! Do not be afraid or discouraged. For the Lord your God is with you wherever you go.*

I looked across the table at Bram. "Do you believe in God?"

Bram's eyes widened and he straightened. "Of course. Don't you?"

"Maybe I need to find out. I'll be the third rider."

"But . . ."

I glared at him.

"Um . . . we can talk about it more in the morning. Maybe you should get some sleep."

"I can't sleep. Not just yet." I returned two of the stones to my pockets, picked up the third rock and threw it into the trash, then pointed to his messenger bag. "Let me see those arson notes."

CHAPTER 19

B ram handed the notes to me. "I appreciate you taking a look."

"I'm afraid that's about all I can do." I stacked the notes neatly in front of me. "Didn't you tell me that two men died in one of the arson fires?"

"Yes, a double homicide."

"But none of the other cases involved the loss of life."

"Right."

I nodded and bent over the notes. "Could I borrow some paper?"

He handed me several sheets. "Coffee?"

"Love some."

Bram pushed back his chair, stood, and walked to the kitchen.

I'd lost my computer, with the programs I used, over the cliff. I wouldn't be able to do a comprehensive report, but I could certainly give Bram, or whoever followed up, a starting point. The lodge continued to settle into a creaking quietness with pings and groans from the metal roof as the night air cooled it. I had no idea how much time had passed when Bram appeared with a steaming cup of freshly brewed coffee.

"Thank you." I took the cup. "How did you make coffee without electricity?"

"Gas stove, old percolator pot, Eagle Scout training." He sat. "How's it going?"

"I'm just about as far as I can go without my computer."

"So how do you make the comparisons?"

"I look for style markers and linguistic variations. The unconscious choices a writer makes."

"For example?" Holly had crept closer and leaned against Bram's leg. He absently reached down and scratched her ear.

"Hmm. A writer can phrase the same object-clause elements in a sentence differently. For example, I can phrase this idea three ways." I held up my cup. "You brought me this cup of coffee. You brought this cup of coffee to me. You brought to me this cup of coffee."

"Sounds complicated."

"Not to me. Your background, culture, education, region, and other factors define your word choices and sentence structures. I also look for consistency in the style of the writing, then determine if it's distinctive enough to tell different writers apart. There's a lot more, but that's the *Reader's Digest* version."

Holly gave a short bark, followed by Maverick, apparently just outside one window. The earthquake barely made the table quiver.

I took a breath, which quickly turned into a yawn.

"Looks like you're finally tired enough to sleep," Bram said.

"Mmm." I held up a note. "This one is different from the others."

He took it from me and read aloud. "'You will never find me. You should make your mindset one of defeat. I am like a vapor—without form and impossible to capture.'" He looked up. "This is the arson note from the double homicide."

"In that case, you might consider looking for two people—an arsonist *and* a killer."

"What about the rest? Did you find anything?"

I couldn't help it. I yawned again. "I'd need to do more research, but there's a markedness in some of the punctuation, the use of the phrase 'no way,' and the length of words."

———

Somehow Bram wasn't surprised to find out the homicide fire was different from the other arsons. The blaze had required more than just a can of gas and a match. When he got back to the department—if he got back to the department—he'd pull that case file and comb through it again.

Darby crossed her arms on the table, rested her head on them, and immediately fell asleep. He wanted Darby to lay her head on him as she drifted off to sleep. He wanted to protect her, keep her from the nightmares that haunted her.

The thought startled him. How could he want order in his life, perfection in a mate, and still want to protect the wounded?

His early life had been chaotic, with an alcoholic mother and absent father. He was in his early teens when his mother died of cirrhosis of the liver. His grandmother took over raising both him and his younger brother, who eventually took his own life. His grandmother had told him he had an older sister with fetal alcohol syndrome who'd been put up for adoption. Maybe this combination of events twisted his thinking so that his desire for Darby was in conflict with his need for perfection. Or was it his grandmother's need for order and perfection?

Even though his grandmother had been gone for five years, her strident voice was a constant reminder. *Don't be like your worthless mother or brother, Bram. It's up to you. Choose the right road. Make sure you do something perfectly or don't bother . . .*

His eyes were now sandpaper-gritty. He checked his watch, stood, and made his way over to Angie and Cookie. One of the three Polish staff members—he couldn't remember her name—gave him a worried glance. He stayed until he could see both injured women breathing.

He thought again about Darby. She said the arsonist used the words *no way*. It was interesting that Liam used those words all the time. He'd have to ask Darby if there was a correlation between the spoken and written words.

When the FBI report had come back, he briefly considered Liam. The profiler wrote they should look for a white male twenty-five to thirty-five years old who had a low-paying job or wasn't employed. Liam was only twenty-two, but he did have a series of low-paying jobs.

To be honest, it wasn't just the age difference that gave Bram pause. He didn't want to consider the sheriff's only child might be a serial arsonist—and if so, chances were high she knew it. Liam's mother couldn't have read "no way" in the letters and not thought of her son.

Her comment about the recall petition being "for the best" also fit with Liam being the suspect. If she was forced to move and take her son with her, maybe she hoped a new setting would curb his desire to set fires.

The problem was that if Liam set fires to get even with her, moving away with him would only change the landscape of the arsons, not stop the arson. Mother and son were toxic to each other.

Where did that leave him? If Liam was the arsonist, it didn't change the facts of their situation. They still needed to ride for help. He'd just need to keep an eagle eye on the man.

He looked at his watch again, then moved to Wyatt, stretched out between an easy chair and ottoman near the back door. "Wake up, old man," he whispered. "Shift change."

Wyatt stood and stretched. "What time are we heading out?"

"The sun will rise around seven. We need to organize who's going and who's staying, then saddle the horses. I'd say give it an hour. There's fresh coffee in the kitchen."

Wyatt moved away and Bram took his chair. It felt as if he'd barely closed his eyes when Wyatt announced, "Wake up, folks, we need to get moving."

The muttering and groaning ceased as each was reminded of their predicament. Wyatt walked to where everyone could see him. "Ladies and gentlemen, listen up. The sun will rise in less than an hour. Three of us, Bram, myself, and—"

"Me." Darby stood at the opening to the dining room.

Wyatt's forehead wrinkled, but he continued. "And Darby will be going for help. We'll be splitting up and riding hard over incredibly rough ground. If all goes well, someone should reach civilization by early afternoon. We need to know who's going and who's staying behind with Cookie and Angie."

"Is *he* still out there?" Grace asked. "Waiting?"

"We will have to assume so, yes."

"Which way are you going?" Peter asked Darby.

"I'm open to suggestions." Darby looked at Wyatt, then Roy.

"You might take the route around the back of the Devil's Pass, then to Targhee Falls," Cookie said. "It's the longest, but fewer obstacles. It's still a hard ride, and anyone riding with you should be prepared."

"I'll go with Darby." Liam licked his lips and grinned.

Bram gritted his teeth. "If you're riding out, you'll go with me."

"But—"

"With me or not at all." He stared down the young man. "We'll go east to Yellowstone Park."

"That leaves me heading north to the town of West Yellowstone," Wyatt said.

Soft murmuring followed the announcement.

"We"—Zofia pointed to herself and the other two Polish women—"will stay with hurt ladies."

"I'll remain behind as well," Roy said.

Grace, Stacy, and Peter looked at each other. "My wife and I will go with the deputy," Peter finally said.

"I believe I'll stay," Grace said.

"Be ready in ten minutes," Bram said.

—

Cookie struggled to her feet and came over to me. "All your clothes were on that wagon, right?"

I nodded.

"You'll need warm clothing to make that trip. Come with me." I followed her to the gift shop, where she handed me a long-sleeved T-shirt, hooded sweatshirt, and water-resistant jacket, all with the Mule Shoe logo. "Put these on. Layers. I think I have a hat and gloves in lost and found." She disappeared behind the counter for a moment, returning with a pair of wool gloves and a knitted hat.

"Thank you, Cookie. I don't think I would have thought about it until I was out there."

She moved closer, wincing slightly as she bumped into

the counter, and lowered her voice. "I don't know how this is going to turn out, but if things go south here, I'm going to make a run for my cabin. The lodge is too big with too many ways to break in."

"Are you sure it's safer there? And that you can make it?"

"I don't know, but just as you're dividing up to increase your chances of getting through, I think we should divide up so we're not all sitting around like . . . sheep, waiting for the slaughter." She patted my cheek. "You be careful out there, and get out safely, you hear?"

I nodded. I didn't trust my voice.

CHAPTER 20

As Cookie and I returned to the lobby, Roy asked, "What about the guns? Who will be armed?"

Everyone looked at Wyatt. He and Bram exchanged glances. "We'll leave the pistol here," Bram finally said. "Wyatt will take the rifle."

"In that case"—Peter stood—"my wife and I will go with Wyatt." He turned to Bram. "No offense, but—"

"None taken," Bram said.

The six of us moved to the center of the room. "I think we should use the same strategy in getting to the barn that we're using to ride out," Bram said. "Wyatt, Peter, and Stacy will go out the back of the lodge. Liam, Darby, and I will run out the front." He didn't have to say that the killer couldn't be two places at once. Unless there were two . . .

"Good idea," Wyatt said. "Darby and Liam." He looked at both of us. "You two can help me saddle and bridle the horses."

"I'll start with the rifle and keep watch while you do that," Bram said. "Peter, you can keep watch at the other side of the barn."

I looked from face to face. Stacy was pale and had her arms tightly crossed. A vein throbbed in her husband's forehead. Liam kept rubbing his mouth. Bram's jaw was determinedly tight, while Wyatt's hands were clenched into fists.

Cookie had disappeared into the hall. She now reappeared with handheld GPS units, bottled water, and granola bars. "You'll need these." After she handed everything out, she said, "What about setting up a diversion?"

"What kind of diversion?" I asked her.

"I can go to the kitchen door and make some noise. That could draw the killer to that end of the building."

"That's a good idea, but be careful." Roy had joined us. "Where do you want me?"

"We'll need someone at each door to block it once we're outside," Bram said. Roy directed the Polish women into place. "Ready?"

As I moved toward the front door, Bram put a hand on my arm. "Darby, can you run?"

I stiffened.

He let go. "I'm sorry, I—"

"Yes, Bram, I can run."

He looked like he wanted to say more, but Wyatt said, "Come on, folks, the time's getting away from us."

Grace took her place by the chair blocking the front door. Cookie went into the kitchen. Wyatt, Stacy, and Peter, along with Roy, moved to the back door.

My mouth dried and stomach tightened. Stuffing the

water bottle, granola bar, and GPS into my jacket, I shook out my hands to try to loosen up. *It's not far. Just run to the barn. Just run—*

A cacophony of banging came from the direction of the kitchen.

"Go!" Grace yanked away the chair and opened the door.

For a moment, I couldn't move.

"Go! Go! Run!" Bram yelled.

I ran, Holly at my heels. Bram and Liam sped ahead of me, weaving to make a harder target. I ran in a straight line, sucking in large gulps of the cold morning air. My back felt naked, exposed. I listened for the sound of gunfire, but I could hear nothing. My vision narrowed, with only the barn door in focus. *Run, run, run!* The words pounded in my head with every beat of my heart.

The world dissolved around me.

I was running toward a line of trees, clinging to a pistol. I heard a voice, *his* voice. "Shoot now, Darby!"

Something smashed into my leg. I pitched forward. The ground rushed up to meet me. I landed hard on my side. The odors of dust and dead grass and the coppery stench of blood filled my nose. My vision narrowed to a small pinprick of light. In the center was the killer.

I raised my pistol to shoot him. My hand was empty.

The killer's face disappeared. Bram came into focus. He grabbed my outstretched hand and yanked me to my feet.

The flashback clung to me like a gauzy spiderweb.

Bram put his arm around my waist and partially carried me to the barn's dim interior. "You okay?"

"I . . . yes . . . sorry."

The dogs had followed us into the barn and immediately began exploring. We were in the side of the barn next to the pasture, on the opposite side of where Riccardo had fallen. Open stalls lined up on the right. While everyone caught their breath, Wyatt handed out bridles, then picked up a bucket and filled it with oats. He jerked his thumb to the right. "Tack room. That door over there"—he pointed to the far end of the room—"is facing east. You'll find a trail that will take you to the top of the first ridge, where the road will split. From that point you can see all of the resort and, just on the other side, the trails. The different directions are well marked for our guests. Bram, you'll take Pinecone Path and keep heading east. Pinecone loops around after a few miles, so keep an eye on the GPS. I'll be following the ridge to the north on Blackfoot Track. Darby, you'll head southeast over the ridge. You'll be going cross-country without any marked trails. All of you, get out of here fast and don't stop until you're at the top of the ridge. Everyone got it?"

We all nodded.

He walked to the door to the pasture and rattled a bucket of oats to draw in the herd. As the horses approached, he'd move aside and let in the ones he wanted, calling out the correct bridle and bit as they passed. "Snaffle on the bay and buckskin, curb on the dun, sorrel, and this bay. Hackamore on the Appaloosa."

After the last of the horses we needed were in, he dumped the oats outside and shut the door. We quickly had the horses in the correct headgear. The saddles were all similar, well worn but in good condition, and all had breast collars and flank cinches with hobble straps. The horses were swiftly saddled. Wyatt added a scabbard to the buckskin's saddle to hold his rifle.

"Bram, you take the dun. Liam, the sorrel. They're both about the same speed so you'll stay together. You two." He pointed at Stacy and Peter. "How well can you ride?"

"We've been taking dressage lessons for years," Peter said.

"Okay, there isn't time to show you the difference." Wyatt handed Peter the reins of the two bays. "These two aren't as picky about their riders."

He handed me the Appaloosa's reins, then led the buckskin to the door and opened it. "Darby, the Appy is my toughest horse. He's stubborn but fast—"

Gunshots rang out, coming from near the lodge.

"Let's go!" Bram yelled.

Without waiting for more instructions, I grabbed the saddle horn and swung into the saddle, ducked through the door, and kicked the horse into a gallop. As more shots rang out, I bent low and prayed a bullet wouldn't find me.

Wyatt was right. The big gelding was fast. He flattened his ears and charged up the hill as if it were flat ground. We didn't slow down until we reached the top of the ridge.

I pulled him up. He wasn't even breathing hard. I, on the other hand, was gasping for breath.

Behind me came the thunder of the other horses. I didn't wait for them to catch up but continued off the marked trails while I checked the GPS. I adjusted my direction slightly right. I needed to head southeast for a few more miles before turning south.

Holly and Maverick seemed overjoyed at this galloping romp in the woods.

I urged the Appy to a trot and instantly regretted the tooth-rattling gait. Another nudge with my legs pushed him into a distance-eating lope.

The sky lightened, but a heavy overcast hid the sun. The ground grew rough and rocky, so I slowed to a walk and let the horse pick out his path. After what I figured was another mile, I pulled out the GPS and checked, then turned south.

The mountain grew steep, though the Appaloosa still navigated with ease.

A soft rumble like a heavily traveled highway grew louder as we continued. The sound resolved into a sheer cliff dropping to a boulder-filled stream far below.

We stopped. The dogs sniffed the air, then the ground. I took out the GPS to look for an alternate route.

The screen was black. Pushing the On button, I waited. A depleted battery symbol flashed on, then off.

Turning the GPS over, I opened the battery compartment and rotated the batteries. *Please work, just for a moment.*

The screen remained black.

CHAPTER 21

B ram handed the rifle to Wyatt and scrambled onto his horse as soon as the shooting started. Darby, nearest the door, had already taken off at a gallop. The rest of the riders followed. The horses stayed pretty much together as they raced up the hill.

They pulled up their horses at the top of the ridge. Everyone was silent. "I don't suppose you checked to see if any of the horses or mules were missing?" Bram finally asked Wyatt.

Wyatt shook his head. "Just the few from when they broke out earlier. I should have thought of it."

"I didn't think of it either." Bram frowned. "So we don't know if the killer will be stalking any of us or will stay at Mule Shoe. I guess I don't have to tell you all to be careful and ride fast." He jerked his head at Liam and turned his horse east, pressing the dun into a trot.

The trail angled downward, then flattened before starting to climb. The path was clearly marked and in excellent condition, and they made good time. Bram checked his GPS often, watching for the point when they'd have to set off cross-country. Finally the trail angled north. "Liam, we need to continue straight."

The young man didn't answer, just turned his mount off the road and down the slope. At the bottom, the trees thinned. A brook with sulfur-laden steam rising from its surface—evidence of the geothermal activity—meandered through the small gulch.

"Liam, we need to bear more to the right—"

"You know, Bram, I'm perfectly capable of reading a GPS. I'm tired of you bossing me like I'm an idiot. Not anymore. No way." Liam kicked his horse hard, sending the little mare into a gallop.

"Liam, slow down!" Bram urged his mount to go faster. "Slow down! We have a long ride! We don't need to go that fast!"

Liam disappeared into the trees ahead.

"I'm gonna catch that little jerk and pound some sense—"

His horse pitched forward, sending him flying over her head. He hit the ground hard, knocking the wind out of him and sending shock waves of pain throughout his body. Sucking in tiny gulps of air, he lay still until he could breathe normally.

Once air was again flowing into his lungs, he took inventory of his injuries. His back hurt, arm throbbed, and shoulder pounded.

Slowly, carefully, he pushed to a seated position. His horse had already righted herself and was shaking off the dust. She took a few steps and sniffed a thatch of grass, appearing to be unhurt.

The reason for the fall was quickly evident. Ground squirrel burrows dotted the field. It was a wonder his horse didn't break her leg. He gingerly tried to push off the ground. What felt like a firebrand slashed through his shoulder. "Aaah!" He dropped back down.

The mare jerked up her head at his voice, danced sideways, then started trotting back toward Mule Shoe.

He clamped his jaw against the pain and stood, swaying. "Whoa there, girl. Come here." He moved after her retreating rear. "Come on. Here you go . . ."

The trot became a lope, then a full-out gallop. She vanished up the hill, leaving only a slight dust cloud.

Bram cycled through every cuss word he knew. The GPS was in the saddlebag, along with his water. He had to be five or six miles from Mule Shoe and a whole lot farther from Yellowstone. He could try for Yellowstone, but without the GPS, he could get lost, not to mention the park was full of wild animals that thought cops tasted just like chicken. And his shoulder was probably dislocated.

He'd have to retrace his ride from Mule Shoe and hope he stayed clear of the killer.

——

I dismounted and led the horse away from the sheer cliff. The dogs looked at me with heads cocked. "Don't worry.

This isn't a huge disaster. We'll head south. The sun is . . ." I glanced up. "Currently in the east. We just have to get around this spot, unless you two have a better idea?"

Maverick stood and started climbing away from the precipice as if he understood completely. I mounted the horse and fell in behind. We climbed for about half a mile before Maverick took a right. We seemed to be on a game trail. Numerous boulders and rocky outcroppings lined the narrow path.

Crash, thump! A startled elk with an impressive seven-point antler shot up the hill. The Appy jerked but didn't bolt.

I looked around for the dogs, expecting them to pursue the tempting chase.

The dogs were gone.

The trees here were ponderosa pines, widely spaced and park-like. I should have seen the dogs easily. "Maverick! Holly!"

I turned the horse completely around, searching. The two canines had simply vanished. "Holly, Maverick!"

The only sounds were the wind rustling the pines and the high whistle of a golden eagle. "This doesn't make sense." I was hoping my voice would give me encouragement. "They're not below me, beside me, or above me. So that leaves . . ." Straight ahead was a solid granite cliff. I took another slow look at the surroundings. Trees. More trees. More trees. Dead tree. Rocks—

My gaze returned to the dead tree. It was partially

blocked by several pines. I backed the gelding several steps. The dead tree was a blackened snag, probably hit by lightning a long time ago. I'd seen that same snag before—in two of Shadow Woman's drawings.

I dismounted and led the horse forward, staring at the ground. Dog footprints showed where the two had run. I moved forward, step by step, approaching the granite wall. When I reached it, I ran my hand over the warm beige surface. The wall ended. My hand slipped around to a narrow opening behind the large slab. Because of the uniform color, the space was all but invisible. I led the horse through, the stirrups scraping against the stone. We emerged on the other side.

A low hunter's shack was tucked into the hillside. Beside the shack was a shed with an overhang to form a covered area for feeding livestock. Currently a very content mule was thinning out the hay supply. A small stream burbled nearby.

The dogs greeted me with mouths wide open in doggy smiles.

I had no doubt in my mind. I'd found Shadow Woman's dwelling.

—

Bram started limping toward Mule Shoe. There was always a chance his horse would stop and graze, allowing him to capture her, or Liam would notice he was alone, but he wasn't counting on either possibility. Hoofprints from their ride out were easy enough to follow.

Even though he was unarmed, returning to Mule Shoe did give him the element of surprise. He could find a vantage where he could see most of the resort. Whoever was out there would be focused on the lodge . . . unless . . . unless the killer had followed one of the three riders. Or there were two of them. If he could easily see the evidence of his passing on the ground, so could anyone else.

The thought slowed his pace. How far behind would the killer be? Could he find himself face-to-face with the stranger?

A branch snapped to his left.

He froze, then slipped behind a tree and listened. He caught the *shuuuuush* of wind through the pines. The chatter of a chipmunk. The stench of a wet dog.

A large black bear sauntered next to a tree, stood on his hind legs and scratched the bark, then dropped to all fours and rubbed his back.

Bram remained motionless.

The bear stopped and sniffed the air.

Bram couldn't tell which way the breeze was blowing. At least it was a black bear, considerably less dangerous than a grizzly.

He looked at his watch. By now, anyone following him would have shown up. At least he didn't have to worry about running into an armed killer.

As the bear wandered off, Bram continued his trek

to the ranch. If nothing else, he could formulate a plan of action.

———

The ground gently sloped in front of the cabin before dropping away to a narrow gully. The roof sagged and the earth seemed to be slowly swallowing the log walls. Other than the babbling stream and panting dogs, silence. No birds chirped or wind disturbed the trees. A slight vapor rose from the creek. A closer inspection showed it was a hot spring.

Shadow Woman visited the store once a month. She could have purchased batteries. Opening the back of the GPS, I confirmed I needed double A's.

I tied my horse next to the mule and entered the house.

Inside, the air smelled faintly of smoke and dust. A single built-in bed, covers tossed into a heap, poked from the opposite wall. A small wood-burning stove on my left seemed to serve as both a heat source and cookstove. A sagging chair rested near the stove. To my right was a white-painted table with a mismatched chair. Shelves made up of orange crates were nailed to the wall. I moved to the shelves. On the bottom one was a Bible.

On impulse, I picked it up and opened it. Inside was written, *To Mae, on your graduation from Sunday school, Pocatello Community Church*, and the date. The pages were filled with scribbled notes. I looked up the verse Scott Thomas had written. Jeremiah 29:11. "'For I know the thoughts that I think toward you,' says the LORD, 'thoughts of peace and not of evil, to give you a future and a hope.'" Mae had underlined it and written in the margin, *Believe.*

"Right now, Scott, I think the whole 'strong and courageous' verse is needed." My voice sounded loud in the quiet cabin. "And a nudge toward batteries."

After returning the Bible, I searched the shelves, then moved around the room. Mae had a whole lot of Old El Paso traditional refried beans and Spam with cheese. No batteries anywhere. I searched again, this time on hands and knees, looking under everything, tossing things to the floor, before standing.

"Flapp-er-doo-*dle*! What's wrong with this lady! Is it too much to ask that she have at least one battery in the house!" I stomped to the door and opened it. I said to the horse, "And while we're on the subject, what's wrong with modern conveniences? Huh?" The horse didn't look up from eating.

"Aaarrrrgh!" I ran outside and yelled at the sky. "I don't know where I am, I don't know where to go, people are dying, and all I ask, God, is for one stupid battery!"

God didn't answer.

Breathing heavily, I waited for my heart rate to climb down out of the stratosphere. *Look on the bright side.* With Spam and refried beans, I wouldn't starve. Just die from the lard and sodium phosphates.

The dogs had watched when I started my rant, their

mouths agape. Now they turned back to peering over the gully.

"Okay, I know that was childish. You don't need to be dismissive." I walked over to see what was more interesting than my temper tantrum and apology.

Ten feet below me, caught in the bushes, was the body of a woman.

CHAPTER 22

My eyes burned and a lump formed in my throat. This had to be Shadow Woman. Mae Haas. I had to know her fate.

I retrieved the rope on my saddle, tied one end to a nearby pine, then slipped the lariat around my waist. I didn't want to get stuck down there. Sitting down, I slid carefully forward toward the body. The slope was steeper than it looked.

The clerk at Sam's Mercantile said Mae had stopped coming to the store six months earlier. She must have fallen at that time, and the condition of her body testified to that. She'd been essentially mummified by the dry air. No sign that a cougar, wolf, coyote, or bear had found her.

I looked up at the dogs, both watching me intently. "That's why it took you two months to make your way to Sam's store. You were guarding her." I thought about the healed scars on Maverick. The guarding had been intense.

Her outward appearance showed no sign of trauma that I could see. Her teeth were in poor shape with a number of them missing. If the brush hadn't caught her clothing, she probably would have tumbled all the way to the bottom of the gorge.

What about the note? And check?

Someone *had* to know she was dead. Someone who didn't want anyone to go looking. "So how did anyone know what happened to you? Did they find your body? Or . . ."

I moved closer, careful not to touch anything. She wore jeans, a red plaid jacket over a stained pink sweatshirt, and thick boots. Six months ago would have been March, when snow would still be present, so her clothing further confirmed the timeline. Her hair had sloughed from her skull and tangled in the branches. Her sightless eye sockets and mouth open in a silent scream made my stomach churn.

Now that I was closer, I noticed something strange about her skull.

Leaning forward, I studied her body. The skin had pulled from her cranium on one side and a tiny line on the bone tracked from the back of her head. That could be a radiating fracture.

I could touch the skull, turn the head, and confirm it.

An involuntary shiver went through me. I'd be touching the body with bare hands. The *forensic* in *forensic linguist* didn't refer to dead bodies. It meant law enforcement or legal proceedings. Paper, ink, computers. Not blood, bones, or rotting flesh.

Wait. I did have gloves, albeit wool. I tugged out the gloves Cookie had given me and put them on. Hands shaking, I reached over and rotated her skull.

Some hair caught on the wool.

I yanked my hand away, ripped off the gloves, and threw them over the gorge.

The back of her skull had been smashed inward.

Looking upward, I searched for a rocky outcropping where she could have hit her head. From here I couldn't see a likely answer.

Gingerly I backed away from the body, then hauled myself to the top of the slope. *Don't fall, don't fall.* If I screwed up my prosthesis now, I'd be in a world of hurt. On all levels. Holly gave me a tail-wagging, rear-waving greeting. Maverick slowly walked over, sat, and leaned against my leg.

"I'm so sorry, big fella." I stroked his head, then scratched behind his ear. "You've shown me your deepest wound. Thank you."

The ground above Mae's body had clumps of dried grasses, a pinecone or two, but no hard surface large enough to have crushed the back of her head.

I widened my search. Near the house, rocks had been placed to create a planter, now overgrown. Evidence of chives and tarragon was among the weeds. One of the rocks was missing. I found it some distance from the old herb garden—a jagged piece of granite.

If I picked up this rock and hit Mae on the head . . . Looking around, I found a small stick, which I pushed into the earth next to the rock, marking its location. The rock had a brown stain on one side, but I had no way of telling if the stain was human blood. I carried the possible murder weapon inside the house. At least it would be out of the elements.

Now what? I could continue riding south, using the sun, to hopefully find civilization, or I could try to retrace my route to Mule Shoe, hoping my horse wanted to go home. Neither sounded like a good plan. I wandered around the room, hoping for an answer, ending up at the Bible. *Maybe God could direct me.* I opened the book at random. The first verse I saw was Judges 1:7. "And Adoni-Bezek said, 'Seventy kings with their thumbs and big toes cut off used to gather scraps under my table; as I have done, so God has repaid me.' Then they brought him to Jerusalem, and there he died."

"Not quite as enlightening as I'd hoped, God."

I couldn't just sit around here waiting for something to happen. Mae had been here six months and no one had found her. There wasn't six months' worth of Old El Paso traditional refried beans and Spam with cheese. There wasn't even a piece of paper to put into a bottle and float down the stream . . . paper.

Paper.

Mae was an artist. I had some of her drawings. Where were her sketchpads? Works in progress? Drawing pencils or charcoal for that matter?

The rock, location of the body, and note she supposedly wrote to Sam saying she was leaving all pointed to murder. I added the missing art and supplies to that conclusion. What about the bounced check?

This search of the cabin was brief. No checkbook.

The dogs began barking. I braced myself. The earthquake caused the logs to shift and rumble and dust to fly. The door of the stove rattled free. This time the barking kept up. Not good. What did they call this? An earthquake swarm?

Still bracing for the next quake, I stared at the stove. *If I wanted to get rid of art and checkbooks, I could burn them* . . . I drew closer, then peered inside. A lump of something was just inside the door. I reached inside.

Warm.

I snatched my hand out and jerked upright. A woman dead six months didn't need a fire. Who'd been staying here?

The dogs' barking became high-pitched. The last time they'd carried on like this we'd had a major quake. The roof of this building already sagged.

I charged from the house, pausing only when I was clear of the structure. The dogs faced me, hackles raised, barking frantically.

No. They weren't barking at me. They were barking at something behind me.

I started to turn. Something smashed into my head.

CHAPTER 23

opened my eyes, then closed them. Nothing changed. I was in absolute blackness.

Night. Dark. Black. *No! No! No!*

I can't remember. Not again. Ground yourself in the present . . . I couldn't stop the PTSD flashback. The sealed section of my memory opened, returning me to that day in Skagit County five years earlier.

"This was the surprise?" I leaned across to see the house better. My dear, sweet husband, Jim Carson, put his truck into park, turned off the engine, then turned to me.

"Are you buying it?" I scrunched my face as if smelling something bad. "Tearing it down? Maybe arresting someone here? I rather *thought* we were going to go look at horses. Horse. Not house. That little mare isn't going to be on the market long—"

"We are." He pointed up a small rise to the modest white rancher surrounded by looming evergreens. "But first, the humble abode of Kirt Walter Daday." Yellow crime scene tape fluttered around the front yard. Jim rolled down his window. The rain-tinged mountain air filled the cab, and the screeching caw of a raven broke the silence. "You worked so hard on this case, Darby. Every so often you should get the chance to actually *see* more than words on a piece of paper."

"News flash. Words are my thing. Forensic linguists *love* words." I touched his face. "But thank you."

He grabbed my hand, rotating it so the emerald solitaire on my wedding ring caught the light. "Like you, the rarest and most priceless stone on earth." He leaned over and kissed me.

I couldn't believe Jim had asked me to marry him. We'd said our vows a year ago. I'd prayed for just such a godly man. My second prayer had also been answered. I stroked my slightly rounded stomach. A son. We hadn't decided on a name yet.

Today could be the icing on the cake—finding my perfect horse, which I would one day ride to a team roping and barrel racing championship. The horse that we'd been on our way to see.

"Darby?" He was staring at my face. "You zoned out for a moment."

"Just contemplating our future." I pointed at the house. "And I do hope it doesn't include buying the Daday place. That's just plain creepy."

"No."

"Then shouldn't we get going?"

"We won't bother anyone. The place is empty."

"That's good." This time when we kissed, I wanted it to go on forever, but eventually I had to come up for air. "I . . . um . . ." I cleared my throat. "I thought Daday had an apartment in town."

"He did, but we found this address when we searched the apartment." He reached over and stroked my now-tangled shoulder-length hair. "Daday would still be killing women if not for your work."

"But my contribution was very small. Infinitesimal." I held my fingers a quarter inch apart. "Just a bit of a nudge on some notes he wrote."

"Hardly—"

"I was just doing my job. Everyone in the department put in overtime, especially you. You should have gotten a promotion after all that."

"Well, I—"

"I'd bet if Daday hadn't committed suicide-by-cop, his trial would have highlighted your investigative work."

"Maybe, but it was your linguistic work that moved the case forward."

"Then there's that whole nickname issue."

He rolled his eyes. "Don't start on that again—"

"It offends me. Of course, naming a killer is disgusting enough, but when the press gives a serial killer a label, they usually do a better job. The Hillside Strangler. The Green River Killer. Jack the Ripper."

"Is there a book somewhere that gives the rules for naming serial killers?"

"Of course not, don't be silly, but the structure should be the ordinary juxtaposed with the dangerous."

"Darby, nobody thinks about the order of the words."

"I do. And how stupid a name is the Butcher of Sedro-Woolley?"

He sighed and straightened. "But that's where his victims lived—"

"And the words *butcher* and *Woolley* don't flow. *Woolley* makes me think of Chewbacca. Wild and woolly. A woolly lamb. Woolly bully."

"I think—"

"Even Chewbacca was a Wookiee, close to *woolly*."

"You and words. Come to think of it, you and talking."

I raised my eyebrows. "Are you saying I talk too much?"

He touched my hair again. "I would never say that. And live." He grinned. "What would you have named the serial killer?"

"Something like the Cascade Killer. Seattle Slayer—"

"He didn't murder in Seattle—"

"Poetic license. They couldn't even call him by his last name, like Bundy or Dahmer. Daday sounds like daddy. The news needed . . ." A movement caught my attention. I peered over his shoulder, then squinted. "I thought you said the house was empty."

He turned and looked. "He lived alone. It should be . . ." He narrowed his eyes.

"Maybe someone is in there collecting souvenirs." My neck prickled and I scratched it.

"This address was never released." He reached for his cell. "But I can tell you're bothered by something. It's possible the forensic team is still collecting evidence."

"Don't bother trying to call." I leaned forward, watching the house. "No service." I rubbed my neck on the other side. "I don't see the forensic van."

His gaze tracked around the house. "I think I see it. Through the trees over there. We should probably let them do their work." He reached for the starter button. "We'll double check when we get service and let the county sort it out." He pushed the starter. "Ready to go look at your horse—"

Something moved next to the house.

It took me a moment to understand what I was seeing. I grabbed Jim's arm in a white-knuckled grip.

He whipped around.

A man was slowly moving toward us. One arm held a woman, mouth twisted in horror. His other arm held a pistol to her head.

Jim jerked. "We're in the shade. I don't think he's seen you yet. Duck down."

"Oh, sweet heaven!" I slid to the floor of the truck. "Who are they?"

"I think she's a forensic technician for the county. Don't know the guy. Is your pistol still in the glove box?"

"Yes." My stomach hardened. I needed to tell him something, but my mind wouldn't focus on what.

Without looking at me, he opened the glove box,

handed me the gun, then slid the cell over. "I'm going to try to talk him down. See if you can get a clean shot."

"But—"

"The phone will vibrate when you have service. Keep trying for backup."

I reached for his hand but he'd raised his arms to show he held no weapon.

He was going to face that armed gunman and trust me to cover him? To save him? My vision blurred.

He lowered one hand and slowly opened the door from the outside.

Can I kill a man? Pull that trigger?

"Take it easy. I'm unarmed. My name is Jim—"

"Shut up!" the man yelled. "I know you. I seen you on TV. You're that cop."

"I'm—"

"He didn't do nothin'."

He didn't do nothin'? I snatched up the pistol. *Wrong. This is wrong.*

Jim slid from the cab, hands again upraised, then shut the door behind him. I used the sound to mask my opening the door on the other side, then slid to the ground.

"I'd like to understand. Please tell me. I'm listening." Jim's legs were visible under the truck. He stepped forward and right, pulling the man's attention in that direction.

I crawled swiftly on hands and knees in the opposite direction, ending up by the rear bumper. I risked a quick glance up the hill at the man.

"Don't come no closer or I'll shoot her." He jammed the pistol harder into the woman's temple. Her eyes squeezed shut.

"I won't. Tell me about what happened." Jim continued to move away from the truck and toward the man. "I understand you're upset."

"Upset?" The man spit on the ground next to him. "Upset!" His eyes were like white marbles. "I told ya, he didn't do nothin'!"

"And I hear you. What did people think he did?"

"Killed them women."

"Are you talking about Kirt Daday?" Jim lowered his hands slightly.

I rested my hand on the bumper and sighted in on the man's head. The pistol shook. My brain kept pounding out, *Terribly wrong.*

"'Course I'm talkin' about Kirt!"

Shoot, Darby!

"He just wrote them notes for me."

I gasped. Daday didn't write the notes? Had I identified the wrong man?

"What do you mean?" Jim shifted his weight and prepared to step forward again.

"I mean you killed the wrong guy." He pulled the trigger. His hostage dropped, pulling him off balance.

Darby, shoot!

Jim looked at me, eyes wide.

Pull that trigger!

233

"Now, Darby. Shoot now!" Jim screamed.

The killer fired again, this time at my husband.

Jim crumpled.

Run! I leaped up and ran toward a line of trees.

Something smashed into my leg. I pitched forward. The ground rushed up to meet me. I landed hard on my side. The odors of dust and dead grass and the coppery stench of blood filled my nose. My vision narrowed to a small pinprick of light. In the center was the killer. In slow motion, he rose from the ground.

I felt around me for my pistol.

The killer walked up to me and raised his gun.

My hand encountered only grass. *I'm going to die.*

He put his gun into his mouth and pulled the trigger.

CHAPTER 24

B ram couldn't believe he'd ridden so far, nor that the ground had been so rough. He felt like he'd climbed uphill for miles. He hadn't been able to come up with a plan for what to do at Mule Shoe other than observe and try to find the killer.

To take his mind off the pain in his shoulder, he returned his thoughts to Liam as the possible arsonist. No one particularly liked the young man. Well, maybe a few females, but he certainly didn't receive what most men, most people, wanted. Respect.

His best bet would be to formulate a timeline of Liam's movements. At best it would be circumstantial, but Liam might confess if he thought there was a witness or other evidence. Yesterday when Bram asked Liam if his mother had met Shadow Woman, Liam mentioned the only fire where someone had been killed. He'd said, "Mom was really upset, but I . . ." Bram was willing to bet his mom was upset because she thought Liam set the fire, and Liam was about to say, "But I had nothing to do with it."

Liam's time of reckoning was approaching fast.

—

Something was hitting me, pushing me, wet, pounding.

My eyes were open, but the blackness did not go away.

The back of my head throbbed. My throat ached from screaming. Something clawed, whined, and licked me. I reached out to push it away. A soft coat, floppy ears. "Holly?"

The dog shivered and nudged me.

Panting and warm air came from behind me. "Maverick?"

The big dog lay beside me and let me hug him before he moved away.

"Good dogs."

I tried to put it all together. I was shot. *Shot! Bleeding!* Reaching for my belt to apply a tourniquet, my hand encountered a small object. I felt it with both hands. Of course, this was the GPS. I wasn't bleeding.

I was . . . wherever this black hole was.

My brain seemed scrambled from the blow and memory. I'd never had such a powerful and detailed flashback. Why hadn't I fired my gun five years ago? Why had I run instead? Did I let my husband . . .

"Stop! Ground yourself in the present. Got that? Okay, my name is Darby Carson. No, Darby Graham Bell. My husband and my baby . . . No!"

Present. Not past. Not another flashback. "I'm soaking wet from sweat. It's hot here and it stinks. The ground is . . ." I felt around me. "Dirt. The dogs are here, so they had to get here . . ." I shook my head, then immediately regretted it. Reaching back, I touched the aching spot. My hand came away wet. "Someone hit me over the head and put me . . . here. Did they put you two here as well? No. Maverick, you wouldn't have let anyone near you. You must have found me or followed me here."

I felt my jacket, then pants pockets, on the remote chance I had a flashlight or match. I found the two remaining rocks Scott had given me. No help there. I reached out and explored the space. Rock. A rock wall was within arm's length.

I shifted to find out what was on the other side. *Something's wrong!*

Ground yourself . . . Another cascade of memories fell.

A thousand bees were stinging my leg. I opened my eyes. In front of me, on the ground, were the remains of the killer. I jerked my gaze in the other direction. My husband lay in the distance. *Nonononono!*

The bees were stinging less. The world was starting to retreat. *Fight this.*

It took all my strength to push to a seated position so I could see. A red lake was forming around my lower leg. My brain felt like it was filled with growing black tar. *Tourniquet.* I unfastened my belt and looped it around my thigh, screaming with the pain. The darkness returned.

I had no idea how much time passed before I regained consciousness. Was I still in the ebony blackness of an abyss, or on the lawn lying next to the killer?

Holly pressed against me. I stroked her head and sat up. *I have to fight this.* The counselors at Clan Firinn had warned me I could go into a dissociative fugue state to escape from the memories, the trauma. I could become confused, lose my identity, wander aimlessly. We'd never get out of here. *Ground yourself.*

"Holly, Maverick, here's the plan." My voice was high-pitched and shaky. "You got in here, so you'll have to lead us out. No voting on this." The earth throbbed slightly and the stench grew. Sulfur.

"We need to move as quickly as possible 'cause it stinks, in case you hadn't noticed. And getting hotter if that's possible."

Something had triggered that second flashback episode. It occurred when I moved my body. Cautiously I felt around. Rock wall to my right. My voice bounced as if in a small space. Holly was on my left. Beyond Holly? Reaching out, I felt nothing. I dropped my arm and touched the ground. Dirt and . . . metal? My fingers explored the object. Rounded top with a lip under two sides. Long—I couldn't find an end to it. A rail? Railroad? That didn't make sense. Could we be in a railroad tunnel? Would a train be coming through soon?

No. The rock wall was within arm's length. A train couldn't fit in here. Something smaller. More like a mine cart.

"Good news. Maybe. I think we're inside an old mine.

To get out of here, we just need to follow the rails. I'm sure you two can figure out which direction."

I started to stand, then froze. A drop of sweat slithered down my forehead. Slowly I ran my hand down my leg. My prosthesis was gone.

I clapped my hands over the scream. *Stop, stop, stop . . . No . . .* Again the memories flooded my brain.

Night. I'd been lying here for hours, drifting in and out of consciousness, hoping, praying for someone to come along. I'd rolled onto my stomach and tried to crawl away from the killer, but I was too weak to get far.

The sound of a car and flash of headlights made me raise my head. *Praise Jesus, thank You, God, someone is here.*

Voices.

"Hey, Matt, Chris, come over here! This is cool. A body!"

"Naaa, really? Awesome!"

"Whatcha think we shood do?"

"Grab his gun, man. 'Nother gun over there."

Approaching footsteps. "Hey, there's a chick here. Pretty. Should we—"

"Naa, man, I ain't that drunk."

They moved away.

Help me! I moved my lips, but no sound came from my throat.

"Check the truck."

The slam of truck doors, then car doors, then the roar of an engine, and they were gone. Silence again descended on the field.

I closed my eyes.

This time it was Maverick, pushing against me and whining, that brought me around. It was hotter than ever, and the sulfur stench punched me in the face.

"Okay, Maverick, okay." Something tickled my brain. Hot. Sulfur. Something Grace said. Something about Yellowstone.

The ground trembled again, lasting longer.

Hot air pushed against my face.

Maverick whined again, then grabbed my jacket and pulled.

Grace. Outside the lodge. Talking with Dee Dee and Angie. *Yellowstone's incredibly fragile geothermal pools and geysers can be destroyed or altered by man. For example, people routinely throw pennies, garbage, even soap into geysers and pools. This can change the direction of a geyser or . . .*

I grabbed Maverick and pulled myself upright. "Right. We gotta get out of here."

Somehow, Maverick knew what I needed to do. The big dog let me put my hand on his shoulder and use him as a crutch. We started forward, he keeping pace with my hopping.

The ground shook and a rumbling came from behind.

I hopped faster.

Heat like a blast furnace plastered my clothes against my body. The rumbling grew louder.

My hops were more like one-legged leaps.

Ahead, daylight.

Rushing hot air pushed us. The rumbling was now a locomotive engine. The ground bounced.

We weren't going to make it. Holly shot ahead and out the mine opening.

I put both hands on Maverick's shoulder and leaped. *Go. Go. Go.*

Steam scalded my exposed skin.

We hit the entrance and vaulted to one side.

Seconds later, the geyser erupted with boiling water and steam.

CHAPTER 25

I lay on my back, gasping in the clean, fresh air. "Thank You, God," I breathed. Maybe I *did* believe in God. *For the Lord your God is with you wherever you go.*

How else would we have made it out in time?

The geyser's outburst stopped, leaving the stench of rotten eggs.

The sun was still shining, a Steller's jay scolded me with a *shook, shook, shook,* and a fly buzzed my face. The world was going on as if nothing had happened.

But something *had* happened. Whoever put me in that mine knew it was an active geyser and removed my prosthesis so I wouldn't be able to run.

Someone tried to murder me.

Would they be watching to ensure I didn't make it out alive?

I jerked upright and looked around. The mine was tucked into a narrow gulch with a creek, now swollen with superheated water flowing down the middle. In front of me rose a steep, rocky hillside where only mountain goats and bighorn sheep would be comfortable. This side had a gentler slope populated with ponderosa pines.

We seemed to be alone. The dogs casually drank from the stream above where the geyser had sprayed.

I exhaled and waited for my racing pulse to return to a somewhat normal rate.

My head ached from the blow and my good leg throbbed from the frantic hopping. I rubbed my leg, then itched my neck. Whoever had taken my prosthetic leg took the liner as well. Phantom pain surged from my missing limb.

The darkness. I'd faced darkness and come out sane. I grabbed one of the two remaining rocks from my pocket and stared at it. "As the saying goes, the only difference between stumbling blocks and stepping-stones is the way you use them." I tossed the rock into the mine opening. *That felt good.*

There was a good chance the would-be killer would return to be sure the geyser had done its job. I had to get moving, but where?

I could hide, wait for the killer's return, and follow him out. Right. He'd never notice two dogs and a hopping woman behind him. *Any more stupid ideas?*

Obviously my brain was still muddy, and the adrenaline rush had left me shaky. "Ground yourself in the present. Come up with a plan. What can you use to help yourself?"

At some earlier eruption, a mine cart had been shoved out and tossed on its side. Black ore and a miner's pick lay in a pile next to the cart.

I pushed up from the ground. Maverick, as if trained since puppyhood to be a service dog, moved next to me. His shoulder was almost as high as a kitchen counter. With his help, I maneuvered over to the cart. The ore didn't appear to be worth the effort it must have taken to haul it out. On impulse I selected one of the smaller pieces and stuck it into my pocket. Peeking out from some of the rocks was something gray. I brushed the stones away. The gray turned out to be a baseball cap.

Leaning against the cart, I took a closer look at the hat. It was still in good shape, so it couldn't have been here for years. Was it evidence of someone mining here recently? How remote was this place?

I called Holly over and held out the hat. "Find. Holly, find."

Holly sniffed the cap, sat, and scratched her ear.

Placing the cap under Maverick's nose made him sneeze. *So much for search-and-rescue dogs.*

Straightening, I examined the area again, this time paying close attention to the landscape.

The area where the geyser sprayed was rocky and without vegetation, which would make sense. A couple of bushes on the perimeter were dead, a few more farther away were dying, and a nearby ponderosa had turned yellow and dropped the needles on the lower branches.

Leaning on Maverick, I made my way toward a flat area of dead grass next to the creek. A round rock about the size of a softball caught my attention. When I picked it up, black soot came off in my hand. I dropped the rock and looked for more. I quickly spotted a number of same-sized rocks scattered around the area. Now that I was closer to the dead grasses, I could see they formed a square.

A campfire ring? The square outline of a tent? But no garbage, cigarette butts, tin cans. If someone had pitched a tent here, it wasn't there long enough to permanently kill the grasses.

So the miner had gotten what he wanted after a short amount of time, picked up, and left, taking care to erase his presence. He would have to have known that mining this close to Yellowstone was illegal.

Of course, the chances of getting caught would be slim to none. If not for the dead vegetation, the opening would be hidden from above and from anyone coming up the gulch. So why—

Dead and dying bushes. If this geyser had been active for a long period of time, there would be nothing growing around it. The ground around Yellowstone's Old Faithful was barren.

A seed of an idea sprouted in my mind. Again I replayed Grace's comments. *Yellowstone's incredibly fragile geothermal pools and geysers can be destroyed or altered by man. For example, people routinely throw pennies, garbage, even soap into geysers and pools. This can change the direction of a geyser or . . .*

Another thing could alter the course. Mining, especially mining that used explosives to loosen the rock. What if someone accidentally blew an opening into an existing vent? Once that happened, there would be no safe way to remove the ore. Maybe that's why this place was abandoned—not because the mine tapped out but because it was too dangerous to work here.

The sun had shifted and was now directly overhead. I needed to move on. The killer could return at any time.

I hoped one of the riders had made it to civilization by now and notified authorities of the situation at Mule Shoe. When I didn't show up, they'd come looking for me. I needed to be where I could be spotted from the air. I'd follow the stream downhill.

A faint path, little more than a game trail, paralleled the creek, heading roughly east. Maverick paced himself to my slow, hopping speed. I had to pause often to give my good leg a rest. I kept my eyes and ears open to any indication of someone returning.

The trail narrowed, with dense bushes pushing in on all sides, and shifted to a southeast direction. I had to let go of Maverick's shoulder and hop behind him. Holly followed me.

The trail suddenly split, the right side following the stream and the left heading north. I stayed with the stream. The path widened but became steep. Not good. A fall at any point would be a disaster, but especially downhill. I sat and continued by scooting on my rear.

The track finally leveled and snaked around a large boulder. I stood, brushed off my pants, and patted my leg for Maverick to return to my side. We stepped around the boulder.

I froze.

I was back at Mae's house.

CHAPTER 26

Bram gazed down at the sprawling Mule Shoe. It had taken him several hours of walking to cover the ground his horse had so swiftly crossed. The pain in his shoulder had settled into a throbbing ache that flared into a branding iron whenever he stumbled.

He could see no sign of movement at the resort. His original plan didn't include the disadvantage of a dislocated shoulder, so he needed a more passive approach now.

If Darby or Wyatt had reached their destination, help could arrive at any time. In the meantime, the barn held the most promise. The hayloft had a large door that opened toward the lodge and cabins. He could hunker down behind some hay bales and hope the killer didn't have the same idea. He'd have to be careful.

The hillside to his left had the most cover. He crouched and moved from bush to tree to fallen log, pausing in the shade of each location to wait for the waves of pain to pass. In the sunlight, the heat pounded down on him. Sweat dampened his back and underarms.

He made it to the barn without raising any alarm. His

runaway dun mare was just inside the door. "How nice of you to show up here," he whispered. He looked inside the open saddlebag for his bottle of water and the GPS. Both missing. He should have looked around the ground after the mare fell to see if they had fallen out. *Dumb, dumb, dumb.*

Using only his good arm, he unsaddled the horse and led her to the pasture door, where he removed her bridle and turned her loose. An astute killer might notice a horse suddenly appearing with sweat-outlined saddle marks, but hopefully the sheer number in the herd would prevent that.

He and Wyatt hadn't moved the body from the last stall, and he hoped he wouldn't be driven from his hiding place by the smell as the day's heat did its work.

He eased over to the stall and looked.

The body had been moved.

———

I blinked. Mae's house. It was as if I'd dropped into the *Twilight Zone.* Or starred in my own version of *Groundhog Day.* Was I doomed to circle endlessly? Or had I actually died in the cave? Was I in a special purgatory? I pinched myself. That hurt.

I was really here, still lost, still without a working GPS. And someone who had tried to kill me was probably wandering around.

I ducked back behind the boulder.

I had no doubt that the killer from Mule Shoe was the same one who hit me and dumped me into the mine. Probably the same one who killed Mae. He liked bashing people on the back of the head. *I'd like to bash his head.*

Before I could stop her, Holly pranced out to the front of the house.

Nothing happened. No shout of alarm, no slamming of a door. I ventured from my hiding place.

My horse was gone, as was Mae's mule.

A sour taste rose in my mouth. My leg grew weak and I slumped to the ground. *How am I going to get out of here now?* I barely made it here from the mine. I would never be able to hop or crawl so far for help. Nor was there any way I could play hide-and-seek from a killer—a killer who would make sure I was dead the next time.

I should just give up. Get it over with.

The words drifted into my brain. *This is my command— be strong and courageous! Do not be afraid or discouraged. For the Lord your God is with you wherever you go.*

I rolled onto my back and stared at the sky. "Well then, God, You're gonna have to get me out of here, because I'm most definitely not strong and courageous right now."

Holly came over and sniffed my hair, gave me a sloppy forehead kiss, then wandered away. Maverick lay down beside me.

God's miracle didn't happen. I wasn't suddenly transported to my old room at Clan Firinn. I was still at Mae's cabin, lost, missing a significant means of transportation, with a killer stalking me, surrounded by mountains and trees . . .

Tree.

I sat up and squinted. The burned-out snag I'd seen just before we found the hidden entrance to Mae's place was visible from this side as well. Mae had sketched that snag in two of her drawings.

I mentally retraced the path we'd taken from the mine. We'd followed the stream heading east, according to the sun, then southeast. The snag was on the highest point west of here. I hadn't seen it from the mine, but I hadn't looked around once we started down the trail.

Was that important? Mae drew the things around her—the people she saw, the dogs by the stream, the landscape. The only unusual things were her portraits, revealing two sides of the face.

And the weird drawing of two men. Two men standing on what looked like a cloud with two lines at the bottom.

I frowned. An elusive idea lurked just out of reach.

The sun, which had been pleasantly warm, was now hot. The killer hadn't returned . . . yet. I needed to move out of the center of Mae's yard and then find a way out of here.

I'd searched Mae's house once before, but I was looking for a battery. I'd try it again. Maybe this time some brilliant solution would come to me. I made my slow way over and entered the house.

If anything, it was sadder than the first time I'd looked. I left the door open to air out the smoky smell. Crossing to the built-in bed, I lifted and shook out the covers, raising only a cloud of dust. I felt grubby. Touching her things, with her body lying so close by, gave me the willies. I moved to the orange crate shelves, this time removing everything and placing the items on the table. Mae should have a knife, maybe even a pistol, somewhere.

I should have realized whoever murdered Mae and so carefully destroyed her art wouldn't leave anything behind. Picking up her Bible, I turned it upside down and flipped through the pages. An old photograph fell out. The image was faded and grainy, but I recognized Mae from the self-portrait. She was much younger, standing under a maple tree. Standing in shadow. I put the photo in my pocket.

One last sweep of the room brought me to the cookstove. It had been warm when I opened it. Someone had a fire in there recently.

Maybe I needed to rethink the idea that the killer had followed me. Maybe he was already here when I arrived. Cleaning up loose ends? Burning art? Making sure that if someone found this place, there would be nothing useful?

But the killer couldn't be two places at once. He shot out a window last night and opened fire on us as we fled this morning. Everyone had been accounted for in the lodge in both cases.

Except for the missing staffer. Or could two people have been on the helicopter? One stayed at Mule Shoe, one followed me to Mae's? Or was my active imagination running loose? Maybe some passing hiker took refuge here for the night.

The house was a washout, but I hadn't looked in the shed. I might find a weapon there, maybe a handy pair of crutches . . . oh, why not? Maybe she had a cell phone with the whole US Army on speed dial.

Maverick waited outside and helped me over to the shed door. Inside, a partial bale of hay and a full bale of straw were along one wall with a small pile of baling twine. A log on one side held a sawbuck pack saddle with double rigging, worn canvas panniers—bags used for carrying supplies—and a rope halter. No guns, knives, pitchforks, hay tongs, or computer with internet access.

The shed had a rectangular opening at about waist height, allowing Mae to place hay into the feeder without having to haul it outside.

The feeder gave me an idea. The mule had escaped from the resort and returned here. Someone could have driven him off, but if he was still loose, maybe I could hitch a ride on him. The lack of a saddle and bridle was a little concerning. All the tack suggested Mae used him to pack in food, not ride. For now, maybe the last of the hay would lure him here. I'd worry about catching and riding him later.

After dumping the hay into the feeder, I sat on the straw bale. From here I could see a hole in the bottom of the shed in the corner. I could slip through the hole and be very close to the mule should he show up. *Good.* I'd bet he'd spook should I come crawling or hopping around the corner leaning on the dog.

I could see the dogs in the yard, stretched out in the shade. They'd let me know if someone showed up. They'd barked at whoever hit me on the head . . . but hadn't attacked. Now that I thought of it, that was strange. They'd taken on a grizzly bear when they thought I was in danger.

Two possibilities. The attacker had a gun and they knew what that meant. Or they knew the attacker.

Holly picked up a pinecone and tried to get Maverick to play. The big dog turned his back on her and lay down.

Mae had drawn some of the people she'd met, who by extension were probably the people the dogs knew. Roy. Sam. The sheriff. Since attaching to me, the dogs had a chance to be around all the staff and guests at Mule Shoe, plus Bram and Liam. *Good. I've narrowed the possibilities to everyone I've met since being here.* That didn't seem to be a promising line of investigation.

I swatted an annoying fly and thought about Mae's drawings, letting my mind whorl around. Drawing. Mae. Art. Angie. Angie's words during lunch. *Art is more than the subject, medium, or application of paint. The artist might be conveying a message . . .*

Mae couldn't speak, but she might have been trying to communicate through her drawings. I closed my eyes and tried to picture the sketches. Each one was signed and dated, although I didn't remember the exact dates, only that they were close to the time I believed she died.

When I'd shown the drawings to Angie, she'd arranged them by date. The first had been the two dogs by the stream, then one landscape, the men in the cloud, Roy, the sheriff, the second landscape, Sam, and the self-portrait.

Think about them in order. Her dogs. Pets? Only friends in the world? Faithful. Loyal. If she drew her pets, her animals, why didn't she draw the mule? So something about the dogs. I picked up a piece of straw and gnawed on it.

Maybe I needed to approach this from another angle. The first drawing in the series was the dogs. Her message started with that. The first thing she noticed was . . .

I threw away the straw, picked up some twine, and wound it around my hand. Forensic analysis of writing was so much easier. I knew words were an attempt to communicate thoughts. I didn't know that Mae was saying anything in her art. She may have just been drawing for pleasure.

I tied the twine into a bow. *I have nothing to lose by assuming a message.*

Back to the dogs. They were by the stream. Was it important that the dogs be by water? Dogs playing in the water, drinking from the stream. . . . the stream that flowed past the mine. I'd followed it down to here.

But the miner had blown a hole in a vent, and now a geyser spewed boiling water and minerals into the creek.

The temperature and taste would have changed, and the dogs would have reacted.

A puzzle piece dropped into place. Either Mae noticed

the dogs' reaction to the change, or she saw it, tasted it as well.

"I did it," I whispered. "I know what you wanted to say."

The next drawing was the landscape with the snag. I couldn't be positive on this, but I'd bet that snag was close to the mine. If so, the second piece of the puzzle was the location of the problem. She would have followed the stream to the mine.

I raised my arms in a Rocky Balboa moment while the opening music played in my brain. *Da da-da da, da da DA da da!*

I pictured the third drawing. It made sense.

My stomach lurched. Two men in a cloud with two lines below. Not a cloud, a geyser. Spraying boiling water over the two men. The lines would be the mine cart rails.

The miners hadn't left because it was too dangerous. The two men were caught in the steam vent. In her searching for the change in the stream, she would have found them. Or maybe the dogs found them first. What would she have done? Buried them? Gone for help?

Something nudged my memory, but every time I focused on it, it would scurry away. Maybe if I moved on, it would come to me.

She'd drawn Roy next. If I guessed correctly that she went for help, then maybe she sought Roy and the Mule Shoe Ranch. Had she sketched the drawings for him? She wrote checks, so she was capable of writing, but based on her note, her skills were primitive. Wait. That note was written to throw off an investigation. She might have only been able to sign her name on a check. Could she communicate a more complex idea? Regardless, Roy said she left without anyone figuring out what she wanted to say. And that she'd been very upset.

Or maybe Roy was lying. He'd locked himself in his office and didn't go looking for Cookie after she told him the staff was AWOL. Because of that, Cookie almost died.

Could Roy have sent for me to uncover any of this?

I was getting a headache and not moving any closer to answers.

Keep going to the next drawing. The sheriff. *Had* Mae gone to the sheriff with the sketches, and the sheriff didn't understand? Understood but didn't believe her? Could the sheriff be tied up in this somehow? After all, someone got off that helicopter. Another hole in the puzzle.

I sighed in frustration. I'd started off well but didn't know enough to decipher the rest of the drawings, and I had more questions than before. There had to be more clues, more evidence, more angles that I hadn't yet figured out. Those answers were at the Mule Shoe.

One thing I did know for sure: whatever Mae had been trying to convey, she'd been murdered for it.

CHAPTER 27

Discovering the body missing from the stall dried Bram's mouth and sent his heart racing. The killer must have moved the corpse, but why? Cautiously he searched the rest of the area, but he could find no sign of the missing man.

When they'd saddled the horses early this morning, he hadn't thought to look over here. For usually being so careful, he'd been overlooking a lot lately. He cautiously opened the door to the center part of the barn. Bales of hay were stacked almost to the beams holding up the tin roof. He saw no sign of anyone lurking behind any of the bales.

He wanted to sneeze from the dust in the air. Pinching his nose, he crawled up the bale-stacked stairs until he reached the top. He stayed out of sight of the door as he lifted and arranged the hay to create a blind. From his perch, he could watch anyone moving around most of the ranch as well as anyone entering this part of the barn. Now all he needed was a tall glass of cold water, a pain pill, and a gun.

The horses were visible to his right, grazing contentedly, not the least worried about missing bodies or hidden killers.

He realized he'd been staring at one horse, a large Appaloosa. It looked like the horse Darby had ridden this morning. He squinted to see better. A saddle-sized patch of dried sweat marked his back.

His throat closed and he clenched his jaw.

It *was* Darby's horse.

———

The sun crept slowly across the sky. I'd grown drowsy when I heard the sound coming from the cleft in the rocks where I'd first slipped through. Hoofbeats.

My heart hammered in my ears. I held my breath. Either the mule was returning, or the killer. I remained still, praying for a mule.

The dogs stood and wagged their tails, staring at the rock opening.

A brown head with large flappy ears appeared. The mule.

I exhaled. *Please come over and eat.*

As if hearing my thoughts, the mule continued to the sheltered feeder and grabbed a mouthful of hay.

"Easy, big guy." I stood up slowly so as not to frighten him.

The mule backed away and trotted to the middle of the yard.

I couldn't let him get away. "Steady there, easy." I fluffed the hay into what I hoped was an appetizing pile.

His ears perked up. Slowly, cautiously, he again approached the feeder and stopped.

I recognized the mule as the one I'd petted at the pasture. He wasn't that shy if he'd come over to the fence. If I picked up his halter, he might stay calm.

If he was only trained for packing, not riding, I could be in for a real rodeo. I needed something to hold on to should he decide to buck.

I studied the sawbuck pack saddle. The design, most like the one Native Americans developed, had a wooden crosspiece, like a letter *X*, in the front and back where the panniers were hung. The crosspieces in turn were attached to a wooden saddlelike structure. It would be dangerous, and incredibly uncomfortable, to try to sit between the crosspieces. Fortunately, the rigging wasn't attached. The double cinches going around the mule's chest were fastened with latigo leather through a metal ring. I unfastened the cinches, then used the latigo to create a single piece of rigging. This would at least give me a chance to stay on his back. I left the breast collar, breeching, and back and hip straps in place so the entire thing would stay put.

There seemed to be no evidence of a lead rope that I could use for reins, so I tied the baling twine together and fastened it to the halter. I stuffed extra twine in my pocket.

The mule had been eyeing me while I created the make-shift tack. After twitching his ears back and forth a few times, he sauntered up to the feeder and started to eat.

An apple or carrot would have been useful to keep him close. I doubted the mule would be thrilled with a slice of Spam. "How do you feel about people hopping up to you?"

The mule perked up his ears at my voice.

"Yeah, that's what I thought." I'd have to slide through the hole in the wall right next to him, stand, and slide the halter over his head, all in one movement. Then slip on the rigging, tighten it, and jump on. *Easy-peasy.*

I slung the cinch over my shoulder, grabbed the rope halter, took a deep breath, and dove through the hole in the wall.

The mule seemed unperturbed by my actions. He continued to eat, which was good. Mules could startle and land with both feet in a person's back.

I stood, looped a piece of twine around his neck, then put my hand over his nose and gently rubbed between his ears. He stiffened at my action, then relaxed. I knew mules had sensitive noses from their donkey side. When I felt we'd reached some level of understanding, I put on his halter. The breeching and hip and back straps were next, which would keep everything from sliding forward, followed by the breast collar, which kept things from sliding back. After looping the cinch and latigo around his chest, I tightened it.

The mule's ears tracked all my moves.

The roof was low enough that should the mule decide to buck, I would be a candidate for a brain concussion or worse. I hoped he wouldn't mind if I hopped around him a few times. He obediently turned and moved free of the shed.

It was now or never. I leaped onto his back.

He didn't move.

That wasn't so bad—

The first jaw-shattering buck almost threw me. I held on to both the latigo and his mane with both hands.

He threw a couple of spine-cracking kicks, gave another buck, then shot toward the narrow slot in the rocks.

I drew my legs up near his shoulders to keep from raking them against the rough stone. Once clear, he galloped hard toward a stand of pines with low-hanging branches.

I pulled on the twine reins, but all I did was tear up my hands.

He slowed and aimed for a large branch.

"You're a rotten, lop-eared . . ." I ducked forward and lay flat on his back, wrapping my arms around his neck.

The rough bark scraped my back. Something ripped, and dried needles showered me.

The mule stopped on the other side of the grove, breathing hard.

"I'm staying on your back like bubble gum on a bedpost. Stop with the nonsense and let's head to Mule Shoe. There's food there, remember?"

He put his ears back to listen to me, but otherwise remained stationary.

Maverick and Holly had kept pace with the mule's wild run. They sat and stared at us.

The dogs had found their way to civilization before. Maybe they could inspire the mule to move. "Maverick, Holly, go home! Come on, guys, let's go home. Kibble? Cookies?"

The dogs perked up at my offer. They stood and began

to walk south. The mule followed. *Praise the Lord! Maybe the whole idea of God needs to be revisited. If I survive.*

I had no idea if we would walk in circles, stroll into downtown Targhee Falls, end up in Yellowstone, or fade into legend—the woman in shadow, riding a mule, with two ghostly dogs ever present at her side. At least we were moving.

My stomach reminded me that the last food I'd eaten was sometime yesterday. The granola bar had disappeared when I was taken to the mine. I was starving. Spam with cheese and refried beans now seemed like gourmet food.

The sun was dropping in the sky. If these animals were heading home, they didn't need the sun and would be able to find it even in the dark. But if no one had arrived to help at the resort, I'd be riding right into the middle of a spree killer's hunting ground.

Of course, if the killer had followed me, as I believed he had, then had he gone back to the resort or after another rider?

We continued south and a bit east. Nothing looked familiar, just ponderosa pines, mountains, mountains, and more mountains. The mule grew sweaty under my legs, and I'm sure my deodorant had given up as well. At least bears, cougars, wolves, and other critters downwind of us would move on.

Thirst joined my hunger. To take my mind off my dry mouth and empty stomach, I thought about the drawings. If I read Mae's sketches correctly, she'd tried to tell Roy, then the sheriff, about the mine accident. Could she have drawn their unequal faces to show their hidden reaction? Roy was too defeated to be of help? The sheriff worried about something?

The thought that had drifted in the back of my head crystallized. What happened to the bodies of the miners? Did Mae give up on getting help? Did she return and bury them? Maybe that square of dead grass wasn't a tent site. Maybe it was a grave.

We'd reached a small gulch with a brook, sulfur-laden steam rising from it, and a cattail-lined pond. The mule carefully picked his way around ground squirrel holes, pausing at the pond where he and the dogs took a drink. I was thirsty, but this could easily be the home of a bevy of beavers.

If Mae did bury . . . No, she disappeared in March. At this altitude there would still be snow on the frozen ground.

One rather nasty thought emerged. Mae had two dogs, and dogs . . . well, she'd need to do something about their bodies. There was no way the dogs would leave them alone. Maybe she dragged their scalded bodies out of the mine and to a snowbank to keep them frozen until—

Scalded.

Just like the men who died in the arson fire. That would mean that in a county of thirteen thousand people, four different men were scalded to death around the same time. Coincidence? *Right.*

What if the appearance of Mae at Mule Shoe and possibly the sheriff's department alerted someone that something had gone wrong?

The story of an exploding hot water tank had sounded hinky from the start. But what if the two men hadn't died that way? What if they were already dead? Fremont County usually didn't perform autopsies, Bram had said, which would have established time of death.

What if someone decided to hide the bodies by staging a fire in the middle of a series of fires? I pictured sitting at the table with Bram, arson notes in front of me. I'd shown him one of the notes and told him it was different. He'd identified it as the fire where the bodies were found.

Why go to the trouble of dragging two stinking corpses into town, setting it up to look like one of the arson fires, even writing the note? So their bodies were burned . . . because . . . because . . .

I was too tired to think, to figure out the answer. Even if the ground were frozen, the chances of someone finding their bodies, outside of someone like Mae, would be remote. People disappear all the time in the wilderness.

The mule finished drinking and started forward. A densely forested hillside was directly ahead.

I'd been assuming the two men would be missed. They could have been transient, and no one might have realized they were gone for months, even years, if ever.

Hopefully I wasn't in the same category. If anyone realized I'd gone missing, they'd look for me. To improve my chances of being found, I'd need to be in a cleared area like this . . .

Search. When someone went missing in a remote area, an extensive search was launched.

The bodies were put in a place they would be found, because if they simply disappeared, people would look for them and discover the mine.

Was the mine at the center of this puzzle?

I patted the chunk of black ore in my pocket. I wished I knew something about geology. Roy had talked about Idaho being the Gem State, about the rocks in his collection, but he said he wasn't an expert. His geologist guest was the expert.

And she was dead. A rather convenient turn of events? The only person in the area who would instantly know the value of what I held in my hand had died in an accident at Devil's Keyhole. Another coincidence? *Yeah. Right again.*

Bram had said something about that accident. I chewed my lip and dredged my memory. We'd been sitting outside under the trees. Bram had smiled, showing those perfect teeth, and placed his hand over mine, then said, "Then we need to work together."

My face grew warm and I clutched the twine reins. *Focus.* I didn't have time to think about feelings. I squeezed the reins harder, digging my fingernails into my already abraded palms until the pain brought tears to my eyes.

Something about maps. The hikers were not supposed to be at the Devil's Keyhole. Bram said that the maps found on them showed they had strayed miles from where they were supposed to be. They were supposed to be east of where they were found, which would place them in the area of the mine.

Mae's second landscape drawing of the old snag showed two hikers. Another coincidence? *Yeah, no.* I wasn't buying it. The hikers probably didn't have an autopsy either.

Their bodies had been found quickly by a Fish and Game officer looking for poachers. Yet a third coincidence?

"I'd bet my last dollar that the officer was tipped off about the location of a poacher. No searching for lost hikers."

A vent had opened into a mine and killed two miners. A domino effect of death followed with the two hikers, who probably found the mine, followed by Mae. Then the death and murder stopped.

Until yesterday.

"The deaths stopped, but someone kept trying to sabotage the Mule Shoe. That's why I was brought here." Somehow, speaking out loud made me feel less alone in the middle of this wilderness.

After I arrived, things began to happen, alleged accidents. Riccardo? I had my doubts from the beginning that his fall was an accident. Dee Dee? Could that wagon brake have been tampered with just before we left? Definite murders of the two workers. Two more attempts with Cookie and Angie. If the dogs hadn't helped me get out of the mine shaft, I would have been another statistic.

Why kill a group of people attending an art class? *Wait.*

If Bram's speculation was correct and a staff member was the intended pitchfork victim, no guest had been attacked. Dee Dee was an accident—even if the brake had been tampered with, no one would have known she'd be in the wagon.

So the staff had been singled out. Why now? Because . . . because something changed? What changed? Roy sold the Mule Shoe. The earlier events—broken pipes, horseback riding accident, hikers' deaths, loss of the insurance coverage—could have been designed to drive down the price of the resort and force Roy to sell. If so, that behavior pointed directly at someone on the staff. An inside man.

Once the resort sold, the next step might be for the conniving buyer to eliminate that inside man and any potential witnesses. And to send the current guests away with tainted water, a dead raccoon, and the threat of a bear.

Madam Sparkles—Stacy—may have wanted a personal source for gemstones. Grace had enough money to buy the Mule Shoe a dozen times over. She might want to turn Mule Shoe into an environmental retreat. Come to think of it, even Teddy Rinaldi could want the resort.

Somehow I had to get to my cabin and go through the papers Roy gave me. If I knew the name of the buyer, maybe I could figure this out.

The biggest question I kept circling around was what was the exit strategy? How was someone going to explain all those dead bodies once the sheriff showed up? What was the ultimate motive?

Think about something positive. Three of us went for help. One, maybe two should have found it by now. Help would be on the way to the resort.

I just prayed the mule and dogs were on their way to the only other places they knew—the store in Targhee Falls or the Mule Shoe.

What if I got to the resort and help *hadn't* arrived?

I could turn around and try to find a phone by riding an unbroken mule through millions of acres of wilderness.

I could return to Mae's cabin and wait it out. Maybe I'd learn to love Spam with cheese. But I doubted the mule, currently my only source of transportation, would hang around once he consumed the last of the hay.

I could hide at the overlook to the resort and wait for help to arrive.

Right. Just me in a thin jacket, without food or water, with night approaching, and a grizzly bear in search of another can of sardines.

If I could get to my cabin, I'd have food and water as well as the kibble I'd promised to the dogs. I could stay out of sight until help came. And I could figure out the three things I needed to know. Why was the mine's content so valuable? I had the mineral magazines Roy had given me. Who wanted it? I could go through the paperwork I had from Roy that I'd left in my cabin, although my notes were gone. How were they going to get away with all their crimes? That would be the hard one.

We'd started up the heavily forested hill, so I ducked. I

didn't want to get brushed off at this point. The dogs found a game trail and the mule followed. The trail itself had numerous footprints. Among them were hoofprints.

I sucked in a quick breath.

The dogs picked up the pace.

We burst through the trees onto a well-groomed path. We'd arrived at one of Mule Shoe's maintained trails. The dogs turned west.

The path crested and a sign appeared noting we were on Pinecone Path. It wouldn't be long before the Mule Shoe came into view. What then? If a helicopter were there, or if people were walking around normally, I could just ride up to the front door.

We climbed until we reached to top of a ridge. The resort lay around the next bend. I leaned forward so I wouldn't be seen should someone look in this direction. We worked our way around the turn. Mule Shoe spread out below us.

CHAPTER 28

The ranch appeared empty. The only movement was the herd of horses in the pasture. I nudged the mule behind a large tree and waited. I didn't have to wait long. A movement in one of the cabins caught my peripheral vision. I focused on the cabin's windows. A few moments later, a curtain twitched.

The killer had chosen the best location to keep an eye on most of the ranch—directly across from the lodge.

To get to my cabin, I'd have to cross the open area where the gunman could pick me off at his leisure. Wait until dark? Try to circumvent the entire resort and come in from a different direction? The cabin would still be difficult to reach without detection.

What I needed was a diversion.

"I don't suppose you dogs would like to go down there and create havoc? No? How about you, mule? Or better yet . . ." My gaze drifted to the horses. They'd gotten loose before and run around the resort in a wild stampede of dust and chaos. If I was in the middle of that on horseback, I could ride right up to my doorstep.

Only two slight problems. I'd have to ride out of sight of the shooter. And I'd have to jump off a galloping horse and not get trampled by the rest of the herd. "Easy-peasy," I muttered. Spam was looking better and better.

I used to do something called the Apache hideaway trick, where I would hang off the side of the galloping horse. That required a special saddle, but I could do a version of it much like the original Native Americans did during war—they used the horse as a shield. I just needed to loop a strap around the horse's neck to hang on to and hook my leg over the horse's spine.

Turning my attention to the logistics of creating a stampede, I studied the sprawling horse pasture. If I rode along the ridge until I was at the end of the field, I'd be out of sight of the cabin. The mule would announce his arrival and bring the herd over to check him out. If there was a gate at that end, I could get in and switch mounts. I wasn't about to attempt trick riding on a green-broke mule. Even if there wasn't a gate, I could climb through the fence.

I had no idea of the time, but the sun was approaching the horizon. I had to get my plan going now or wait until the middle of the night. I was pretty sure I'd conquered the PTSD trigger of night and darkness, but I didn't much relish the idea of stumbling around in the dark.

The ridge and the field both ended. I didn't have to turn the mule. He'd already decided he was home. He called out to his equine buddies with a loud grunting whinny, followed by an *aw ah aw.*

A number of horses returned his call and galloped toward us. So far, so good.

—

Bram's mind played a dozen scenarios of what could have happened to Darby. She could have been thrown like he was. Was she hurt? God forbid, dead? Or had she turned around and returned? Had she found her route too difficult?

Did the killer follow her?

That last thought left him twisted in knots. They never should have gone separate ways. He should have insisted Roy be the third rider.

Had he finally found someone he wanted in his life, only to drive her away emotionally when he found out about her leg, then physically when he let her go for help alone?

She insisted she wanted to be the third rider.

He should have hung back this morning to be sure they weren't followed. He folded his hands and bowed his head. "Lord," he whispered, "protect Darby. Keep her safe. Bring her back to me. I promise I'll never leave her. I'll love her for all she is, a beautiful woman, a child of God." He blinked to clear his vision and swallowed hard.

Shhhhhhhhh.

He looked up.

The sound came again. The shuffling of hay.

Bram's pulse quickened. It could be an animal. Or . . .

"Bram." A whispered voice, little more than exhaled air.

Bram jerked upright, winced from the pain, and scanned the interior of the barn.

"Bram, help me."

His heart jackhammered in his chest. "Darby?" he whispered back.

"Over here."

Thank You, Lord. Praise Jesus. He stood and gingerly moved toward the door leading to the horse stalls. "Darby?"

"Here."

She had to be in the stall area. He hurried, trying to ignore his shoulder. The horse stalls were in darkness. "Darby?"

Something smashed into the back of his head. Blackness.

———

The mule chose this moment to try to dislodge me. He bolted toward the horses, kicking as he went. I clung to the rigging, hoping he wouldn't dump me before we reached the fence.

He finally stopped at the fence line. I couldn't see any gate, so I put plan B in motion. I dismounted on a shaky leg and looped the twine over the top rail. The horses had gathered and were checking out the newcomer. I removed one of the twine reins, slid through the fence, then stopped.

The Appaloosa I'd ridden to Mae's place was here.

"Hello again, big fella." I patted him on the shoulder, then wrapped the twine around his neck and led him to the fence. After slipping back through the rails, I removed the rigging from the mule along with the halter, then quickly returned to the pasture side, placed the halter on the Appy, and held tight. As expected, the mule took off, kicking up to celebrate his freedom, and the rest of the herd followed on their side of the fence. The Appy pranced in place, wanting to join in the romp. I untied him, grabbed a hunk of mane, and leaped to his back. He didn't need encouragement. Ears back, he joined in the race.

I held on to him with my legs, bent forward over his neck to keep a low profile, and tied the twine into a loop. I hoped I wouldn't have to hold on long when I dropped to his side. The herd had reached the fence nearest the lodge. Keeping low, I guided the big gelding to the gate. Someone was moving away from the barn.

I pressed myself against the horse's neck and remained motionless. The herd's restless stomping made it difficult to hear. I finally lifted my head and tried to see what was going on in the gathering dusk.

The figure had disappeared.

Which side of the horse would hide me? If the killer had moved toward the lodge, I needed to be on the horse's left side. If he were in the cabin, the right side would conceal me.

I wrapped my arms around the Appy's neck and waited.

The herd soon lifted their heads and flicked their ears forward. I risked a quick peek. I couldn't see anyone, but the horses were staring toward the cabins.

I bent toward the gate, removed the latch, and pushed.

The Appaloosa moved through at a walk, which quickly became a lope. The rest of the horses shot through behind us and raced toward the lodge.

I grabbed the twine on the gelding's neck with one hand, his mane with the other, and dropped parallel with his body. My residual left leg stayed on his back, hooking onto his spine.

It had been years since I'd tried this trick, and I'd been in top physical shape. Dust from the pounding hooves choked me, the twine ripped into my already-torn palm, and the musky odor of sweaty horses filled my nose. I couldn't see anything. The horses pressed closely together. If I dropped now, I'd be trampled to death, but I wouldn't be able to hold on much longer. *Oh, dear Lord!*

I'd have to sit upright and pray we'd passed the killer's cabin and were somewhere near my own.

I slid my leg farther onto the horse's back while pulling up from the side of his neck.

The gelding spooked, lurched sideways, and pivoted.

I lost my grip and flew off his back.

CHAPTER 29

Bram opened his eyes. It felt like someone was hammering the back of his head and holding a hot poker to his shoulder. Something was in his mouth. A mixture of odors, all bad. He tried to move, shift to relieve the agony.

His arms were stuck.

He blinked, then tried to yell. The thing in his mouth was a gag.

The last thing I remember . . . Closing his eyes, he tried to reconstruct how he got here . . . wherever *here* was . . . His horse fell, he'd been thrown, walked for miles, hid in the barn. Been attacked.

Now he was lying on his side on something soft, arms tied behind his back. The smells made him want to vomit—an act that would surely kill him with the gag.

He moved his legs. *Tied together.* Opening his eyes, he focused on the surroundings. Bunkbeds on the far wall and side, a table in the middle, worn dressers. The men's side of the bunkhouse.

Using his tongue, he tried to push the gag out so he could yell. It held tight.

He tried to loosen the binding on his hands, but that brought blinding pain to his shoulder.

Maybe he could stand, hop if need be, to find help.

Trying to find help had gotten him into this mess. At least whoever had knocked him out had placed him on this bed and tucked a pillow under his head. He could have been left outside, tied to a tree, or left on the floor. This didn't make sense.

Why here? Why the bunkhouse? It was out of sight from most of the resort. It would, however, eventually be searched when Wyatt brought help.

Unless Wyatt's group ran into problems as well. Liam could also be bringing help. He hadn't bothered to stop when Bram was thrown.

A thought stopped him cold. Had Liam been given a GPS? Or just the three main riders? He couldn't remember. Liam could even be one of the suspects.

The stench grew.

The back of his throat burned. Sucking in air through his nose, then holding his breath, he swung his legs over the side of the bed, then let the momentum swing him to a seated position.

The room twirled around him. Sweat broke out on his forehead. He waited until the world stopped spinning.

Now he could see there were people in the other beds. Motionless people.

The odors sorted themselves out. The reek of dead bodies. And the pungent smell of gasoline.

—

I landed, rolled, and kept rolling. A hoof clipped my hip. Another set of hooves thundered past my head. I stayed in a fetal position, arms over my head. The ground rumbled under me. *Oh, please . . .*

The drumming moved away. I remained curled up just in case a straggler came along. When it seemed the herd had passed, I uncoiled and checked for injuries. I'd have some doozie bruises, and I didn't even want to look at my hip, but otherwise I was in one piece.

I'd landed between my cabin and the next one. I could clearly see the window where the killer had stood. I couldn't see anyone standing behind the curtain. I'd bet he was still watching the horses. That wouldn't hold his interest for long. The dust was just settling from the stampede and I needed to put a tree or two between the killer and me.

My canine crutch, Maverick, was nowhere in sight. Crawling would be faster than hopping. I wasn't even sure my good leg would hold me up. Rolling to my hands and knees, I crawled as fast as I could to the nearest ponderosa.

Leaning against the craggy bark, I was shaking so hard my teeth chattered. Twice today I'd faced death. I tried to calm my racing heart and slow my panting. *Be strong and courageous! Do not be afraid or discouraged. For the Lord your God is with you wherever you go.* I wasn't strong or courageous. I *was* afraid and discouraged. But the strength to get out of the mine, ride that unbroken mule, and get away with fancy trick riding after a five-year hiatus wasn't coming from me. *Thank You, Lord.*

The sun had set, and nightfall drew close. For the first time since I woke up in that hospital room with a full-blown case of PTSD, darkness would be my ally.

I planned my next move. I couldn't crawl diagonally to the next tree—the one nearest my cabin. I'd be exposed the entire way. I needed to keep this ponderosa between the killer's window and me by crawling straight away until parallel with the next tree. A fast ninety-degree turn and I'd be behind it. From there it was a straight shot to my cabin.

Holly found me and gave me an enthusiastic greeting.

"No, Holly," I whispered. Holly continued to circle me, tail wagging. "Holly, go away, go." She became more excited at my whispering. The killer might easily see Holly reacting to something and come out to investigate. He'd find me.

I swatted her.

Holly backed away, tail now still.

My vision blurred. A massive lump formed in my throat. "Go now!" I whispered.

The dog trotted away, turning every so often to see if I'd changed my mind. To see if I still loved her.

An anvil rested on my heart. I wanted to call her back, to love on her. To ask for forgiveness. Instead I pointed away when she looked.

Someday, somehow, if I lived through this, I'd make it

up to Holly and Maverick. They'd saved me from a bear, from my nightmares, from death in the mine.

I wiped my eyes and nose with the sleeve of my dirty sweatshirt and started crawling. When I'd gone beyond the next tree, I moved over slightly to see if anyone was watching from the window. I felt naked, exposed, and helpless now that I didn't have the shield of trees.

No one was at the window. *Go now.* I scurried over to the next pine. My cabin was tantalizingly close.

My palms were on fire from the rough twine and from crawling on stiff pine needles. My jeans had a hole in one knee. All of my muscles ached. My residual leg ached and pinged. I waited a moment, then moved toward the cabin as fast as I could.

Finally I arrived at the small porch. I used the handrails to pull myself up, then hopped through the door with Maverick close behind, closed it, and leaned against its wooden surface. In the gloomy darkness, I could see the room hadn't been touched since I left. Crossing to the table, I picked up the binoculars still resting next to the fruit basket and moved to the window. No one was moving around that I could see. With the exception of the window shot out last night, the lodge looked the same. I scanned the building from end to end and was about to turn my attention to the rest of the resort when something stopped me—the tiniest glint coming from the corner of the lodge. It took me a moment to find it again.

A knife was jammed sideways into a large crack in the

logs. Only the back edge of the blade showed and the point extended slightly beyond the log. That's what had caught the last rays of the sun. Surrounded by all the places someone could hide something, a crack in a log seemed odd. The good news was that the handle, which might have fingerprints, was protected from the elements.

A final sweep with the binoculars revealed that the horses, having had their run around the resort, had returned to the pasture and were calmly grazing.

After pulling the drapes tightly closed over the window, I did the same for all the windows. A chair jammed under the doorknob blocked that entrance. I could barely see. I turned to the dog, who'd sprawled in the middle of the room. "Maverick, this is the deal. We're stuck here until help arrives, and you have to guard me if anyone tries to get in, just as you guarded Mae's body from predators up there in the mountains. Okay?"

Maverick thumped his tail on the floor. A bowl of dog food sealed our agreement. I wished that my luggage, including my iWALK, hadn't gone over the cliff.

A glass of water and several chocolate pieces later, I was ready to go to work. One final check of the resort with the binoculars revealed light seeping around the curtains in the killer's cabin. If I needed a light, I'd have to be somewhere it wouldn't show. The bathroom was at the back of the cabin and had a single window with a blackout blind.

I sought the book Roy loaned me from the International Gem Society, a handful of books from the bookshelf, the stack of magazines, and the packet from Roy. I put everything on the bathroom floor, shut the door, and placed a towel along the crack at the bottom. I made sure I had matches in my hand before pulling the blind. The room disappeared into total darkness.

After lighting the match, I lit the row of candles on the shelf behind the tub, grabbed the two largest, placed them on the floor, then sat. Placing the lump of ore on the rim of the tub, I started with the gem book. Page after page showed beautifully cut colored gemstones. The rock in front of me hardly looked like any image. I had no idea if this was what, say, a Yogo sapphire looked like in its natural state. Or even if this was a raw gemstone. It could be gold, or silver, or just a rock.

I slammed the book closed in frustration.

Maverick bumped against the door.

"I'm okay, Maverick. Just keep guarding."

Two of the titles from my bookshelf drew my attention— one on the mining history of the region, the second on regional lore.

The rock looked nothing like any of the precious metals in the mining book. *Three strikes, you're out.* The legend book, under different circumstances, might have been interesting, but contained nothing about rocks or gems. I did find the same map that was in the lodge. Mae's place was probably along Beryl Creek.

I closed the book, but the word stayed with me. *Beryl.* I had seen that word in the gemstone book. I looked it up in the index, then turned to the correct page. "A mineral colored by trace amounts of chromium and sometimes vanadium. $Be_3Al_2(SiO_3)_6$. Emerald."

One of the most precious gems in the world.

CHAPTER 30

My hand shook as I picked up the stone. According to the book, emeralds of lighter green shades were classified as green beryl.

I put together a new theory. Someone had discovered emeralds on the protected border of Yellowstone and began mining them illegally. Just finding the raw stones wouldn't be enough. What would need to happen next?

I returned to the book on gems. Emeralds weren't addressed specifically, but in general, raw stones could be taken to a cutter to be faceted, then sold to jewelers.

The *Rock & Gem* magazine had ads for various services, including cutting of gemstones. One was in Montana, not far from here. Another said they sent the stones to Sri Lanka for faceting. Either way, raw gems could go from a mine, to a cutter, then be sold to jewelers.

A very nice little operation.

I'd found the answer to the first question—what was so valuable that would drive someone to murder? Question two was who wanted it? I carefully reread the resort offerings. Nothing new jumped out at me. The lowest offer did carry the initials SD, but I didn't know if that was the agent or potential buyer. Question three would also remain unanswered—how did they plan on getting away with all their crimes?

A door slammed in the distance.

I awkwardly stood, dropped the ore into my pocket, then blew out the candles and opened the blackout shade. Very little light came from outside. Closing my eyes to accustom them to darkness, I opened the door, moved to the window, and peered out. A figure with a flashlight was moving toward the lodge. He carried something under his arm.

I grabbed the binoculars from the table and trained them on the figure. The physical outline of the person was indistinct because of a hat and coat, but the object under his arm wasn't. He was carrying my prosthesis.

I almost dropped the binoculars.

When he'd disappeared around the back of the lodge, I turned and studied the cabin for signs of a second killer. The lights were off. Taking a breath, I opened the door and softly called Maverick to my side. As quietly as possible, I followed the man.

With Maverick's help, we stayed fairly close. We reached the corner of the lodge and spotted him walking away, now no longer carrying anything. He had to have stashed the prosthetic leg nearby. Unless he threw it into the woods, the only other place would be the staff quarters.

I waited until I could no longer hear his footsteps.

Before I could start toward the staff house, a thin line of fire wrapped around the edge of the wall, moving swiftly. I couldn't take my eyes off the blaze. It raced to the front of the building, which burst into flame.

A *whoomph!* and then a crackling sound. Smoke blew into the room.

The building was on fire.

Bram's gut tightened. He struggled to get to his feet, then pitched forward onto the floor. Already the room was hot and filled with smoke.

The air down low was clearer, though still choking him. Using his body and feet, he started to worm his way toward the door. He was moving toward the fire, but there was no other escape from this room. If there were fire alarms or a sprinkler system, they didn't seem to be working.

Clearly no one was going to call the fire department or come swooping in to rescue us. The only advantage I could possibly have over this killer was surprise, but with only one leg, I could neither run nor really fight.

I'd never be able to get through the front door or even the front windows of the staff house. If my limb was in that building, I would have to go get it.

Maverick didn't want to approach the blaze. I urged him around the side and to the rear. Two small windows were on either side of the chimney with a stack of wood under one. I crawled up the wood and did a chin-up on the window ledge to see.

My prosthesis lay in the center of the room.

Movement drew my eyes to a door leading to another room.

I squinted, trying to see through the smoke.

Someone was in there, someone trying to get out.

A burst of adrenaline shot through me. I wanted to scream, call for help, but that would only alert the man who set the fire. He had to have known someone was in there. Probably Spuds, the missing ranch hand.

There was no way I'd be able to break and climb through this window. My cabin, however, had a small opening where someone could place logs next to the fireplace without coming inside the building. The door was about two feet square. If the same contractor built this building . . .

Dropping to my hands and knees, I eased off the wood pile to the ground and hopped to the other side of the fireplace. No small door.

I frantically searched for a way into the building. More windows were on my left, but that end of the structure was already engulfed in flame.

On a hunch, I started grabbing the stack of firewood and throwing it behind me. The top edge of the opening came into view. "Yes!" I breathed. I yanked the wood away faster.

The fire had grown so large I could clearly see what I was doing now. Just a few more chunks of wood—

The door was nailed shut.

Biting back a scream of anguish, I pounded on the surface.

The wood moved slightly.

I got as close as I could, lay down on my back, and kicked at the door. Kicked again. And again. On the fourth blow, the wood splintered.

Smoke and heat poured from the opening.

I didn't wait, didn't stop and think. I ripped the last of the wood free and dove through.

The heat was furnace-hot, the smoke almost overwhelming. I stayed on hands and knees, feeling for the person I'd seen. Could anyone still be alive in here?

Encountering my prosthetic leg, I tried to retrieve it, but it was too hot to handle. I kicked it behind me toward the opening and kept crawling.

I couldn't breathe, couldn't see. My exposed skin was raw. I wouldn't be able to save anyone. I needed to turn back now—

Turning around, my leg touched something. I reached around. A body. I briefly touched the head. Short hair. A day's growth of beard.

A gag in his mouth.

No time to remove it. Hooking an arm around his arm, I tugged. He was heavy. A deadweight. *Tug.* Was he dead? *Tug.* No time to check. *Tug.* The heat was unbearable.

Smoke saturated the air and clogged my throat. Panic coiled around my brain.

The flames shot up the wall by the door and lapped at the beams.

Crying openly now, I pulled the prone figure farther, just a little farther. *Please, God!* Again I found my artificial limb. I picked it up and threw it toward the opening, burning my hands. I prayed it made it through.

The air from outside fed the fire. The conflagration roared like a locomotive. My strength was gone, each tug on the body moving him less and less. I was afraid my hair and clothes would catch fire. *Be strong and courageous!* I couldn't see where I was going.

Reaching forward, I groped for the small opening. My hand found nothing. Had I gotten turned around?

Something grabbed my arm, bit down, and pulled. I slid forward a few inches. My arm was released and I waved it, smacking into the edge of the opening.

I turned around and backed through. The first gulp of frigid air sent me coughing.

Reaching through, I grabbed the man under his arms and pulled. He moved forward, but not fast enough.

It looked like his legs were on fire.

Gritting my teeth, I put my leg on one side of the opening to brace myself and pulled with all my might.

The man's body slid out. His pants were on fire.

I jerked off my sweatshirt and smothered the flames.

I was almost afraid to see who it was. And if he was still breathing.

With the fire out, I looked at his face.

Bram. Soot rimmed his nose and mouth.

I gasped, then untied the gag with trembling hands and placed my fingers against his neck, praying for a pulse. It was there, weak and thready. His breathing was shallow.

The fire had fully engulfed the roof. We had to move. Waves of heat enveloped us. I looked for Maverick to help me move. He was nowhere to be seen, but Holly stood nearby. Holly had helped pull me from the flames.

"Help me, Holly." My voice was wheezy, my throat inflamed.

She somehow knew what I wanted. She approached and grabbed onto Bram's jacket. I took hold of his arm. Together we pulled, shoved, towed Bram far enough away from the inferno to be safe. I gave Holly a brief but hearty hug before checking Bram again.

He was pale and clammy, but now breathing a bit easier in the fresh air. His arms and legs were tied. I rolled him on his side and worked on the knots. My hands were burned from the fire and badly scratched from the twine.

Holly sat next to me and gravely watched.

After working for a few moments, I had to stop and give my fingers a rest. I spotted it.

My prosthetic leg lay near the burning building.

"Holly, go fetch." I pointed.

She wagged her tail.

"Holly, fetch."

She moved closer.

A section of wall collapsed, sending sparks flying. My prosthesis now lay under the burning timbers.

Something twisted within me. I'd be back on crutches until I could get a new artificial limb. People would again stare.

Bram moaned.

"Bram, can you hear me? It's Darby. I'm trying to untie you." I attacked the knot holding his hands together.

Holly growled. She jumped up and raised her hackles.

I glanced in the direction she was staring.

Sam, pistol pointed at my head, glared at me.

CHAPTER 31

The little hairs on my arms lifted. *Breathe.* Of course. It would have to be Sam. Mae had practically shown his motive in her drawing by placing the expression of schadenfreude on one side. Taking pleasure from someone else's suffering.

I worked up enough spit in my mouth to speak. "You don't want there to be any more killing, do you, Sam?"

"Shut up, Darby. What's done is done."

"You took a huge chance flying out here on the chopper. The pilot will remember you—"

"So what?"

Bram was lying on his side between Sam and me. My hands, out of sight, continued to work on the knots.

Sam must have noticed. "Put your hands where I can see them."

Before I raised them, I gave the knot one final tug. I could feel the rope loosen. "Those emeralds—"

His head jerked backward and gun shifted slightly.

"Yes. I know about the emeralds. The mine. And so will others soon enough. You can't keep killing people who might stumble on the location."

Sam pulled back his lips, exposing his teeth more like a snarl than a smile. "You're crazy, Darby. Cleanup. That's all I do. Cleanup, but you don't have to worry about it. It doesn't matter anyway. The mine tapped out shortly after the accident that killed the miners."

With an ear-shattering *whoosh*, the roof of the staff quarters collapsed.

Sam moved closer to us. I could feel Bram working on his bindings, but his face was a mask of pain.

Bram won't be able to help. It's up to me.

"Don't concern your pretty little head about it. What we did find there were world-class stones. We found an investor who took the whole lot."

An investor? Someone who loved cut stones. Like a husband and wife named Stacy and Peter? Who left with Wyatt to get help.

Had all the riders failed?

A sour taste filled my mouth. I lowered my hands.

"We just had to keep the source of the stones hidden for a bit. And, of course, take care of the loose ends."

"Loose ends? Like when you killed Mae, then covered up with the note?"

"No one killed Mae. She moved to Pocatello."

I stared at him a moment. "I found her body. At the cabin."

His gun wavered slightly before he retrained it on me. "You're a liar."

"No. You went to the cabin and tried to kill me."

"Darby, you're a liar and crazy. I never tried to kill you. I was off on my timing, but that was an accident. I meant I bought Mule Shoe." He raised his pistol.

I was going to die.

I dropped my head, but something he said sent my mind spinning. The miners died six months ago. I had thought all the deaths were directly related to the mine's discovery, but if that wasn't an issue . . .

"Now, Darby, about you."

I closed my eyes. *Heavenly Father, forgive me—*

Crack!

I jumped. The sound hurt my ears. Was I dead? Or . . .

Opening my eyes, I reached for Bram and looked up.

Roy stood outlined by the fire, Bram's Glock in hand. Behind him stood Grace, two of the Polish ladies, and Cookie.

Sam sprawled on the ground, motionless.

"Snake." Roy spit at him.

I wanted to scream, cry, pray, vomit. I remained motionless until the waves of emotion passed. When again I could get control of myself, I helped Bram to a seated position leaning against a tree stump.

Was it over? Really over? I pushed to my feet and hopped over to Sam's body. I knew everyone would stare at me, at my missing limb. I didn't care.

Sam's partially open eyes stared at eternity.

The pistol Sam pointed at me was the same kind of weapon I'd owned, the last gun I'd touched since the shootout five years ago. A Sig Sauer 9mm. I reached for it, hesitated, then picked it up.

A memory opened. I gasped. *A memory, not a flashback.* I remembered grabbing the gun from the glove box. I'd thought something was wrong. *Wrong with the gun.*

Jim had been talking to the serial killer. I was supposed to cover my husband. I'd sighted in on the man's head, but I didn't shoot. My brain had kept pounding out, *Terribly wrong.*

"Now, Darby. Shoot now!" Jim had screamed.

The killer had fired. Jim had dropped to the ground.

I had run. I hadn't taken the shot. *I'm a coward.*

A heaviness settled in my chest. I'd failed to correctly interpret the killer's letters, lost my husband and baby, and finally lost my leg, all because . . . I shook my head.

No. Something else. The gun. I kept coming back to the gun. My flashbacks and dreams had returned to the Sig Sauer. Why hadn't I pulled the trigger?

I looked down at the weapon in my hand. *Could it be?* I turned my back to Roy and the staff, then ejected the gun's magazine. No bullets. *Just like my gun five years ago.*

I'd known then that the gun's weight was off. I knew that weapon, handled it every day. In the mind-numbing terror of that day, I'd known something was wrong but couldn't figure out what. When I'd been discovered by that group of teens, they took my purse and the weapons. I remembered their voices.

"Hey, Matt, Chris, come over here! This is cool. A body!"

"Naaa, really? Awesome!"

"Whatcha think we shood do?"

"Grab his gun, man. 'Nother gun over there."

Approaching footsteps. "Hey, there's a chick here. Pretty. Should we—"

"Naa, man, I ain't that drunk."

When they'd stolen my pistol and left me to die, they'd also stolen the one way I could have known I wasn't a coward. I wasn't running away—I was running for help because the gun was unloaded.

"Darby, are you okay?" Roy asked.

"I'm better than okay. I'm exonerated." I slid the action back slightly and stuck my finger into the chamber, then quietly closed it.

"It's finally over," Cookie said.

"Yes." My neck started to itch.

Something had fallen from Sam's pocket. A walkie-talkie.

The itch grew. What had Sam said? *The mine tapped out shortly after the accident that killed the miners. We found an investor who took the whole lot. No one killed Mae. She moved to Pocatello. I never tried to kill you. I bought Mule Shoe.*

I knew the answer to question two, who wanted it. Just one problem.

We. Sam had said "we."

My neck was on fire. I still needed to figure out who he was working with. Roy? He was the one who shot Sam, but he wouldn't drive down the price of his own resort. Cookie? Possibly someone had found out about her PTSD and stint at Clan Firinn. *Yeah right.* Then she'd somehow stabbed herself in the back and hit herself over the head. Spuds, the missing staffer? Open to bribes? Wyatt? He'd been in prison and was strong enough to have carried bodies into the building and set it on fire. He'd also ridden out to safety . . . and freedom.

"Roy." Cookie put her hand on Roy's arm holding the pistol. "We need to have a mindset for resolution here. Sam was the killer." She gently removed the weapon from Roy's hands.

Mindset. The arson note had that unique phrasing. *You should make your mindset one of defeat.* Wyatt had used a similar phrase when we were trapped in the lodge. *We want you to adopt the survival mindset.*

And Roy had written the welcome greeting in the brochure. *You should bring to Mule Shoe your mindset for success.*

It wasn't unusual for people who lived and worked together to pick up each other's unique dictionary of words and phrases. I'd have to figure out something else. Some clue I'd overlooked. Where had everyone been? What had people said?

I bought Mule Shoe. Probably the lowest bid, which was SD. Sam . . . Dankworth?

Words written. A note. *As per our tradition.* The note from Scott Thomas to me. *Gift.* The puzzle pieces dropped into place.

I knew who, and I knew what I had to do. I just hoped it wouldn't kill me. *Be strong and courageous! Do not be afraid. God is with you.*

"Are you okay, Darby?" Roy asked. "You have a strange look on your face."

"I just figured out the answer to question three. What was the escape strategy? How could someone possibly get away with all these murders and still end up with the mine and Mule Shoe? You simply blame everything on Sam, then kill him. If you're the closest relative, you inherit everything. Resort, emerald mine, the whole enchilada. Who was he, Cookie? Your dear brother?"

CHAPTER 32

ookie's face blanched and she shook her head. "No, no, no! Why are you asking me about Sam? I only order supplies from him. I would never otherwise associate with someone like him."

"Multiple denials, answering a question with a question, and claiming to be morally unable to do something." My stomach felt rock hard. "Three signs of deception."

"I'm not going to stand here and be accused of something I had no knowledge of. He attacked me!" Her hands formed fists. "Did you forget he hit me on the head and stabbed me?"

"No, I didn't forget. Earlier tonight the setting sun glinted on the tip of the knife extending from a crack in a log. You jammed the knife tightly into that crack, then backed into it. That's why you received more of a cut than a stab. The rock you used to hit yourself on the head was right where you dropped it."

"Nonsense. Sam did it. You heard him." Cookie's face had gone from pale to flushed. "You all heard him."

"We did hear Sam confess," Grace said to me.

"He confessed to what he called 'cleanup.' And he said he was off on his timing, which was an accident." I wiped my sleeve across my face, trying to get the smoky stench out of my nose. "What needed to be timed? The slide at Devil's Keyhole. I'd bet Sam's military experience had to do with explosives."

No one spoke.

"But Sam also said 'we'—plural. He had help. It had to be from someone who worked here, and so they had to die. The plan must have been to seal the exit route by blowing it up, but the timing was off and the route was closed before we could get out.

"Cookie called Sam on the radio just before she destroyed it. He knew he had to catch the helicopter and that things were coming to a head. She outlined the plan and kept in touch with him with a walkie-talkie."

"Ridiculous!" Cookie almost yelled. "He killed the three men here on the ranch to hide his presence, then went after you and tried to kill you—"

"You're making more and more mistakes, Cookie." I didn't take my gaze off her. "How could you have known someone tried to kill me? How could you have even known where I'd be?" I let her mistake sink in. "Because you were the one to suggest the route I would take, and you gave me a GPS with a low battery. You couldn't know how long the battery would last, but you knew the dogs would head straight for Shadow Woman's house, and I'd go after them.

Besides, Sam didn't follow me. He left for the mine as soon as he got here. You sent him ahead."

"You're crazy." Cookie looked at the others. "She's crazy."

"You should have told Sam not to light a fire in Mae's cookstove. Yet another mistake. It was still warm. You told Sam to put me in the cave because you knew darkness was a PTSD trigger for me—"

"How could I have known that? I don't know you that well."

"You knew I had PTSD. You saw my reaction to the darkness my first night here. You offered a lantern to Wyatt and Bram to get me to the cabin. You were hoping I'd get lost in the cave, go into a fugue state, or die in the geyser." My voice shook. Putting her plans for my death into words sent chills down my back. "But Sam had no idea what I was talking about when I accused him of trying to kill me. He didn't know about the geyser. *You* did. Mae couldn't get her message through to Roy, but you were there. You understood. You moved the miners, set that fire, then murdered Mae."

"No!"

"He believed the mine tapped out because *you* told him. *You.* His beloved sister. His only family."

"That's horrible." Grace looked at Cookie now as if she were the devil incarnate. Which she was.

"You told Sam to remove my prosthesis and bring it here. You probably said that would slow me down. You had him put the prosthesis into the building, which you'd then burn. You hoped no one would question what happened to the rest of my body."

Roy had stepped away from Cookie and was staring at her. Now he looked at me. "That can't be right, Darby. Sam was here all last night and today. You were in the dining room when Sam shot in the window! And this morning when you rode out, Sam was shooting at you. He couldn't have been two places at once."

"He didn't have to be," I said. "Cookie was doing the shooting. I'd bet she placed the missing stash of guns next to the kitchen. She conveniently went to the kitchen for water last night. She had plenty of time to move the chair holding the door shut, shoot out the nearby window, hide the gun, replace the chair, and tuck herself under a table where I found her. Remember we were all scrambling for cover."

"What about this morning?" Grace asked.

"Once again Cookie offered to create a diversion, again from the kitchen door."

Cookie almost sputtered. "You're accusing me of killing three men, stabbing Angie—"

"Another mistake, Cookie." I wiped my sweaty hands on my jeans. "We haven't found the third ranch hand. So he's dead too?"

"I didn't mean it that way."

"You wanted Sam to buy Mule Shoe, so you started by getting the insurance dropped with the horseback incident and the hikers' deaths. That dropped the price and changed the cash flow. Then came the 'accidents,' like a trap set so someone would fall through the loft onto a pitchfork. Mixing up reservations. Attracting bears. Planting dead raccoons and contaminated water. You destroyed the art room. Sam wasn't around for any of it, and none of that would have been necessary if the mine were tapped out."

Cookie pointed at me. "You're delusional. Suffering from PTSD. You had to get rehabilitated at Clan Firinn, like me. I'll be sending Scott Thomas my report. You need to be treated—"

"You were never *at* Clan Firinn. That was the best lie you could have told, because you knew I'd trust you." I wanted to spit as Roy had done. "You expect an enemy to lie to you, but not a friend. That's what took me so long to suspect you." My voice cracked and I swallowed, then continued. "You knew all about Clan Firinn because you read Roy's mail. And you found my note from Scott hidden in the art room. That was your biggest mistake, Cookie."

Cookie didn't answer.

"Scott wrote in my letter that he was sending me a gift that was 'as per our tradition.' That meant everyone got the same thing from the beginning. The gift was three rocks, representing the three stumbling stones I'd need to overcome, my PTSD triggers. But you had no idea what I was talking about when I showed you the rocks. You didn't know what the gift was. I bet you thought I was asking about another kind of rock—the kind with emeralds in it."

Cookie's eyes narrowed to slits.

"I have just one question for you, Cookie. Why did you try to kill Angie? Unlike the ranch hands, she didn't see Sam get off the helicopter."

"I caught her snooping in my room. She knew too much. And so do you."

I lifted Sam's pistol and pointed it at her.

She laughed, high-pitched and shrill. "Your gun is empty. I unloaded it before giving it to Sam."

I kept my gun aimed at her.

Cookie laughed again, even more maniacally, and raised the Glock. "You're a fool, Darby."

I pulled the trigger.

CHAPTER 33

ookie screamed and dropped to the ground. Roy raced to her side and yanked the pistol from her hands, then bent down and checked her. "You'll live," he said to her.

I knew she would. I hadn't gone for a fatal shot. "I'd still tie her up."

Roy pulled off his belt and used it to tie Cookie's hands. The bullet had gone through the fleshy part of Cookie's hip—painful, but not life-threatening. "Maja," he said to one of the staffers, "there's a first-aid kit in the lodge. Bring me that and a blanket."

The woman left.

"I thought she said your gun was empty," Roy said to me.

"She emptied the clip but forgot to check the chamber." I was suddenly exhausted, in need of sitting down before I fell down. I hopped over and sat next to Bram.

"How bad is it?" I tried not to look at his burned legs.

"Bad." He winced. "My legs . . . and I think my shoulder is dislocated."

I started to stand and called for Roy.

He grabbed my hand. "No. Don't leave. I wanted . . . want to say I'm sorry."

"For what?"

"For not believing you were perfect from the start."

"Thank you, Bram. I'm not perfect."

Maverick came up to me and lay down, keeping a wary eye on Bram. I put my arm around the dog. A calm settled over me.

"He's finally trusting you," Bram said.

I stroked his silky ear. "He's coming around."

Bram shifted, then winced. "The dogs led you to Shadow Woman—"

"Mae. Her name was Mae Haas. Her dogs guarded her body for as long as they could."

Maja returned with the first-aid kit, water bottles, and blankets. She left the kit and one blanket with Roy, then brought the water and second blanket over to Bram. We covered him and gave him the water.

Grace joined us. "You said you were exonerated." Grace sat on the other side of Bram. "From what?"

I held up Sam's empty pistol, then placed it on the ground beside Bram. Reaching into my pocket, I removed the last stone and set it on the pistol. "For feeling responsible for losing my unborn baby, losing my leg, and losing my husband. That day five years ago, my gun wasn't loaded."

"That wasn't your fault," Bram said.

"Yes and no." I shrugged. "I guess I'll always feel guilty,

but who'd believe they needed to be armed when going to buy a horse?"

"I read that you weren't found until hours after the shooting," Bram said.

I nodded. "Sepsis had set in on my leg, which made me miscarry."

"And your husband died," Grace said.

I stared into the fire for a moment. "No," I said softly. "He was hurt, but he recovered. He blamed me. For . . . everything. He divorced me. That's what put me over the edge."

Grace leaned forward. "So Shadow Woman wasn't really Mae Haas. It's really *you* who's been living in the shadows."

I nodded. "The shadow of guilt, fear, and shame."

In the distance came the most wonderful sound in the world, the *chuff, chuff, chuff* of helicopters. "Help will be here soon," Grace said, then stood and walked over to Roy. The two of them left to direct the arriving officers and medical staff.

Maverick jumped to his feet and trotted into the night.

Bram reached over and squeezed my hand. "What now, Darby Graham?"

My eyes blurred. I knew what he was asking. "I don't know. Maybe see what God has in store for me. Check out the promise of Jeremiah 29:11. Hope and a future."

The helicopters were close enough that speaking was difficult.

All that had happened seemed like a dream. Someone *had* been able to ride for help. Peter and Stacy? Wyatt? Liam? Whoever it was, uniformed officers and EMTs soon swarmed us. I was grateful when Roy and Grace explained what happened. I was too exhausted to talk.

The EMTs checked Cookie, then Bram. I scooted away so they could have access to him. They called for stretchers, and Angie, Bram, and Cookie were whisked away to the medivac chopper.

An officer finally came over to where I was still sitting on the ground. "The sheriff is going to have a lot of questions for you."

I nodded.

He bent down and lifted me as if I weighed nothing. "Come along then." He didn't put me down until he had me strapped into a police copter.

EPILOGUE

EIGHTEEN MONTHS LATER

MULE SHOE RANCH

W hy are those dogs barking?" The teenage girl stared at Maverick and Holly, now howling under a pine tree.

"You'll soon find out." I held up my clipboard. "Name?"

The earthquake hit before she could answer. She squealed and sat on the ground clutching her rolled-up sleeping bag. All of the young campers grabbed each other or their assorted luggage while the ground briefly shook.

When the quaking stopped and the dogs ceased their barking, I blew a whistle to gain their attention. Grace, wearing khaki Bermuda shorts, hiking boots, and a *Camp Mule Shoe* polo shirt, stepped forward. "Welcome, campers. Don't worry about the earthquake. They're common here. We're less than five miles from the edge of the Yellowstone caldera, the so-called Yellowstone supervolcano."

One young girl raised her hand. "What's a supervolcano?"

Grace gave her an approving nod. "A supervolcano, by definition, must eject at least 240 cubic miles of material and is capable of measuring a magnitude eight or more on the Volcanic Explosivity Index . . ."

While Grace gave her favorite end-of-the-world-erupting-volcano speech, I did my final count of participants. This would be another good week. We had a full house.

To offset Grace's obsession with supervolcanos and the sudden destruction of civilization, I'd had the photograph of Mae Haas along with the second verse Scott Thomas sent me laminated, and I carried it with me every day. *"For I know the thoughts that I think toward you, says the Lord, thoughts of peace and not of evil, to give you a future and a hope."*

The quiet purring of one of our electric shuttles announced a visitor. I handed the clipboard to the nearest counselor and strolled over to greet the newcomer. Bram stepped out.

My breath caught in my throat. My heart rate shot off the charts. I hadn't seen him in over a year and a half.

He was as handsome as ever, maybe even more so with the touch of gray at his temple.

My face warmed. I was wearing the camp uniform of khaki shorts and polo shirt, my leg exposed for all to see.

He reached into the shuttle and pulled out a cane, then grinned at me.

Grace had stopped speaking and I realized all eyes were on us.

I moved closer. "Welcome, stranger."

Holly couldn't contain her joy at seeing her buddy. She ran over to him, jumped up, and planted a sloppy kiss on his cheek.

Lucky dog.

I could hear the campers near me whispering.

"Who's that?"

"I think it's a movie star."

"He's hot for an old guy. He must be at least thirty."

"Positively ancient. One foot in the grave," I muttered and nodded toward a picnic table out of range of the teens. As I walked over, I quickly yanked the clip holding my hair up, fluffed it, and bit my lip to give it some color. A quick finger check found no leftover lunch stuck between my teeth. We sat across the table from each other, then both spoke at once.

"I thought you—"

"How are you—"

"You first," I said.

"I left the sheriff's department."

"I'm sorry to hear that."

"Don't be. The scandal when I turned over the evidence to have the sheriff's son arrested as the serial arsonist pretty much meant we all had to leave. I figured the judge would be more lenient on Liam because he was the one who got help for all of us, but he still got a hefty sentence."

"Did they ever figure out why he set the fires?"

"Pretty much what I'd worked out. Get even with his

mom, move out of Fremont County, end up in a bigger city. But he'd also found he liked setting fires. Didn't you follow all that in the news?"

"No." I traced the wood grain on the tabletop. "I returned to Clan Firinn until Cookie's trial—"

"I thought for sure I'd see you then."

"They kept me pretty much sequestered. And the defense attorney was brutal . . ." I looked up and smiled at him. "Let's talk about better things. What are you doing now?"

"I'm between jobs, but I have an offer I'm considering." He glanced around. "I see a lot of changes here."

"Cookie couldn't benefit from her crime, so the place went back up for sale. When Grace bought Mule Shoe, she turned it into a summer camp for challenged teens. Each week is a different group. This week it's amputees. The cabins are for staff, and we added tepees for the campers to sleep in. The kids love it."

"Well, what kid wouldn't want to sleep in a tepee?"

Maverick wandered over and sat beside Bram. "Well, hello, Maverick." He tentatively patted the dog on the head, then looked at me. "This is new. When did he start letting people touch him?"

"He's coming around. Anyway, we still don't allow cell phones or electronic devices, but now we have electricity, internet service, and outdoor lighting. And batteries. Lots of batteries."

Bram gave me a questioning look before asking, "And you?"

I grinned. "I teach western riding. And have a book club featuring dog stories. What else?"

The counselors had sorted out their campers by now and were escorting them to the different tepees. Grace strolled over to us. "Bram! Good to see you!"

"Good to see you, Grace. Quite the adventure you have here."

She sat. "We only run this in the summer, of course, as a camp. During the winter we have retreats with snowshoeing and cross-country skiing. Booked solid for the next year and a half." She patted me on the back. "Darby here has had a lot of good ideas."

"Do you hear from Roy?" Bram asked. "Or Angie?"

"Roy moved to Alaska," Grace said. "He claimed Idaho was getting too crowded. I lost touch with Angie."

"What about Wyatt, Peter, and Stacy?" he asked. "And Riccardo?"

Grace glanced at me. "Riccardo's fine. Started college. Wyatt hung around a bit. I think he was hoping Darby would . . . well, anyway, he finally took a job in Montana. Big resort north of Missoula."

Heat had started in my neck and rushed up my face. I cleared my throat. "Peter and Stacy went home. They were Sam's gemstone investors but believed everything to be legit."

"Did you ever find out why those three didn't get help for us?" Bram asked.

"They tried." I shook my head. "No one would take

them seriously. Three people on horseback claiming a murderous killer was running loose at a resort? They thought the three of them were doing some kind of a stunt for the local mystery theater."

"You know, Darby," Bram said, "if you hadn't put it all together, Cookie just might have succeeded. Either way, Sam would have been blamed."

"Mae put it together. I just followed her message." I shrugged. "Would you like a tour? Or . . ." I glanced at his cane.

He picked it up. "Just temporary. I twisted my ankle shooting hoops at the Y."

I didn't know how to ask him about his burns.

"I was in the hospital for two days." He laughed at my expression. "Remember I told you I was a mind reader. Anyway, a little rehab, some scars, but otherwise I healed up just fine." He stood. "I guess we all ended up with a few scars."

We slowly made our way over to the lodge. Behind us, the cheerful calling and laughter of the children filled the air. Holly had taken her favorite ball and found a camper willing to throw it for her. We came to a newly installed sundial. Engraved on the top, it read In Memory of Mae Haas. No Longer in the Shadows. I'd had the photo of her from her Bible enlarged and sealed behind glass in the base so everyone could see her.

"Very nice," Bram said. "Fitting."

"We had her remains scattered over the mountains she loved," I said.

Inside the lodge, Grace had doubled the size of the dining room and added long tables. "Where the original staff quarters stood"—Grace pointed straight ahead—"we have an indoor pool and arts and crafts center. There's a new chapel up by the pond. I remodeled the triplex and made it a duplex where Darby and the new art teacher stay. The old art room is now the manager's office." She turned to Bram. "What do you think?"

"Mule Shoe was breathtaking before. Now? Yeah."

"Good. You start in a week."

"Wh . . . wh . . . what?" I was having a hard time breathing.

"Bram just agreed to be the new manager," Grace said. "You two will be working together." She smiled and sauntered away.

"What do you say, Darby?" Bram asked. "Think you could work with me? I have some big plans."

"Depends."

His forehead furrowed. "Oh."

"Did you ever add unlined five-by-seven mint-green index cards to your selection of papers?" I thought for sure he'd laugh.

Instead he pulled a rock from his pocket. "Hopefully I've done better than that." He held up the stone.

I recognized it as the one I'd left sitting on the pistol that awful evening, the last pebble given to me by Clan Firinn.

"My grandmother used to say . . . Never mind what she

said. I've carried her enmity for far too long." He crossed to the door, opened it, and threw the stone away as hard as he could.

I slowly joined him, pulling a lump of ore from my pocket—the one I'd found in the mine. I didn't know why I'd kept this one all this time. *You know why.* I swallowed hard. *It's time.*

I dropped the rock, crushed it into the ground with my prosthetic foot, then looked up at him. "What are those plans you have?"

"I think you know. Plans for a hope and a future."

THE END

A NOTE OR TWO FROM THE AUTHOR

Whoa, you made it through another story. This time I wanted to try a bit of an Agatha Christy angle with elements of my usual forensic art and, of course, dogs! I hope and pray you enjoyed this book!

I also wanted to continue the story of members of Clan Firinn that started in *Relative Silence*. I invented Clan Firinn as a retreat and rehabilitation place for first responders based on my close friendships with so many in law enforcement. As a forensic artist, I experienced some of the truly awful things that happen in this fallen world. My heart goes out to those who are in the field.

Targhee (pronounced Tar-gee) is a real place—not the town but the location in Idaho. For this story I wanted to bring my experience growing up here on our ranch in Northern Idaho. My dad was a champion bareback bronc rider in college and grew up on a cattle ranch near American Falls, Idaho. Mom also grew up riding horses and my folks met in college at a mounted patrol club. When we moved to The Ranch (that's all we ever called it) we had horses, cattle, and, of course, dogs. Dad taught me how to train horses and I spent my every waking moment on horse-back or showing my dogs. I speak from experience when I describe getting thrown, bucked off, or falling off a horse. Also bitten, kicked, and stepped on. Growing up around horses is both wonderful and at times painful!

I'm always delighted to hear from my readers, and I answer your emails: carrie@stuartparks.com.

ACKNOWLEDGMENTS

This is now my eighth novel for HarperCollins Christian, and I'm thankful every day for the honor and privilege of working with such a warm and caring publishing house. Amanda Bostic, my editor and publisher, as well as friend, is sheer joy to work with. The dog, Holly, in this story is in honor of her dog. My marketing team of Nekasha Pratt, Kerri Potts, Matt Bray, Margaret Kercher, and Marcee Wardell are all the best in the business and I'm thrilled to have them.

I'm so blessed in having the award-winning editor and bestselling novelist in her own right, Erin Healy, as my editor. She polishes my words until they shine and I'm so grateful for her keen insight.

Karen Solem, my agent, is the most awesome, perfect, delightful, wonderful (I could keep adding here for another hour) lady that I've had the honor to know. She listens to me and gives me solid, sound advice every time. She joined our brainstorming crew to hash out the elements of this story along with the fabulous Colleen Coble, Robin Caroll, Lynette Eason, Voni Harris, and Pam Hillman.

ACKNOWLEDGMENTS

I thank my dear husband, Rick, for reading and giving me suggestions on the book. He still wants me to place a book on a river cruise so he can do the research. Dream on, Toots.

Thank you to Sheriff Len Humphries of the Fremont County Sheriff's Office for letting me interview you, and to Jeff White of J. L. White Fine Gemstones of Kingsport, Tennessee, for the information on fine gems.

Finally, the most important thank you of all to my Lord and Savior, Jesus Christ, in whom all things are possible.

DISCUSSION QUESTIONS

1. The Mule Shoe Resort is a fictional location with parts loosely lifted from Double Arrow Resort and Paws Up Resort in Montana. Have you ever gone to an all-inclusive resort or retreat?

2. Darby had three stones, representing her still-present hurdles she had to get over. If you wanted to give yourself a physical reminder of a challenge you might face this year, what would you choose and why?

3. If you were at the resort and needed to get help, what would you have done? Ride out with one of the characters, stay behind, or another solution?

4. Darby was given two Bible verses, both of which she repeated to give her comfort or strength. By the end of the book, she believed in the source of that comfort and strength. Do you have a Bible verse that has helped you through rough times?

5. What did you think about the drawings that Mae

did? Did you figure out their meaning before they
were revealed?

6. Have you ever heard of a forensic linguist? What
   types of forensic specialists have you heard of?
7. Have you ever visited Yellowstone National Park?
8. Would you like to see Darby return in another
   book?
9. Do you have suggestions for an interesting location
   for another book?

ABOUT THE AUTHOR

Andrea Kramer, Kramer Photography

Carrie Stuart Parks is a Christy, multiple Carol, and INSPY Award–winning author. She was a 2019 finalist in the Daphne du Maurier Award for excellence in mainstream mystery/suspense and has won numerous awards for her fine art as well. An internationally known forensic artist, she travels with her husband, Rick, across the US and Canada teaching courses in forensic art to law-enforcement professionals. The author/illustrator of numerous books on drawing and painting, Carrie continues to create dramatic watercolors from her studio in the mountains of Idaho.

Visit her website at CarrieStuartParks.com
Facebook: @CarrieStuartParksAuthor